WORLDS DON'T COLLIDE
BOOK 9 OF THE VALKYRIE BESTIARY SERIES

BY KIM MCDOUGALL

Hardcover ISBN: 978-1-990570-42-1
Paperback ISBN: 978-1-990570-38-4
eBook ISBN: 978-1-990570-39-1

Version 3

FICTION / Fantasy / Urban
FICTION / Fantasy / Paranormal

About This Book

Critter wrangler rule #24: When the gods come knocking, don't answer the door.

Kyra has been charged with a sacred duty—to wipe every filthy, blood-sucking vampire off the face of Terra's earth. Starting a war with the vamps means she needs help, but her allies are scattered and squabbling amongst themselves.

When the vampires attack Montreal and Kyra's family is threatened, she has no choice but to start the fight that will change their lives and the very shape of their worlds forever.

Worlds Don't Collide is the exciting conclusion to the Valkyrie Bestiary Series.

PROLOGUE

October 13, 2084
Vioska Ward

Ichovidar dressed carefully that morning. He chose a waistcoat of fine black wool. Its fashion was dated, but it wouldn't hurt to remind the others of his true age and the power those many centuries gave him. The lace cuffs of his pristine white shirt brushed the backs of his hands. He opened a walnut cabinet to display a range of fine blades—silver, steel, and obsidian—all embedded with jewels. His long fingers trailed over them as he decided on one to compliment his dress. Many were too ornate for real battle, but he kept them relentlessly sharp anyway. His gaze rested on a silver ceremonial blade with a snake etched into the flat edge. The snake's eyes were emeralds. Its ruby-encrusted tongue curved along the blade like a flame. It was a blade meant for sending sacrifices to God. And today would be a day of sacrifice. He looped it onto his belt without a sheath. It was his only nod to ostentation.

As he entered the great hall, he spied the Zaubers lined up like statues along one wall. These were his men. The top mages in the city. They respected and feared him because there was no greater mage in the history of the opji.

The sun was setting through blood-red stained glass windows that washed the Zaubers in a macabre light. Ichovidar did so love a dramatic setting.

He nodded to Menno, the most proficient of his mage acolytes, as he strode into the room toward a massive table made of holly, a wood so white it seemed to glow. Eight black-robed figures sat around the table—The Council of Elders.

Ichovidar's lip trembled with the temptation to sneer as he examined their stoic faces.

Elders. Not one of them could match his years, not by half. This is what their grand and glorious race had been reduced to. The opji were once God's favorite children, made not in his image but in his blood. For thousands of years, they had been scions in the greatest houses of the world, confidants to kings, and leaders of industry, hiding their rare magic and bloodlust under a thin veneer of humanity. And then that witch god flooded the world with magic, made it commonplace. To make matters worse, she tore down cities and filled them with trees. Fucking trees! She forced humans and fae to cloister themselves in wards, and the opji struggled for every drop of blood that was their sacred birthright.

The rage that had filled Ichovidar's veins in those early days of the Flood Wars never left him. It didn't take much to let it boil to the surface.

She had taken everything from them. Humans might whine about being restricted to wards, but the opji were the real victims of the Flood Wars. They needed blood to survive. Human blood. And when Terra woke the world and confined their blood source to warded cities, the opji suffered.

At first they fought back, and their numbers dwindled. Then they survived on the blood of beasts. The very thought of it made his fists clench. The insult! Ichovidar of the ancient house of Erazm surviving on the blood of rats and deer.

It was beyond shame.

And it nearly proved fatal. So many opji were lost during that time. Their race could barely survive, let alone flourish, without the rich magic of human blood.

And so, Ichovidar had lobbied the Council of Elders to expand on the work of Filip Vidar, the founder of Vioska. Vidar had proposed the *gazgroda* or holding policy. It was a revolutionary way of farming, but they wouldn't be planting crops or raising sheep. They kept humans.

Before his death, Vidar implemented the new plan on a small scale. He raided human settlements, took captives, and built farms to keep them. But the frail humans proved to be terrible livestock. They were unmanageable and without honor. The thing they did best was die—from disease, from cold or hunger or even suicide.

Upon Vidar's death, the project was almost abandoned. The Council of Elders at the time fought for a return to beast blood. But Ichovidar proposed an expansion of the gazgroda. Instead of simply holding the humans and using them until they died, the opji began breeding them. It was an ambitious project, but the Elders sanctioned it mostly because the lower ranks were restless. Raiding homesteads gave them purpose.

So for forty years they built their farms and bred their krowa, the human cows that served and fed them. But the krowa had proven to be as intractable as ever. They fought the opji at every chance. They fought amongst themselves when they had no other outlet for their pathetic human rage. And they sickened, dying in huge numbers that made the whole project unsustainable.

How had these feeble creatures come to rule the world? Ichovidar would never understand, but it didn't matter. Human life was insignificant. The time of the opji had come.

The failure of the holding project had been a blow to his authority. The Council had pushed him aside for years. But Ichovidar was patient. Biding his time in seclusion had given rise to his most ambitious plan ever.

Today he would make a god live, so he could kill her.

Today they would burn the mightiest of sacrifices and ignite the ancient magic of the *gadzic*, a rite that would trap the witch god in her corporeal form. She would be as frail as a human. Powerless.

And with the witch god out of his way, Ichovidar would be free to implement his most ambitious plan, a new brand of magic that wasn't found in the ancient texts, a rite he was calling the *brechzen*—the great breaking.

Wards would shatter. Worlds would collide. The chaos would be terrible and glorious. He would prove to the witch and the watching world that he also had the power to change reality. The unnatural order that favored the lives of trees and vermin would be put to right, and in the breaking the opji would finally be free to harvest blood from all creatures.

The opji would reign as God had originally intended.

Though he had the full backing of the mages, the elders knew only about the gadzic—the part of the plan where they ousted the witch queen from her safe haven. That magic came at a great cost, and he would not push the fragile accord of the elders by revealing the full extent of his genius. For now, their ignorance served his purpose.

The elders watched in silence as he took his seat. There would be dissension, of course. Audo in particular would object, but then Audo would object if you told him the sun rose in the east. Ichovidar would let the dissenters have a voice. On this day, he would let them pretend they had a claim to power.

And then he would do what must be done.

The room was silent as a tomb. The squeaking of a chair broke the stillness and Audo rose. He'd once been a great warrior, but age comes even to the opji and Audo stooped under the weight of it. His raised hand trembled and lips quivered as his tongue and palate struggled to form words. His rheumy eyes were glassy and unfocused.

Ichovidar clenched his fists under the table to keep from lashing out at this despicable show of weakness.

Audo cleared his throat and spoke with a phlegmy whine.

"In the past year we have burned five hundred hectares of forest—"

"Trees are weapons of the witch god." This from Waldar who sat beside Audo and had a gift for proclaiming the obvious.

Audo spoke over the grumbling. "I do not weep for the witch god's children. The burning was necessary. I only suggest that we may not have enough accessible fuel left to perform the gadzic. I propose that we take more time to investigate other options before committing so many…ah, resources to this last desperate act."

The air in the room seemed to grow cold as the elders took in a collective but silent gasp.

Had Audo just called Ichovidar desperate?

Even Audo realized he'd crossed a line. His trembling hand flapped against his chest.

"That is…I mean…we should be certain that our focus is clear, that we will succeed before…"

The mages ranged along the wall began to shift. The sound of their heavy robes rubbing together was like the slither of a giant serpent. Many of them would die in the rite that would expose the witch god. And that was all right. They accepted their fate with dignity and honor. But to doubt their focus—

their very loyalty—called Ichovidar's ability to govern into question. It was beyond stupid.

Ichovidar studied each face around the table. The council was about to discover that their claim to power was a sham. The Zaubers held the real power here. And they were loyal only to him.

He leaned back in his chair and smiled at Audo. The councilman jerked to his feet, knocking over the chair. His body went rigid. Veins protruded from his throat as he strained against Ichovidar's spell. His hand slapped his hip as he searched for his blade.

He fights me.

Ichovidar redoubled his efforts and pushed out more magic. Audo's fingers gripped the blade's hilt and he lifted it from his belt. His hand rose. The knife point quivered as it fixed on Ichovidar.

Ichovidar's grin flattened. This defiance grew tiresome. He flicked his fingers as if shooing a fly.

Audo's back arched. Breath wheezed from his chest. His hand slowly bent until the blade pointed inward. His eyes bulged as he swiped a line across his own throat.

Menno stepped forward and jerked Audo backward to avoid staining the table. Ichovidar appreciated his forethought, but blood sprayed across the table and adjacent elders anyway.

Audo crashed to the floor. Menno took the blade from his still fingers and sliced through the remaining bone and sinew to separate his head from his body. The true death.

Menno tossed the head aside and stepped back in line, wiping the blade with the hem of his robe.

The room was silent. Two krowa servants appeared. One dragged the body away while the other collected the head. Ichovidar waited for them to finish, then turned his attention back to the elders.

"Are there more protests?"

His question met stony gazes. Waldar licked Audo's blood from his lips and shook his head.

Good. Let them remember who was really in charge. Let them tremble at the power of his ancient bloodline and the magic that ran in his veins—magic that would bring a god to her knees.

Ichovidar smiled. "Then we adjourn until the hour of the moon when the world will finally appreciate the true might of the opji!"

Fists pounded on the table like thunder coming down the mountains.

THE SUN SET AT 6:21pm that day, Friday the thirteenth, and the full moon was already cresting in the sky. Ichovidar wasn't superstitious, but the mages assured him that all the auspices pointed to a successful gadzic.

An early snowfall blanketed the ground and crunched under cart wheels as they traveled over a narrow road. For miles in every direction, charred tree stumps jutted through the snow. It was beautiful. Black and white as the world should be. No room for indecision.

The cart drew up to the site and Ichovidar jumped down to study their preparations. The mages had cut hundreds of fresh trees from the witch god's breast and arranged them in giant bundles. A thousand krowa were crowded into a pen around these prepared bonfires.

When the fires were lit, the flames would be so great, they would wash out the light of the moon. The screams of the dying krowa would fill the night with a transcendent song that the witch god could not fail to ignore.

A stone obelisk had been erected in the middle of this pyre. It rose fifty feet into the air. Metal rungs were pounded into one side. Menno gripped the first one and began the slow ascent. The waiting elders and mages were silent and watchful. Wind lashed Menno's cloak as he approached the apex. He placed a crystal spirit jar on the head of the altar, then climbed down and bowed to his master. Ichovidar smiled.

When the screams of the dying kindled the gadzic, the god's essence would be pulled from her realm and captured in that jar like a fish in a bowl.

Dozens of carts pulled up alongside Ichovidar's. Every able-bodied opji had come out to witness their triumph.

The krowa had been sedated, but the drug was wearing off now, and they stumbled around their enclosure, gaping at the great piles of kindling or weeping for their obvious fate.

A thousand krowa. More than half their stock. Would it be enough? Menno had assured him it would be. Any more would deplete their blood stores too much to recover.

That hesitation spoke of weakness. If they succeeded—when they succeeded!—the world would once again become their feeding ground. To hold krowa in reserve suggested failure was a possibility.

There could be no failure.

Ichovidar motioned for Menno to walk with him. Menno's second, the mage Leon, trailed a few steps behind them.

"Tell me how you will proceed." Ichovidar waved a hand toward the preparations. "The fire must burn hot and quick. There can be no interruption."

"Of course, my lord." Menno bowed. His hands were hidden in the long sleeves of his mage's gown. A black beard, just starting to turn white, hung to his chest.

Menno had been the one to find the gadzic in the ancient text and bring it to Ichovidar's attention. He knew the rite by heart. They all did. But he didn't hesitate to go over the plan once more.

"We—my fellow mages and I—will be the catalyst to light the fire. As we chant the sacred song, the witch god will hear. She will taste the flesh burned in her name and respond. She will have no choice. The magic will compel her."

Ichovidar did not disagree. Magic was power. The gadzic was as ancient as the first opji, drawn from their Book of Blood, as sacred as the zycha rite that stilled their blood lust at puberty and brought them long life. Unlike the zycha that was performed dozens of times every year, the gadzic had never been done. They'd never had need like they did today.

"Is it enough?" Ichovidar waved toward the babbling krowa and waiting logs.

"By my calculations, it is more than enough, my lord." Menno bowed.

"Add the carts. And the cart handlers."

Menno pinched his lips and glanced back at the dozen carts that had brought them from Vioska.

"Of course."

Waldar overheard and complained. "But...my lord. How will we return home?"

Ichovidar turned his gaze to the elder. Sometimes he wondered if Waldar wore his idiocy like a shield.

"Are you afraid to walk, Elder Waldar? Perhaps you would prefer to camp here in the light of the bonfire."

"Of…of course not, my lord."

"Good. Then take two carts and ride back to the city. Bring two of the demons to add to the pyre."

Waldar's mouth gaped open, but he wisely shut it without comment, then hurried away.

Menno was made of sterner stuff, and while he never outright questioned his master, he was fond of the unasked question. He didn't meet Ichovidar's eye as he spoke.

"The demons were meant for the coming fight against the humans."

Ichovidar gave his mage the courtesy of considering his concerns, but then dismissed them. The humans and fae would come. That was inevitable, but no army could stand against the opji might and Ichovidar's magic. And they had three demons—pulled through the veil at great expense. He'd keep one in reserve for the coming fight. Let it never be said he was rash.

He flicked a hand toward the bonfire preparations. "This is the greater need. Add them to the fire. There can be no mistakes tonight."

"Yes, my lord." Menno bowed and hurried away to give commands to the other mages.

Within minutes, the waiting opji lifted the carts onto the prepared bonfire. The krowa cart handlers were tossed over the fence into the waiting crowd.

Ichovidar watched with satisfaction. Waldar returned. More carts hauled metal cages that held two of Ichovidar's prized demons. He'd be sorry to see them go. The demons were marvels of hidden power, and he'd enjoyed poking them with magical sticks to see how they worked. But everyone would be sacrificing something tonight. The demons were his contribution.

A light wind rose. The full moon smiled down on them. Five of his best mages, including Menno and Leon, stood at intervals around the great pyre that was now piled high with human, demon and forest sacrifices. Archers waited with flaming arrows to light the bonfire.

Menno's voice rose in the silence. He sang the ancient words of the gadzic—words put down in blood on pages made from the skins of humans by their ancestors. Ichovidar could feel heavy magic in the song and he added his voice. The other mages joined it, filling it with harmonies and power.

Magic swirled around them like fog. Archers launched their burning arrows. They hit the prepared logs and kindled the first flames. The krowa began to panic. Why could the damned humans never be still? Their yelling and thrashing wouldn't diminish the power of the rite but they ruined the aesthetic of the occasion.

One of the demons bellowed as it began to roast. The metal cage warded with runes would keep the demon contained until it died. There would be no chance for it to jump into a krowa host.

Ichovidar blocked the noise and focused on the chant as it rose to a crescendo. Krowa screams filled in the harmony, and flames brought the sweet smell of burning flesh and wood.

The bonfire exploded.

Ichovidar fell backward in the blast wave, light and heat washing over him. His head hit the ground, and time suddenly had no meaning. The world was dark and hot and full of pain.

He had no idea how long he lay there. When the night stopped spinning, he pushed up on one elbow. Sound seemed to be a solid thing in his ears, and he tasted blood. He wiped tears from his eyes. The stink of burned hair and skin filled his nose. His ribs ground painfully in his chest, but the wounds were minor and already healing.

The bonfire had been razed to the ground. The krowa, kindling and demons were nothing but ash and bone. The five mages lay dead. That was a shame, but they'd known it was a risk.

The explosion had blasted burning wood and body parts into the forest and now the trees were alight. Good. Let it all burn.

He felt a growing sense of wonder and urgency. The gadzic had worked. He felt it in his blood.

"You!" He pointed to Waldar then to the stone obelisk. "Climb up there and fetch me my prize."

Waldar gaped at the burning hot obelisk but wisely kept his mouth shut. He tore the singed robe off a dead mage to wrap his hands. Even so protected, he screamed as he gripped the first scorching hot rung. But still he climbed. Wind blew smoke around the obelisk. Waldar coughed and sobbed but continued. Ichovidar grew impatient for his prize.

When Waldar finally fell to the ground, the rags on his hands had burned away. So had much of his skin, but the spirit jar lay on a cord around his neck like a jewel.

Ichovidar grabbed it. The jar was no longer than his little finger and shaped like a fang. He held it up in wonder and gazed at the green substance swirling inside it. Such a small thing to hold so much power.

He'd done it. He'd stolen the essence of a god.

The witch god was alive.

Magic in the power of so many deaths had compelled her. She would walk in his world now, and Ichovidar would find her. He would bend her neck over a rock and drink her until she gasped her last breath. And then the opji would truly be free.

Yes, his plans were finally coming to fruition. First the witch god. And then the great breaking. He would have it all.

ON THE WINDY SUMMIT of Mount Trembles, Terra woke under the full moon, naked and cold and very, very afraid.

October 13, 2084
Dorion Park

I lugged a box of books from my van and dumped it just inside the front door. Shar came tumbling over the carpet with Holly right behind her. My daughter flung arms around my legs and shouted, "Mama!" The shar-lil hopped on her pudgy feet, waiting to be lifted up.

It was the best welcome home ever.

Holly's blond curls were a snarled mess and her cheeks were an over-heated pink as if she'd been wrestling. Standing on four sturdy legs, Shar was as tall as my knee. Her round lattice-work shell protected a body covered in sleek brown fur with big intelligent eyes and a three-pronged snout.

I knelt down to hug them both. "Shouldn't you two be studying with Mister Ludger?"

The puckwudgie in question, sauntered around the corner of the fireplace that filled the center of the living room. He wore his usual waistcoat that had seen better days and short pants that showed off hairy feet and ankles. His features were goblin-like but with paler skin and large ears that dipped at the tips.

He bowed. "Mistress Kyra."

Ludger had been tutoring Shar since we returned from Bosk with Holly in September, but I couldn't convince him to let go of this formal greeting, which was odd, considering his penchant for stealing from us. To be fair, he seemed to suffer from a compulsion, as if his fingers nicked silverware, small statues or anything not bolted down without his brain's permission. He usually brought his stolen booty back the next day, so I mostly overlooked this foible because he was an excellent teacher.

"We're finished for the day," he said. "They have no attention for studies, so I let them tumble for a piece."

That explained Holly's hot and scruffy appearance.

"Okay, thanks. I'll take them out for some fresh air after dinner." I paused. "How are things going at the camp?"

Other than tutoring, Ludger had become our de facto estate manager since the goblins had left. He was overseeing the few refugees who had made camp outside our ward. These were mostly displaced homesteaders that Mason or I had invited to join our coming fight with the opji.

The vampires had been burning forests, killing homesteaders and taking captives for their krowa breeding pens for years. The homesteaders were scared, angry and lost. None of them needed much persuading to kill vampires.

"Most are settling in nicely." Ludger's fingers brushed over a soapstone sculpture of a bear on the table beside the front door. "Your Cricket friend arrived with a couple of hidebehinds. I gave them space near the apple orchard to settle in."

The hidebehinds would be a nice addition to my budding militia.

"Okay. Let me know if you run short of supplies." An army runs on its stomach. I'd been worried about being able to support any sized squad for long, but this morning I'd received an unexpected windfall courtesy of Nesi's estate.

Ludger said his goodbyes and slipped out the door. The soapstone bear went with him.

I hefted the box of books and set it on the desk. I really wanted to dig into it and see what treasures it held, but Holly was clinging to my pant leg and whining while Shar butted the back of my ankles like a goat.

Raven appeared in the hallway that led to our bedrooms. Since the summer, he'd sprouted like a sunflower. He now topped six feet. His black hair was glossy and hung in shaggy curls past his chin. The one white lock at his forehead gave him a distinguished air beyond his fifteen and a half years. Princess, our hell hound, followed him with a yawn.

"I'm finished my homework. What's for dinner?" He swiped the bangs from his eyes. I wished he would let me cut them.

"Smells like spaghetti to me. There are more boxes like this in the van. Can you bring in a couple? I'll find out about supper."

Raven ducked outside without a coat. I bit my tongue before cautioning him about the cold. He was old enough to judge the weather for himself.

Sigh. Being a parent to an almost-man had just as many pitfalls as parenting a toddler. There were just different traps to fall into.

Dutch, our live-in man-Friday, came down the stairs and headed for the kitchen. "Spaghetti okay for supper?" he said over his shoulder. Holly started screaming "Spetti! Spetti!"

"Sure." I grabbed one book from the box and followed Dutch into the kitchen. Holly climbed onto a chair and reached for the bowl of apples in the middle of the table.

"Spaghetti first." I pushed the bowl out of her reach. I tied a bib around her neck and settled her in the seat. Dutch placed a bowl and spoon in front of her and she immediately dug in. Shar, who didn't eat any food as far as I could tell, tumbled away and bumped right into Jacoby. The dervish appeared bleary eyed and rumpled.

"Were you napping?" I asked.

"Uh-huh." He yawned and climbed onto a chair. Holly flung a spoonful of spaghetti that smacked Jacoby in the face. He just scooped up the noodles and swallowed them.

Raven returned just as Dutch was serving up plates of steaming noodles and sauce for the rest of us.

When I'd first moved in with Mason, I'd resisted the idea of having someone cook and clean for me. It had seemed decadent to relinquish those chores, but Dutch was a much better cook than me, and I'd learned to appreciate his quiet efficiency rather than tiptoe around him. And his wild boar bolognese could win awards.

I thanked him with a smile as Dutch sat with his own plate. We wouldn't wait for Mason. He had a big day in Parliament and I didn't expect him home any time soon.

During dinner, Raven chatted about his new homework project, an alchemical design for a water diviner. Then Raven and Dutch talked about Elf Stones, their favorite online game. Holly chanted a new rhyme that Ludger had taught her and Jacoby imitated her. I followed the conversation with only half my attention. My left hand kept straying to the book that lay on the table. My fingers caressed the leather cover. A symbol was burned into it, a tangle of vines with serpent heads. The symbol meant nothing to me, but it felt…important, the way a crest stamped in wax feels important. And the book had magical weight. It was subtle, like it was intentionally minding its own business, but I keened power in those pages.

Holly flung a wad of noodles that landed on the book. I winced and brushed the mess aside. Oh, how Nesi would rant if he saw his library so sorely abused.

There comes a tipping point in any meal with a toddler when more food ends up outside the plate than in the mouth. That's when you know dinner is over.

"Let's get you cleaned up." I rinsed a cloth in warm water while Raven and Dutch cleared the table. I was mopping up Holly's fingers and face, the floor, table and chair, when Raven said, "Wow! Look at those snowflakes. They're huge!"

From my crouch, I turned to the big bay window. The sun hadn't yet set, but the evening was gray and fat snowflakes drifted down. They were already covering the patio stones.

Jacoby rushed over to press long fingers against the glass patio door. "Snows!"

"It's a bit early, isn't it?" Raven asked.

I nodded. "The weather has been weird. It probably won't stick around."

Holly squirmed out of her seat and joined Jacoby at the window.

"Fwakes! Fwakes!"

Gods my kid had a set of lungs to rival the gods'. I glanced at Nesi's book. All I wanted was to sit and sift through my unexpected treasure trove.

Holly's screams ratcheted up a level. Shar hopped up and down, adding her impatience to the mix.

"All right! But we're not going anywhere until you settle down," I admonished.

Holly held in shrieks and breath until her face turned red. All the leaves on the nearby spider plant shot straight into the air.

I sighed. We needed to work on patience and control.

"I can take them out," Raven said. "You sit and read that book you're so curious about."

I could have kissed him. "You are a saint! I will sing your praises to the god of…saints!"

Raven laughed. "You're so weird."

The next ten minutes were devoted to encasing an impatient toddler in a snowsuit, boots, hat and mitts. Whenever we danced this dance, she seemed to grow more limbs. By the time I had her wrangled into her clothes, I was sweating and Holly wanted to take everything off.

Raven popped on a coat and didn't bother with boots or a hat. Again, I decided it wasn't a hill to die on, and motioned him out the door.

"Not too long," I called after them. "It's nearly bedtime for Holly."

Raven raised a hand in acknowledgment. His other one clasped Holly's mittened hand as she navigated the slippery steps.

A few minutes later, I had the house to myself, except for the cats. Grim and Willow had ignored all the commotion and slept by the warm hearth. There was nothing for me to do but pour a glass of wine and curl up beside the fire with my book.

Dutch passed through the living room as I dragged one of the boxes toward the couch.

"Do you need help moving those to the basement?" he asked.

"Not yet, I need to go through them. They're from Nesi. It seems I inherited everything in his shop."

Dutch raised one eyebrow, then grinned. "No wonder you were so distracted through dinner."

"Yep." I plunked myself on the couch and raised the book. Dutch took the hint and left me to my reading. I ran my fingers over the cover again anticipating the wonders inside those pages. I had dozens, possibly hundreds of books to go through, and each one would be an adventure.

Nesi had owned a shop of arcane goods, books and creatures in Abbott's Agora Market. I'd been going to him for years to re-home certain critters, buy specialized feed, and gather information. He'd thought I was a princess from a distant galaxy. I'd thought of him as more than an acquaintance but not exactly a friend. It turned out he didn't have any living family, so he'd left me his entire estate which included books, trinkets, gems and a decent sum of money.

Nesi's lawyer had put all his effects in a storage unit, and this morning, after I got over the shock when she read the will, she gave me the key.

The storage garage was piled floor to ceiling with boxes, and I'd selected a few to bring home and sort through. I planned to sell most of the gems and artifacts. They would go a long way to equipping and feeding our growing army, and I thought Nesi would approve. But mostly, I wanted to get my hands on his books. Nesi had the best occult library in the city, but he'd been miserly about sharing them.

Now they were all mine.

I gently opened the cover, mindful of not cracking the spine. The ink of the hand-written text was faded and brownish-red like old blood. I flipped through it looking at the few sketches. These were arcane symbols that ranged across a variety of cultures. I recognized an Egyptian ankh, an ouroboros and a sun cross. Others were a mystery to me.

Hmm. This would be harder than I thought. I didn't recognize the language. I wasn't even sure it was all the same language. I'd need to find someone I trusted to translate. Maybe I could ask Almarick, the priest from the New Terran Church. He might at least recognize the language, but I wasn't ready to entrust Nesi's library with anyone yet. Not until I had a better understanding of its secrets.

I closed the book and rested my hand on its cover as if I could absorb some of those secrets by touch. The next book in the bunch was a straightforward grimoire with some odd spells. I flipped through the pages, reading ingredients for a spell that would turn your lover's feet into snakes. I wasn't sure why anyone would want to do that. Another potion touted its benefits as "healing the humors and purging bile."

I put that one on the dubious pile. It was more of a collector's item than a book with any practical use.

The next book was a treatise on weapons, specifically knives. It was written in old French, but I understood most of the text. I spent a few minutes admiring detailed sketches of beautiful blades.

The front door was thrust open and a tumble of kids and critters burst in. I glanced out the window, shocked to see the sun had already set. I'd lost nearly an hour with my nose in the books.

Raven's shoes and pants were soaked up to the knees. The fur on Princess's butt and legs was crusted with ice balls. Holly's cheeks were bright red and snot glistened on her lips and chin. Only Shar seemed unaffected by the cold and wet. Snow slid right off her otter-like pelt and she was snug inside her shell.

I sent Raven to get changed. Jacoby went with him to help soak the ice off Princess. The cold seemed to invigorate Shar and she rolled around my feet like a drunken bowling ball. Holly fussed while I undressed her. She was tired. As I stood her up to pull off her coat, she thrust her head onto my shoulder, smearing snot and tears onto my sweater.

This was why I didn't have nice things.

"How about a hot toddy before bed?" I smoothed damp curls from her face.

"Toddy?" Her expression perked up.

In a world where chocolate was more expensive than gold, we adapted. Holly's favorite come-in-from-the-cold drink was warm milk with a dash of honey and nutmeg.

"Come on." I took her tiny hand in mine, intending to lead her into the kitchen but she suddenly went rigid. Shar stopped mid-roll, then resumed tumbling at a frantic pace, bouncing off furniture and the fieldstone hearth. Holly started to cry. Every plant in the house stood on end.

And then I keened it too. Not magic, exactly, but…something.

Outside, the banshee wailed.

2

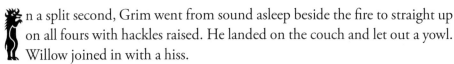n a split second, Grim went from sound asleep beside the fire to straight up on all fours with hackles raised. He landed on the couch and let out a yowl. Willow joined in with a hiss.

Outside, Gita's cry quickly escalated to something that could break sound barriers.

Raven rushed out of his room, a towel in one hand and his wet hair sticking up.

"What's going on?"

"I don't know," I yelled over the noise of screaming toddler and banshee. "Stay with the kids!"

I threw on a jacket and ran outside.

Wind thrust me back toward the house, and I fought against it to reach the driveway. The snow had stopped. Clouds scuttled across the sky, but the full moon haloed the barn in silver light.

And perched right on the peak was my banshee with her head tilted back and long hair thrashing in the wind.

Her voice filled the night. Thunder cracked. It sounded like a mountain breaking. Clouds slid over the moon. I lost sight of Gita, but her cry lingered on.

If my agoraphobic banshee was standing on a roof, singing the song of her people, something was terribly wrong.

Angus, the Captain of the Guardian gargoyles, ran through the front door of the gatehouse and joined me on the driveway.

"By the gods, that woman can scream. What's she on about?"

"I don't know." Banshees usually wailed to signal a death in the family, but Gita had proven in the past that her voice was more than a prophecy. It could be a weapon too.

I keened an odd and shivering upset in the natural order. And Gita's keening was better than mine. To her, the sensation must have felt like a punch in the gut.

I called out but she ignored me. Her cries scratched on my psyche like nails on a blackboard. I was just about to get out the ladder and climb up to her when the ground began to shake.

Angus stumbled backward. I grabbed his arm as the earth rose under my foot, knocking me off balance. Worms, centipedes and beetles erupted from the snowy dirt and swarmed over my shoes. The ground was alive with writhing, glistening bodies.

Angus made a retching sound and danced to shake bugs off his feet. Rain pelted us, cold and sharp as ice. A flock of geese took off from their migratory roost in the old cemetery and filled the night sky with honks and flashing wings.

I lurched back to the door as the ground gave one last shake.

"Is everyone okay?" Inside, picture frames had fallen from the walls and ornaments toppled from the mantle. Raven had his arms around Holly, Shar and Jacoby, like a shield. Princess stood guard by his side. Her lip curled and a growl rumbled from her chest.

"We're okay." Raven looked panicked but he was holding it together for the kids.

"Stay here."

I ran back outside to find the other Guardians had arrived from the main gate.

I grabbed Berto's arm and pointed to the roof of the barn.

"Gita's up there!" I yelled to be heard above the screaming storm. Berto's duck-billed face was hard to read, but I thought he looked worried. He crouched, then launched into the air, showing off an impressive wingspan. He swooped over the barn, grabbed Gita in his arms, and landed on the churned up snow.

He let her go, then caught her up again when Gita crumpled to the ground. I ran to her side. Her wails had quieted to soft blubbering that I could barely hear over the wind and rain.

"Get her inside."

Berto picked her up again and ran for the house. I followed, slipping on the wet ground. The night crawlers had already sunk back into the earth. I had no time to wonder about the significance of it all. My only thoughts were for Gita, whose head flopped over Berto's arm.

I ran ahead to open the door.

Raven was still protecting the kids, but Holly had stopped crying and even the cats had decided the evening's excitement was over. They curled up beside the hearth again, butt to butt, though Grim's eyes didn't close.

"Raven, can you put Holly to bed? Maybe read her a storybook?"

Raven nodded.

"I'll be down to say goodnight as soon as I get Gita settled."

"Will she be okay?" His expression told me that he worried about the old banshee as much as I did.

"She'll be fine. The earthquake just upset her."

Upstairs, Berto had laid Gita on the bed in the spare room next to Dutch's bedroom. He watched her with worry plain on his face. The gargoyles had adopted Gita as their grandmother and honorary Guardian. They would do anything to keep her safe.

Gita lay on her side, curled in a ball. Her eyes were open, but her expression was blank.

"Please ask Dutch for some towels," I said. Berto nodded and ducked out of the room.

Gita began to shake. Gently, I sat her up and wrapped the blanket around her thin shoulders. Dutch arrived with a pile of towels and set them on the bed.

"I'll have tea ready in a few minutes."

I nodded my thanks and he left.

Gita seemed lost in some inward-gazing dream. Her lips moved but no words came out. Tears mixed with rain ran down her craggy cheeks.

I unfolded a towel and dried her hands, face and hair as best I could, then I unwrapped her and pulled off the soggy dress. She was painfully frail underneath. I lifted her arms into a clean, dry shirt, fitted her legs into sweatpants, and pulled fluffy socks onto her feet. She let me manipulate her limbs like she was a living doll, not fighting me, but not helping either.

When she was dry and dressed, I bundled her in a fresh blanket and propped her up in the bed.

I took her wrinkled hands in mine. My banshee was ancient. There was no overlooking that fact anymore.

"What happened?" I brushed a thin strand of green hair from her face. Her eyes finally focused on me. "Did someone die?" I prodded, not really wanting an answer. My family was home and safe—everyone but Mason.

I pulled out my widget to call him but Gita gripped my hand. She pulled me close to whisper, "Death, yes…but *life* too! She's coming."

"Who?"

But that was all I could get out of her. She wilted against the pillows and her eyes fluttered closed.

She's coming.

I had no idea what that meant, but I was more worried about the waxy hue of her complexion.

Dutch returned with tea. I held the cup to Gita's lips. She roused enough to take a sip, then turned her face away. Her eyes closed again and her breath made soft keening sounds like wind through the trees.

I let her sleep and called Mason. The call went right to voicemail. I tried not to panic.

Jacoby appeared in the doorway, clutching Shar in his arms.

I patted the bed. He climbed up beside Gita.

"Is Gita-lady sicks?"

"I don't think so. I think she's just tired. And being out in the cold was too much for her."

"I's tired too."

He curled up in the crook of Gita's legs. Shar rolled. All four feet stuck straight up and I kissed the liver-colored toe pads.

"You stay here with Gita while I go check on Holly."

Jacoby made a sleepy noise. I turned off the light, but left the door open.

I met Raven as he tiptoed out of Holly's room.

"She went out like a light," he said.

"The fresh air and then all that commotion did her in. Thanks for helping out." I squeezed his arm.

"No problem." He smiled and ducked his head. "What was that all about anyway? I've never seen Gita react like that. Or Holly. Was it just an earthquake?"

"I'm not sure." Both Gita and Holly had off-the-charts keening. It was possible the earthquake had simply overwhelmed their senses.

We returned to the living room and flipped on the vid screen above the desk. The news was full of interviews with people retelling their experience with the earthquake that had rocked the ward earlier that evening. After watching them for a few minutes, I realized they had nothing of merit to add and I turned it off.

Raven yawned. "I'm going to bed."

I'd tried to call Mason twice more with no answer.

I sat and opened Nesi's book again, then closed it and walked to the window by the front door. The night was calm. I straightened a frame on the wall, then made a circuit of the room, straightening toppled knick-knacks.

Grim's thoughtful gaze followed me as I paced and fidgeted. I glared at him and his green eyes slow-blinked.

"You have something to say?" I asked.

"Worrying won't make him come home any faster."

I let out a snort. Cat logic.

"What you should be worrying about is what it all means."

"And you would know?"

"I might." He licked a paw as if he didn't have a care in the world. I resisted the urge to shake him. Finally, he said, "It was a cracking. A fracture."

That told me precisely...nothing.

"A cracking of what? An egg? My last shred of patience?"

"You humans are adorable. You fill the space around you with trinkets and walls. You make nests of blankets and pillows to hide in at night, as if any of that can keep out the real monsters."

"Grim," I growled out his name. "If you know something, tell me now."

The grimalkin sighed as if he was sorely put upon.

"That wasn't an earthquake."

"Thanks. I figured that much already. Have you ever experienced anything like it before?"

"Once, in the Nether where such things are accepted. As I said, it was a cracking of the empyrean." He held up a paw when I tried to protest. "A fracture in both time and space. It was the birth of a god."

"A god?" By the All-father, we didn't need another one of those hanging around. And besides, all gods were not created equal. There were pantheons filled with creatures like Odin, Zeus or Ngai. These were human creations, but no less powerful for that. Faith was potent magic and it gave power to the gods it created. But there were other gods who existed outside of human belief. They just were. Their might shifted winds and tides. It shaped mountains and drained seas. They existed whether anyone believed in them or not.

Terra was such a god. And she had proven that she didn't need human reverence in order to remake the world. Shar was a great spirit too. Her magic would eventually be too big to fit into our world. What if this newly birthed god was like that? What if this night had borne something immense and terrifying?

The front door opened. I jumped and hugged my arms around myself. Mason stood in the foyer, shaking rain from his hair.

"I'm sorry. They closed the bridge after the earthquake. Apparently one of the Apex towers was damaged and the phone lines were down."

I didn't care that he was soaking wet. I rushed over and laid my head on his shoulder. He wrapped his arms around me and we just stood there, quietly enjoying the closeness. After the past year, I would never take any moment with him for granted again.

He kissed the top of my head and pushed me gently away to see my face. "Was anyone hurt?"

I shook my head. "Just some upset. Gita was affected the worst. She's sleeping upstairs."

"And you?" He gripped my shoulders and peered into my face.

"I'm fine. Just wound up." I smiled. "Better now that you're home safe."

"And I have news."

I squinted at him. "Good or bad?"

"A bit of both, I guess." He rubbed the back of his neck and I knew he'd had a wearying day.

"Bad news first."

"I resigned. It's official. Ramona will take over as Prime Minister until the next election."

Oof. I'd been expecting this, but it still hit me like a punch to the gut.

Mason had been away from Parliament for months while the demon ran around in his body and again when we'd traveled to Bosk to bring our daughter home. The Alchemists had managed without him, but they'd lost confidence in his commitment to the party, and a minority faction had forced his resignation.

It was a shame. Mason hadn't wanted to be Prime Minister. Oscar and I sort of browbeat him into it, but once he took office, he warmed to the job. He made a difference. He shaped party policy to be more inclusive and more forward-thinking. Alchemists were notorious navel-gazers. Instead of only reacting to problems, Mason had forced them to become part of the conversation that looked for change. I knew he would miss it.

"So what's the good news."

He grinned. It changed his appearance completely. The perpetual crease between his brows smoothed out and a light danced in his eyes.

"I did it. I pushed through that piece of legislation we talked about. My last act as Prime Minister was to free the bluecaps from Grandill Prison."

My grin matched his and I hugged him. We'd been working on this bill for weeks.

Fifty years ago, the bluecaps had been imprisoned for treason when they quite literally undermined the creation of the ward by digging a tunnel under it to the outside world. They'd been sentenced to 151 years on the prison island, a punishment that did not fit the crime.

"There's something else." Mason's expression darkened again. "Is Raven still awake?"

"He said he was going to bed, but he's probably playing Elf Stones on his widget. Why?"

"One-eyed Jack died."

"Oh." I didn't know what else to say, except "We'll tell him in the morning."

I thought of how helpful and grown-up Raven had been lately, but he was still just a kid. We'd let him have one more night as a child before we told him his father was dead.

CHAPTER

3

Two days later, I woke early sensing that shadows loomed on the horizon, but in this moment I was content. I snuggled into my blankets, willing the peace to continue. Mason was sprawled on his stomach with one arm dangling over the edge of the bed. He was always a furnace at night and had flung off his half of the covers. This left me with a clear view of his tawny, muscled back and boxers pulled tight over his butt. It was a nice butt. My fingers trailed along the waistband of his shorts, considering the idea of waking him up.

I let him sleep. He'd earned it.

My eyes roved over his smooth unmarked skin. A few months ago, his whole body and head had been covered in black tattoos, but when Terra returned him to me, they'd been erased. All except one on his wrist. For whatever reason, Terra had left that as a reminder.

I didn't pretend to understand the ways of gods.

That brought back thoughts of the earthquake, which led me to worrying about Gita, and all contentment slipped away.

I rose and pulled on a robe and slippers. I peeked into Holly's room first. She was still sound asleep. Shar had crept into Holly's bed during the night. As I entered, she yawned and rolled over, snuffling and shuffling the blankets into a cozy ball. I quietly closed the door and headed for the kitchen where I found Gita at the table with Raven. I glanced out the dark window then back to Raven.

Yesterday, we'd broken the news about Jack's death, and he'd taken it

29

surprisingly well. Apparently, Thunderbird had already told him. I didn't really understand his relationship with the Great Spirit that was both part of him and a separate entity that he could converse with. However the relationship worked, it seemed to bring him comfort and confidence. Even so, if my teenager was awake this early, something dire was happening.

"It's Saturday and it's still dark out. Why are you up?" I asked.

"I just thought I could, you know, help with chores. Get them done faster." He took a bite of toast and tossed the crust at Princess who snapped it out of the air like a croc snatching a bird.

I squinted at Raven. He gazed at me with innocent eyes.

Something was going on here. Raven never volunteered for chores.

"You promised him some driving time today." Gita's voice was raspy.

Of course. Raven would turn sixteen in March. He'd just earned his learner's permit and was eager to start driving. The gods were shaking the world, but teenagers were still teenagers. The thought actually gave me some small comfort.

The world would go on.

"I'll take you out after breakfast. But that means you have to help with the feedings, and…"

Raven was already putting on his coat and disappearing out the back door with Princess jumping at his heels.

"…and clean the cages!" I called after him.

Gita sniffed. "I can feed the little ones. Been doing it for almost ten years, you know."

"I know. But I want you to rest today." The memory of Gita's unending wail from two nights ago still brought shivers. She'd slept most of the day yesterday, and I wasn't convinced she was recovered.

"I'd like you to stay inside one more day."

Gita preferred the close walls of her tack room hideout in the barn, but I wanted to keep an eye on her. She poured herself more tea and dumped in a good dollop of honey.

"I'm fine." She lifted her chin. "You don't need to fuss over me."

"Maybe you can help me then. I have boxes and boxes of books to go through."

"Books?" That perked her up.

"Not fiction. As far as I know. Mostly arcane stuff. Some grimoires, journals, histories. That sort of thing."

"I suppose I could spare a few hours."

She made it sound like her dance card was overflowing, but I let it go. I'd learned a long time ago it was better to give in to Gita's little illusions, but I wasn't forgetting about her weird rooftop serenade.

"Can you tell me what happened? What made you go up on the roof?" I asked softly. When she didn't answer, I pushed. "Grim called it a cracking of the empyrean."

"That's as good a description as any." Gita sipped her tea and watched the sky lighten outside the window.

"You said it was a death but also a birth. How is that possible?"

"Don't know." She sniffed. "I felt the land die. And I felt it reborn. At the same time." Another longer sniffle. "It shouldn't be possible, but there it is." She laid her open hands on the table and stared at them as if the answers could be found in the lines of her skin.

The death and birth of the land. Of Earth. Could she mean Terra? I sighed. Of course it was about Terra.

Critter wrangler rule twenty-four: When the gods come knocking, don't answer the door.

I'd last seen the god on the summit of Mount Trembles where the veils between her world and ours overlapped. She'd given me my heart's desire. She'd returned Mason from a hellish captivity in the bloodstone—returned him whole and demon free, but this act was a bartering, not a gift. In exchange, I pledged my life and Mason's to her service to defeat the opji vampires who were destroying the forest and enslaving humans.

And now, according to Gita, Terra was dead. And not dead. Like the cat in that famous experiment. How would I know which was true? And did it matter? Did Terra's death relieve me of my duty to stop the opji?

No.

It was that simple. Terra wanted the opji dead, but so did I.

Holly started chattering in her room, and a moment later, Mason entered the kitchen carrying her with Shar tumbling along by his feet. Jacoby arrived right behind them, yawning and scratching his ear with one long finger.

Holly saw me and started to squirm in Mason's grip. Her little arms shot straight out, reaching for me, and her whines ratcheted up to cries.

My heart twisted. While I was off chasing the demon that wore Mason's skin, my grandmother had taken Holly to Bosk, the dryad stronghold. Since returning home, my toddler had been experiencing some separation anxiety. Added to that was the burden of guilt Mason still felt over the violence the demon had committed while wearing his body. His mind told him they'd been separate entities, but his muscles and skin remembered every life he'd taken, every hurt he'd caused. For weeks, he wouldn't even pick up Holly because some part of him feared he would hurt her. Holly felt that rejection. She wasn't able to articulate it, but she felt it.

Mason was working through his issues, but it was slow going, and when Holly pushed him away for me, I felt guilty on several fronts. But Mason was a grown-up. He would deal with his feelings. Holly was a toddler fueled by emotions she didn't understand and had no tools to cope with. So I took her in my arms and soothed her. Mason's expression was carefully neutral as he turned for the pantry and fridge to take out muffins, fruit and cheese.

Breakfast wasn't a quiet affair. Holly chattered the whole time, and Jacoby regaled us with a very long-winded description of his dreams.

"And then the pooka chases me. I rans away and away and away. But I wasn't scareds. Not one bits!"

With a mouth full of muffin, I made a noncommittal noise. Shar's shell rumbled as she rolled across the floor.

Mason turned on the vid screen beside the stove and the low burble of the newscast added to the noise. Scenes from the recent earthquake flashed across the screen. Montreal was still cleaning up after that upheaval.

"I was thinking of visiting Almarick," I said. "I'd like his take on the pseudo-earthquake."

"Good idea," Mason said, "but you should wait a few days. The church is probably inundated with panicked pilgrims today."

I nodded. "I promised to take Raven driving. Maybe you could watch Holly this morning?" My pitch rose at the end of that question, as if it were a painful thought. Seven months ago, I wouldn't have had to ask.

He glanced uncertainly at our offspring who was currently smearing blueberries in her hair. I could see the calculations going on in his head. His dark eyes softened as Holly grinned and smashed a fistful of berries into her mouth, but the line of his shoulders never relaxed. His posture was battle-ready all the time, like he could just as easily take up a sword as a cereal spoon.

"I guess she needs a bath," he said.

"Baff!" Holly screamed and flung blueberries across the floor. Shar pounced on the mashed blueberries and snuffled them, interested in the smell, if not the taste.

Sigh. "You get the bath ready. I'll pick up blueberry mash before Dutch sees what we did to his clean floor."

Mason picked up Holly. She screeched, "Mama! Mama!" and Mason's back tensed, but he was made of stern stuff and he kept walking. Soon I heard the sound of bathwater flowing and Mason's deep voice as he sang her a silly French song about a lonely beaver.

Listening to his deep voice and Holly's shrieks of delight, I knew my family would be just fine.

Driving lessons went well, mostly because there was no traffic on the service roads around Dorion Park. Raven easily picked up the skills for zooming around curves and skidding to a stop. I hoped he'd eventually temper those with common sense.

When he finally parked the van beside the barn, I inspected myself in the mirror on the visor.

"What's the matter?" Raven asked.

"I'm looking for new gray hairs."

"Aww. It wasn't that bad. Driving is just like flying."

"No, it really isn't."

"Whatever. Same time tomorrow? I've got homework to finish."

"Sure. Help me bring in some of these boxes first."

I had homework of my own in Nesi's stuff.

Raven grabbed a stack of two boxes with little effort, while I lugged in a third. Raven plunked his boxes on the floor beside the other three before heading into the kitchen for homework fuel in the form of Dutch's fresh-baked oatmeal cookies.

I'd already set Gita up in the spare room with a pile of books to go through. I added another few to her stack from one of the new boxes.

The next box was nearly too heavy to lift onto the desk. Until now, the boxes had been made of plastic. This one was a sturdy wooden crate. It had a tight fitting lid with a metal latch, and the number thirty-one was burned into the top and on all sides. I glanced at the other boxes and realized the plastic ones also had small numbers taped to them.

Inside the wooden crate I found three black stones. Two were almost as big as bowling balls. The third was about the size and shape of a coffee mug. I picked it up and hefted it in my hand. It was a lodestone.

Mason came from the hallway that led to our bedrooms. I looked up distractedly when I heard him, and then lost all interest in magic relics. He wore only thin cotton pants and a white t-shirt. His hair was damp from the shower and tousled over his forehead. He couldn't have looked sexier if he'd been dressed in a designer suit.

He came over, wrapped his arms around my waist, and nuzzled the space between my chin and ear. His skin felt like velvet against mine.

"You shaved!"

"Mmm. Didn't want you to suffer through beard burn." He turned me around and kissed me.

"You plan on doing a lot of that today?"

"A lot." He went back to nuzzling the secret places on my neck and collar bone. My hand holding the lodestone went limp and it fell to the desk with a thump.

"So Holly's finally napping?"

"Oh, yes. I bribed her with a second reading of The Monster at the End of This Book, and Grover knocked her right out. And that means," he paused to nip my ear which made me squirm like it always did, "we have at least an hour to ourselves before she wakes up shouting for attention."

"Mmm." I turned so he could circle me in his arms. He pulled me against his chest. His mouth continued to find little caverns of sensitivity along my neck, places I hadn't even known I possessed until I met Mason. A little thrill zinged through me. A few months ago, I thought I might never feel those arms around me again, never feel the heat of his mouth on me, or...

"Oh, get a room already." Raven crossed in front of the hearth making for his bedroom. He balanced a glass of milk on a plate piled high with cookies. The kid ate more than an ogre. He also wore a look of pure adolescent disgust that was meant to shame any parent into celibacy.

"Mind your business, whelp!" Mason picked me up and set me on the desk. "And if you don't hurry, you might witness the conception of a little brother or sister."

"Ewww!" Raven made a face then grinned. Of all of us, Raven was the one Mason seemed to feel most comfortable around since his return. They spent hours together in the alchemy lab in our basement. I suspected that Raven's new Thunderbird magic had something to do with it. Mason probably felt like Raven was safe. Even a demon wouldn't mess with Thunderbird.

But, of course, there was no more demon. I sometimes had to remind myself of that fact. I suspected Mason reminded himself daily, if not hourly.

Raven pretended to hurry from the room with a horrified look on his face. I hid a giggle against Mason's shoulder.

"That ought to keep him from barging into our bedroom at night," Mason said.

"Now if only you could teach that to Holly."

"Maybe we'll save the birds and the bees talk for her fourth birthday."

He kissed me, taking his time to make me feel his need, but also his control. There would be no daytime nookie on the desk. Sigh. It was the price of parenthood.

He pulled away and smiled, though his lips dipped downward at the edges as if the smile was against his better judgment.

"Thank you for knowing what I need better than I do." He kissed my forehead.

"What do you mean?"

"I mean that you knew Holly would eventually break down my reserve."

"You can't resist that face for long."

"It's just hard for me to let go of the feeling that I might hurt her. That my mere presence is a danger."

I turned and laid my head on his chest. "It's not and you won't. Kester confirmed it. The demon is gone."

Kester was our friend from Manhattan and the only other person we knew who'd been possessed by a demon. In fact, Kester still fought his demon every day.

"I know." Mason spoke into my hair and pressed his lips to my head. Something was digging into my hip and I started to squirm.

"What's that?" He picked up the rock.

I jumped off the desk.

"A lodestone, I think. Aren't they used in alchemy a lot?"

"Yeah. Magnets are useful in some recipes."

"You can have it." I paused, a new worry making an appearance in my mind. "But you should know that these boxes are from Nesi."

His smile froze.

"What do you mean?"

I took the lodestone and placed it on the desk. "I meant to tell you yesterday…" I trailed off and glanced at the two open boxes and a third on the floor.

"Kyra, why do we have Nesi's store inventory in our living room." He spoke slowly, like that could forestall the answer he didn't want to hear.

By the One-eyed Father, I hadn't thought this through. What an idiot I was! Of course Mason would be upset by Nesi's stuff—stuff that was only here because Nesi was dead. The demon might have done the deed, but he'd used Mason's hands to do it. Mason's eyes had borne witness. And Mason's heart would never forget.

"It…uh…turns out that Nesi had no family and, surprise! I'm his sole heir."

"You? He left everything to you?"

"Yep. There are more boxes in the van, plus a full storage unit. The entirety of his shop. And some money."

"How much."

"A lot."

Mason hurled the lodestone. It smashed against the hearth and fell to the rug. Willow shot from the chair by the fire. Her feet skittered against hardwood as she barreled from the room.

I turned my shocked stare from the hearth to Mason. Lowered brows hid his eyes in shadow. His hands were fisted at his side as if he contemplated more violence.

But I wasn't afraid of him. Mason would never hurt me. He just needed to remember that himself.

I laid a hand on his chest and he jerked away as if burned.

When he spoke, his tone was a low growl. "I don't want any of that stuff

36

in my house." And then he stalked off to our bedroom and slammed the door.

I reined in the urge to follow. Better to let him cool off and come to the realization that he'd overreacted on his own.

My hands were shaking when I picked up the lodestone. It was intact, but the fieldstone hearth had a jagged chip blasted out of it.

I looked toward our bedroom. The house was silent. I took a deep, steadying breath and forced myself to continue the inventory of Nesi's boxes. The sooner I did that, the sooner those triggers could be hidden away.

The last two were neatly packed with more books. All the spines faced outward for easy reading. I recognized the diary of Maffeo Polo, one of the few in his collection that Nesi had been willing to share with me. As my fingers brushed over the spines, one book tingled across my keening.

That had happened before, last summer when I borrowed the Polo diary. I'd itched to read this mysterious book then, but Nesi had been in the throes of paranoia at the time, and I hadn't wanted to goad him into any more violence.

The book practically vibrated with magic. I plucked it from the box. The spine cracked like old bones when I opened it. Several pages were stuck together and the book opened in the middle to a text written in Franglais— not quite French and not English either, but a garbled version of the two that was understood by most Montrealers. I read the page over, then read it again, trying to focus on the words that seemed to be about a trip through the Inbetween. That meant the book wasn't an antique. My fingers traced a drawing of a river, without taking much in.

I was worried about Mason. I sighed, shut the book and drummed my fingers on the cover. I wouldn't be able to concentrate until I put my mind at ease. Mason had been sulking for long enough. Time to face up to the demons of our own making.

I quietly slipped into the bedroom. He sat in the chair by the window. The afternoon light made his face seem ethereally pale.

"I'm sorry," he said without looking at me.

"I know." I sat on the bed. "Do you remember when the peyochip stung me and you sat in that chair all night until I woke up?"

He nodded.

"You were so mad."

"I hated seeing you hurt."

"But you never left me. I would do that too. For you. I won't leave just because you're hurt."

"I'm trying. I really am. This morning…with Holly…and then with you…it all seemed so normal. I could almost forget. And then something reminds me."

"Nesi."

Finally, he turned to me. His eyes were full of pain. "He begged for his life. My hands were around his throat and he begged me not to kill him."

"Not you—"

"I know. The demon." He waved a hand in the air as if Nesi's true killer was of no consequence. "I just don't need the reminder. That's all. And I don't want us to benefit from Nesi's death. That won't sit well in here." He held a hand over his heart.

"I agree." I sat on his lap and took his hand in mine. "But Nesi left everything to me because he had nobody else, and I'm going to use his gift." I held up a hand as he started to protest. "We have one hell of a fight coming. We'll need an army to defeat the opji. An army needs to be fed. It needs weapons and vehicles. I won't keep the money, but I'll use it to pay for our freedom. And I know Nesi would be proud to be part of that fight."

I let the words sit with him for a moment. Then he nodded.

"I shouldn't have brought the boxes here," I said, "but I really need to catalogue them. And my office…isn't secure." We'd shied away from talking about Valkyrie Pest Control too, since the demon had burned it to the ground.

Mason dragged a hand through his hair. "I want to apologize for that too."

"Don't. You know…"

"I know. The demon. Not me. I tell myself that a hundred times a day."

"Does it help?"

"Not yet." He gave me a small smile, then reached for my hand. "I promise that as soon as this opji thing is over, I'll build you a new office, bigger and better than before."

I nodded but felt a prickle in my eyes. We both knew there was a good chance we wouldn't be coming home from any battle with the opji.

"In the meantime, why don't you set up in the gatehouse. There's an office that's never used."

"I guess so." Being in the gatehouse with the Guardians was the best solution. It would keep Nesi's affairs out of Mason's sight.

He saw my frown. "I don't mean it like that. I'll help you sort through it, if you need. It'll be good therapy for me. But you need space to sort through his effects."

I looked him in the eye. He meant it. Accepting Nesi's windfall cost him. Sorting through it would be like picking at a scab that would never heal, but he'd do it for me. For us.

"Thanks. There's some heavy-duty stuff in those boxes and I could use an alchemist's opinion."

Our sleepy-eyed toddler appeared in the doorway along with our shar-lil, the little world seed. Holly took her fingers out of her mouth long enough to shout "Daddy!" Shar bounced. And for the next hour, while my little family had tickle fights and cuddles in the big bed, we forgot all about demons and gods and vampires.

CHAPTER

4

Our house had once been an inn along the old highway. Over a hundred years ago, a more modern highway had become the main thoroughfare into Montreal and the inn had been forgotten. Mason claimed it after the Flood Wars, and the Guardians moved into the Gothic-looking gatehouse built near the property's original entrance.

I hauled one of my many boxes up the two stairs leading to the main doors of the house. It was dark inside. The day was overcast and no one had bothered to turn on the lights. Gargoyles didn't need light. I dumped the box in the office just off the foyer.

Angus sat by the tall, narrow window in the office. He'd made a good attempt at cleaning out the space for me before the sun turned him to stone, but there was still a lot of dust on the one long table and the empty shelves along two walls. I dumped my box on the table, then went in search of a broom, dustpan, and dusting cloth and found them in a closet off the kitchen.

Back in the office, I chatted to Angus as I worked. His face was turned to take in the pale light from outside. The brambly beard and hair had lightened from woody brown to stone gray, and his eyes had lost their spark of life.

"Thanks for the office space." My voice was a little too loud and a little too cheery in the quiet house. "I'm just going to give the place a quick wipe down before I get started." Even as stone, Angus would hear me.

I hummed a little tune as I swept and tidied. Jacoby arrived, lugging a box of books. I was always amazed at the strength in his slight frame.

"Just put the boxes along there." I pointed to the only wall without shelves.

"We'll use the table to unbox and the shelves for sorting."

"Okey dokeys!" Jacoby skipped out the door.

Finished with my cleaning, I opened the first box. Until now, I'd been just scanning the treasures within, like a kid in a candy shop, jumping from delight to delight, too excited to settle on one. Now it was time to get serious. My inheritance wasn't just about funding the vampire-slaying army. There was an even bigger treasure in these boxes: knowledge. I wasn't sure exactly what I was looking for. A panacea to cure vampirism would be nice. Barring that, a weapon that could take out an entire village of bloodsuckers.

And something for Shar. A talisman that would let my baby stay on earth even as her spirit grew to divine proportions.

I gave a little huff of a laugh. Truly, I wasn't expecting a magic bullet for all my woes, but the books and the artifacts still had to be sorted.

The first box of the day held only books, neatly lined up with spines facing out. I picked one with a soft leather cover embossed with the symbol of Nesi's store. There were dozens of these journals in the box. Nesi obviously referred back to them often because the covers were ragged and discolored. I flipped through the pages of the first one. It was full of odd rantings, poems, drawings and lists of numbers that sometimes went on for pages. I closed it and picked up another. More of the same.

The newest looking book in the bunch was only half full of writing. I turned to the first page to see when he'd started it and stopped. Right there, on the inside flyleaf, it said: For Princess Pleiades, then a line of jumbled numbers and letters.

Princess Pleiades. That's what Nesi called me. He joked that I was royalty from a planet around a distant star. "Joked" was the polite version. He'd been obsessed with the idea, but Nesi's obsessions had been myriad and outrageous and more than a little tongue-in-cheek. I'd never been certain if he was serious or just having a laugh at my expense.

I sighed and set the book on top of the stack. At some point, I'd have to read them all, but I wasn't sure I could survive their contents with my sanity intact. I put the lid on the box as Jacoby came in with another one.

"Put that right on the table," I said. His tongue poked from the corner of his mouth as he hoisted the box. I caught it before it slipped from his fingers and crushed him.

"Why don't you use the wagon from the barn?" Jacoby nodded and hopped away. It must be nice to have so much energy.

I opened the next box. This one was full of office supplies—some precious paper and pens, more blank journals, plastic tags with hemp strings attached and markers. There were even some fresh colored pencils. I put those aside for Holly to enjoy under strict supervision. The rest was full of trinkets, silly things of no real value except that they'd meant something to Nesi, including an old crocheted dog with one ear nearly chewed off and a kitschy tourist-attraction Eiffel Tower from before flash bombs had decimated most of the world's wonders.

I closed that box and picked up the first one Jacoby had brought in. Like the box with the lodestones, it was made of wood. This one had the number twelve burned into it. I opened the latch and pulled back the lid. Magic leaked out like a stench. I slammed the lid and sucked in a breath as I built up my wards. I lifted the lid again and examined the interior of the box. It was lined in null material. Whatever was in here, Nesi wanted it protected. And hidden.

Items were bundled in unbleached cotton rags and nestled in wood shavings to protect them from breakage. I lifted out the first bundle and unwrapped it to find a tiny chalice of dull metal. I suspected that once polished, it would turn out to be silver. A plastic tag hung off it by a hemp string. On the tag, Nesi had scrawled: Waterman Cup, DB: 1879.

Huh.

"What do you think? Is that a date of creation? Or maybe it was a baby gift with a birth date?"

Angus didn't answer, of course.

I picked up another object. It was an ankh about the length of my hand and carved from bone or ivory. Another tag: Amon Cross, DB: 1225.

I continued unpacking and found a heavy velvet bag containing milky gems, an old-fashioned quill, a brass mantle clock, and four bronze shoes from a tiny horse held together with a chain. Each item had a tag attached. Magic slithered from the box, but with my personal wards in place, it was hard to tell which items were the most potent.

Errol could have helped me with that, but the little bodach had gone to the Cape Breton Ward with Cece for an extended visit. He'd promised me it wasn't a permanent vacation, that he'd be back one day. I missed him, but I was glad the old hedge witch had some company.

The last item I unwrapped was a stick, about a foot long and honed to a point like a spear on one end. The other end was an eagle head, made from brass. The tag read Dornud Vidar (Thorn of Vidar) DB: 0953.

Mason arrived while I was still inspecting the stick. Jacoby followed him in. He dumped his box and headed out for more. Mason examined the items spread out on the table.

"Is that a vampire stake?"

I gripped the spike and made a pretend stabbing motion. "I guess so. But look." I gripped the stake and the wood parted at the handle to reveal a wickedly sharp blade. "Pretty fancy for killing vampires. It's got a name and everything." I showed him the tag. "See this? Each of the relics has a tag just like this, with a name and a number. The name is obviously the relic's name, and I thought the number might be a creation date."

Mason shook his head. "It's a database number. We use a similar system on Perrot Island for our relics."

"A database? So there should be a logbook."

"More likely a computer file."

That had me sorting through the box of office supplies again. I pulled out a surprisingly new, high-end laptop. The battery was still good and it turned on without a problem, except for the blinking cursor asking for a password.

"Damn." I almost shut it down again, then remembered the journals. I found the newest one with my name in the flyleaf and typed in the password written below it.

The screen launched into desktop mode.

"It's like he prepared all this for me," I said.

"Maybe he did. Maybe he knew what was coming. You said he ranted a lot. Were those actually rants or glimpses into the future?"

"Mostly, I just thought he was crazy."

Mason rubbed the back of his neck. "One person's crazy is another person's precognition."

"I guess."

Mason frowned. His eyes were dark and guarded. I knew what it cost him to sift through the remnants of Nesi's life, but he'd agreed to help and he wouldn't go back on his word. I dared to hope that the exercise might even prove cathartic.

I opened the applications listing. "Do any of these look like databases to you?"

Mason pointed to an icon. "That one. It's a standard Black Hat database. We use the same program."

I clicked the icon and a blank screen opened. Across the top was a simple menu: Account, Ledger, Help. In the middle of the screen there were three empty fields: Title, Keyword, DB#.

I picked up the ankh first and entered the number 1255.

Nothing happened.

"This is the kind of program that needs a boost," Mason said. He meant a magical boost. I could do that. Alchemists used a magic generating device to boost their computers. I only needed to send a little zing to my fingertip as I hit "Enter" again. Magic pulsed through me and connected us to the lww—the ley-line net. It was like a dark web for those with enough magic to access it. On the lww, you could find black markets in magic relics, spells and potions, chat rooms for fae fetishes, and all manner of arcane listings. Along with the more mundane web, I published my blog to the lww so I could reach those with knowledge of otherworldly beasts.

As soon as I hit "Enter," two listings appeared on the screen below.

Amon Cross. Box 12, 1225.

New World Relics, Anton Osman, published 2043. Box 4, 0560

I clicked the first listing and a pop-up window showed the listing for the Ankh. It included four images of the cross from different angles, then a detailed description, written by Nesi along with the date and manner in which he acquired it.

The second listing brought up a summary of the book, *New World Relics*. Box 4 was still in storage, so I couldn't check on it, but I assumed the volume mentioned the Amon Cross or Nesi wouldn't have linked the two.

We inputted several other relics and found similar entries.

I leaned against the table, already worn out from the morning's work. The extent of Nesi's catalog was starting to feel a bit overwhelming.

"I can't believe Nesi was so diligent about cataloguing all this stuff."

"He had to be," Mason said. "There are potent relics here. He'd have to submit his catalogue to the Black Hat Bureau."

"You mean this database is linked to theirs?"

"I don't think so." He clicked a few keys, delving into the account portion of the program. "No, look. It's housed on a private server. But this database outputs a tidy report that he would be able to submit to the bureau."

"Lucky for us. It'll make investigating his collection a lot easier."

Mason gave me a half-grin. "You think so? How many boxes are there?"

I glanced around the room that was already filling up with boxes. "I have about twenty here and in my van. But there's a whole storage unit full of them." I saw what he meant. It could take months to go through everything. "Maybe we could just start with these boxes. And I'll ask Emil to help with the others. As long as Valkyrie Pest Control is closed, he's got nothing to do anyway."

"And I guess that's our evenings sorted for the next few weeks."

"I'm sorry. But I really think this is important."

Mason pretended a long suffering sigh.

"If we're going to do this, I need coffee."

"Make that two."

It turned out that romantic evenings come in all shapes and sizes. Mason and I enjoyed many, many hours over the next weeks cozied up on the couch, sorting through Nesi's massive and eclectic collection. I made notes about relics and books that I thought might help us in our fight and lists of items to sell. We made several trips to the storage unit, taking out more boxes and returning others. After two weeks of this, I hadn't found the silver bullet that would wipe out the opji without any loss to us and our allies, but I kept coming back to that first box, number twelve, with the Thorn of Vidar.

It was so obviously a vampire-hunting weapon, but that wasn't what interested me. The listing for the relic brought up a book called *Vidar's Journey*. It had a publish date of 2035, but I couldn't find it listed in any other library database. As far as I could tell, Nesi's copy was the only one.

Unfortunately, the book's tag listed it in box three, which was deep in the storage unit. It took me two weeks to clear enough stuff to reach it. Once I did, I sat and read *Vidar's Journey* in one day. Mason found me that evening, propped in bed with the book closed in my lap.

"You look thoughtful." He gave me a gentle poke when I didn't answer. "Good book?"

"Hmm?" I glanced up. My hand still rested on the book. "Just finished it. A horrible and yet, utterly fascinating story."

Mason climbed into bed and tucked me into the crook of his shoulder. "Tell me."

And so I did.

"Filip Vidar was the first opji king to settle in these parts after the Flood Wars. He established Vioska Ward and began the practice of keeping humans—or krowa—so the opji would always have a food source. They fed from the krowa until they weakened and then turned them into wojaks. To the opji, he must have been a revolutionary."

Mason huffed. "Sure, about as revolutionary as Joseph Stalin."

"Not all revolutions are good revolutions."

Mason grunted his agreement and I continued Vidar's story.

He not only established the krowa pens, but he led the first raids on Montreal before the ward was ignited. He was a sorcerer of some renown, and he laid the first anchors for the ward around Vioska. He also perfected cunning and lethal weapons that helped opji raiders easily cull the homesteader populations.

One of those was a staff that let an opji pass for human by affecting a glamor to mask their magic signature. The end of the staff had a beautifully carved raptor's head. When removed, this carving hid a thin blade.

Vidar infiltrated many villages under the glamor of this weapon. He made the villagers trust him until he learned their defenses, then called in his army to kill or capture them. His journal, *Vidar's Journey*, detailed this ruse and its devastating consequences over five years.

Until he met Malvina Wilkins.

By Vidar's account, Malvina was almost painfully beautiful. His meticulous journal turned into a rambling stream-of-consciousness nightmare after her introduction.

"The shift in tone is so striking, it makes me wonder if Malvina was also a witch."

"You think she enthralled him?" Mason asked.

"I don't know. It's just that his ramblings sound so much like Gerard Golovin and his obsession with Polina."

"Hmm." Mason's brows were scrunched together. I absently ran a finger over his forehead, smoothing out the wrinkle as I continued.

Vidar found Malvina alone at her homestead. Most of her family had gone into the city to trade, leaving her with only a bed-ridden aunt as company. The writing at this point was still pretty coherent, and Vidar had a knack for description. In my mind, I pictured a homestead like the Hewitts' where I'd first met Soolea hiding from opji.

Vidar approached their farmhouse as a simple journeyman, begging for a hot meal and a place to sleep. Malvina let him stay in the barn. For two weeks, they waited for her family to return. It was unclear from the journal what happened during this time, but Vidar became completely infatuated with Malvina.

When her family returned, the opji descended on the little homestead and took everyone prisoner.

By this time, it seemed that Vidar was completely mad.

I paused, considering something. I'd locked the thorn and other relics in the gatehouse office, but I wished I had it in my hands now. In fact, I'd walked over there three times today, just to look at the thorn, as if it had some kind of hold on me.

"His madness might not have been Malvina's influence. The thorn's magic might have twisted him somehow."

I turned my head to peek at Mason, to be sure he was still listening and hadn't fallen asleep. He was watching me with those deep, still eyes.

"Why do you think that?"

"There's another account of the thorn from someone named Brent Pastor. He's the only known survivor of the krowa pens. In 2039, he escaped Vioska and returned to Montreal, bringing the Thorn of Vidar with him. Nesi bought it from Pastor for $225."

"A steal."

I agreed. "Nesi already had the journal, though its origins aren't listed in the database. It's one of the first listings too."

We were silent for a moment as the weight of all this history pressed on us.

"Is that the end of Vidar's story?"

"Not quite. He brought Malvina back to Vioska, but didn't put her in the krowa pens. She convinced him to keep her alive long enough to bear the child in her belly. Apparently, she became his guest in the opji stronghold."

"That probably didn't go over well with the other opji," Mason said.

"I wouldn't think so. If she was a witch, her power wasn't enough to save herself. When her child was born, Vidar took it." I squirmed a bit, not wanting to think about what a vampire might do to a baby. "And Malvina, now enraged and fearing for her own life, stabbed Vidar through the heart with the blade from his own walking stick. What we now call the Thorn of Vidar."

"What happened to her?" Mason asked.

"I don't know. Vidar's journal obviously ends before that. We know about his death from what Pastor told Nesi. I suspect Malvina was made into a wojak."

"How did this Pastor guy escape?"

"Again not clear. The entry about Pastor is from Nesi's account of meeting the man. He says only that Pastor was a servant in the opji stronghold, nearly five years after Vidar's death. He stole the blade and used it to fight his way out."

"So this thorn has killed more than one opji, including their first king."

"Seems so. You think that makes it more potent somehow?"

Mason considered the question. "Not magically, but symbolically, yes."

"Do you think Ichovidar took his name from Vidar?"

"It's possible. From what I understand, the opji have no home nation. Their language is a bastardization of Polish, Hungarian, German and a few other dialects thrown in. Icho could be a corruption of *ich*, in German."

"So Ichovidar is *I am Vidar*?"

"Or *I am King*, if they've glorified the memory of Vidar to represent all kings."

"Seems a little arrogant."

Mason gave a quiet laugh. "The opji aren't known for their subtlety."

"No, I guess not. But do you think the thorn can be used against him?" I was still looking for that silver bullet.

"Probably as much as any blade. But its power lies in its history. The opji will either fear it in superstition or revere it as a relic of their lost king."

"Either way, I can use it to my advantage."

"We." He turned so that I was forced to sit up and face him. "*We* will use it to *our* advantage. There is no you or me in this fight. Only us."

"Only us," I agreed.

t was time to put plans into motion. We needed allies, big and small. We needed the fae's support and Hub's if we were going to have any chance of defeating the opji. That meant delicate negotiations on our part. I already had feelers out to some rather unorthodox allies, such as the godlings and even the Knackers, the gang of underworld thugs who hosted fights to the death between humans and fae. It was a long shot, but I had nothing to lose.

The most troubling news had come that morning. It was troubling because we couldn't get any news about opji movements in the Inbetween. Without Mason's Prime Minister credentials, he was left out of the loop in terms of military tactics, but even Ramona, as acting PM, couldn't get the information we needed. That left us wondering if someone was shielding the opji. It wouldn't be the first time someone in a position of power thought they could manipulate the opji for their own ends. History had proven this tactic always failed.

From a practical standpoint, it meant we had to consolidate our allies now, before there were sides to take.

Thoughts of upcoming negotiations with Hub and Merrow, Prime Minister of the fae, had me distracted as I drove into the parking lot of what was once Valkyrie Pest Control. The demon had set it on fire last summer, and the ruined building was a blackened eyesore.

"You shoulds build it again," Jacoby said from the front seat. He leaned forward and peered through the windshield.

"Maybe."

I parked my van and stared at the ruins. The whole left side that had been our office and Emil's apartment had collapsed. The upstairs apartment too. I'd checked on Mr. Murray after the fire. He was living in a fae retirement community in the east end of the city, probably spying on his neighbors and getting into trouble for it.

The garage section was mostly intact, and I planned to store some of Nesi's boxes there, since the estate lawyer insisted I move them out of her storage unit by the end of the month. The more magically volatile stuff would have to be kept at the Guardians' gatehouse.

I got out of the van and opened the trunk just as another truck pulled into the parking lot. That would be my contractor.

"Start piling those boxes in the garage," I said to Jacoby. He hefted a box over his head and loped off.

I turned to meet Adam Marat. He'd been the foreman at the Golovin Industrial Complex before Mason and I blew it up to fulfill our pact with Terra. Adam had lost his job that night. Parliament was still dithering about whether or not they should rebuild the complex, but either way, they wouldn't put their confidence in the man who'd let it be destroyed.

Adam stepped out of his pickup truck already wearing a hard-hat. I'd never seen him without it, and I wondered if he slept in it.

I lifted my hand in greeting and he nodded curtly. His boots crunched the broken glass and debris underfoot as he approached. His face was stern and he kept his hands behind his back as he studied the half-fallen, burned out structure.

"I was sorry to hear about the Golovin thing." Offering my condolences on a disaster of my making brought up all kinds of guilt. In the dark of night, when I couldn't sleep, I convinced myself that I'd had to destroy the complex. It was Terra's will and the construction was in violation of the pact the human-fae-alchemist coalition had made with her at the ward's inception. But standing beside Adam, I was faced with the real-world consequences of my actions. It was an uncomfortable feeling.

"It'll work out for the best." Adam said. "I like being my own boss. And I found some backers willing to take a chance on a new enterprise. Seems there's good money in reclamation and construction these days."

I made a vaguely affirmative noise.

Oscar had quietly set up some investors for Adam to start his own business. We were one of his first customers.

"How long do you think it will take to tear it down?" I asked.

Adam rubbed his chin and considered. "Depends. Do you want to rebuild? And can we save that garage? I don't know."

"The fire inspector said the garage was stable, but you'll know better. I'd like to keep it as storage for now. If you need to knock it down, let me know and I'll move everything out." He didn't have to know that it was full of weapons and now the arcane effects of a dead man.

"And rebuilding?" he asked.

I guess the coming battle will decide. There was no point in spending money on a new building that I might never use. Again, that wasn't Adam's problem.

"I would like to rebuild eventually. When I can afford it. For now I just want this eyesore cleaned up." This wasn't exactly an affluent neighborhood, but I was certain the neighbors were tired of looking at the ruin of my life.

"Fine. I'll make an assessment today and let you know a timetable and cost. I'll need the guy off the roof though."

"The roof?" I tilted my head back and shielded my eyes from the sun. Emil was hunched on the garage's sloping roof like a gargoyle.

A wave of déjà vu washed over me. I'd thought Emil was over his futile end-of-life gestures.

"I'll take care of him."

Adam shrugged. "As long as he's gone before we start the demolition." He took out his widget and began taking pictures of the building.

I texted Emil.

You coming down?

I saw him shift on the roof as he pulled out his widget. A second later, I got a response.

No.

I could use help moving those boxes inside.

No answer. Sigh. Emil wasn't done punishing me for Gabe's death, but I was glad to see him. I'd put off asking him for help with our vampire problem because I knew his inner turmoil would make him jump on any rash or dangerous plan I suggested. I'd hoped to give him time to mourn Gabe before I asked him to jump into the fire. But I was running out of time.

I found the ladder and laid it against the side of the garage.

"Why is Kyra-lady climbings?" Jacoby asked as he deposited the last box.

"Emil's on the roof. He won't come down."

"Crazy vampire." Jacoby shook his head. "Kyra-lady needs 'prentice on the roof?"

"No, but you can tidy the garage for me if you're bored."

Jacoby picked up a broom and started swishing it around. He hummed a tune from one of Holly's favorite cartoons as dust and ash clouded up from the floor.

Half the battle of having a dervish apprentice was keeping him busy.

Adam found me as I put my foot on the first rung.

"You going up there?" His hard-hat was tilted back on his head, giving him a surprised look.

"Just going to say hi to my friend."

"He climbs on the roof a lot?"

"Too often."

"You want me to get him down?"

I could see that Adam didn't want to leave a helpless woman alone on a roof with a maniac.

"It's okay. He's harmless. Really."

Adam hesitated, then he gestured with his widget. I've got everything I need. I'll send you a quote later today and if you agree, we can start the demolition next week."

"Thanks." I watched him get into his truck and drive off before continuing the climb. At the eaves, I managed to get my leg onto the metal roof and hook my toe on a rivet. From below, the slope seemed gentle. Up here, it felt treacherous. I grabbed hold of a vent pipe and scooted sideways until I sat beside Emil. His arms were wrapped around his knees and he seemed as comfortable as a squirrel in its nest. A gentle wind caught his auburn curls and tossed them around his head.

"You shouldn't be up here." He attempted a scowl. His boyish face made it look more like a pout.

"Neither should you." My foot slipped and I skidded down the slope. Emil's hand shot out, grabbed me by the collar and hauled me back up.

"I won't splat like a bug if I fall," he growled.

"You will. You just won't care." I'd seen Emil's healing abilities in action. They were the only blessing from his opji heritage. Emil had been abandoned by the opji or possibly kidnapped from them when he was only a toddler. The story wasn't clear. His fae mother spun several tales about how he'd come into her care.

Opji vampires go through a rite—the zycha—when they hit puberty. It's a magical ritual that slows their heartbeats to nearly undetectable levels, which prolongs their lives. It also cools the bloodlust that rages unchecked in young opji. Without this rite, Emil had battled that bloodlust all his life. He was the only opji allowed inside Montreal Ward thanks to a special dispensation bought by his high-ranking mother. As a condition of that grant, he was not allowed to drink fae or human blood. Emil existed on pig's blood mostly, and when I'd first met him on a roof similar to this one four years ago, the bloodlust was driving him mad.

I worried that Gabe's death was causing him to regress to this state.

"You're not thinking of throwing yourself off, are you?"

"No point, is there?"

"Not really."

A fall wouldn't kill him. He might break some bones, but they'd heal.

I was suddenly glad I'd left my sword in the van. It had been many years since Emil had begged me to use my Valkyrie magic to end his life. I didn't want him taking up that call again.

"It's all futile," he said.

"All is a big word."

"Okay. My life is an exercise in futility. How's that."

"It doesn't have to be."

His chin rested on his drawn-up knees and he turned his head to look at me. "Are you going to rebuild?"

"Eventually. Probably. Will you be here if I do?"

"I don't know. Seems so pointless."

"Helping people is never pointless."

"Is that what we do? Help people?" He snorted. "I know a few people we didn't help."

Gabe. It always came back to Gabe. I let the comment go even though it stuck like a barb in my heart.

Emil sighed. "I just feel so rudderless, you know. Like I've come untethered from my life."

"Maybe you need a purpose."

"Sure. I'll pick up a six-pack of purpose on my way home."

"I have one."

Emil frowned.

"A purpose, I mean. I'm going to wipe every blood-sucking opji off the face of the earth."

"High marks for ambition, at least. But you'll never do it."

"Maybe not. But I have to try. It's Terra's will."

"I thought blowing up the industrial complex was Terra's idea."

"That was just an opening act of goodwill on our part. To show that we honor the original pact she made with the founders of Montreal."

Emil sneered. It didn't do nice things to his pretty face.

"I didn't take you for a god lover."

"I may have no love for Terra, but I made her a promise that I can't go back on."

Terra had never been explicit about the consequences of backing out of our deal. But she'd pulled Mason from a hellish eternity inside a bloodstone, and I had no doubt she could take away that freedom just as easily.

"You should never promise the gods anything," Emil said.

"I had no choice." I pounded a fist on my knee. "I'm raising an army to fight the opji and I want your help."

And in a low voice, I outlined my tentative plans for building an army to wage war. His eyebrows slowly raised as he listened. When I was done, he was silent for a moment, then he said, "You're either incredibly brave or incredibly stupid."

"Maybe a bit of both. Are you in?"

He straightened. "Of course. If you're killing vamps, I'll lead the charge."

More than me, Emil blamed Nici—and by extension all vampires—for

Gabe's death. I was pushing on this pain point to suit my purposes, and I'd add that to the list of my guilts when I lay awake at night. But right now, I needed Emil. He was a crucial cog in my plan.

"I need you to infiltrate the opji and bring back intel—their movements, their weapons, how many wojaks in their army and anything else you can tell us."

"You want me to go to Vioska?"

"Yes. Mason believes that someone high up in Hub ranks is working with the opji. We can't trust any information they feed us. I need someone on the inside."

Emil's mad smile faded. "They'll know right away that I'm different. They'll be able to sense that I haven't undertaken the zycha. It may not be obvious to you, but to an opji I would stand out like a flowering bush in the middle of a desert."

"That's exactly why you're going in as a human."

From my backpack, I pulled out the Thorn of Vidar.

"What is that smell?" Emil wrapped his arm around his face, but I knew from experience there was no getting away from the swamp-gas stench.

"We're close to the Laval Flood Plains." I nodded to the marshy landscape outside the car's window.

"And Oscar actually lives here?"

"Not right in the swamp. You'll see."

We drove over a causeway. On either side of the car, black water lay in pools around islands of green. Cedar trees leaned at desperate angles and moss grew on their already shaggy trunks so they looked like giant hairy beasts stepping through the bog.

I slowed the van as magic prickled over my skin. Even Emil felt it. He shot forward in the passenger seat and stared at the road ahead.

"What's that?"

"Just a ward." I texted a note to Oscar and the magic popped as the ward came down. We drove on.

The swamp ended as we climbed a hill. At the top, a gate stood open, giving us access to a large gravel yard. Oscar's mansion stood in the middle of this yard like a Regency era crown. The drive circled around a manicured garden and I parked in front of the massive oak doors.

"Now what?" Emil asked. "We wait for the butler to greet us?"

"No butler. Just Oscar."

"He really lives in this place all alone?"

"Not lives. Works. It's more of a laboratory than a home."

"More of a lair, you mean. You sure he isn't an evil genius?"

"Nope. Just the ordinary kind of genius."

I reached over to shake Jacoby who'd fallen asleep in the back seat. He woke with a shout.

"I didn'ts take the cookies!" He saw me grinning and wiped his mouth on his arm.

"Dreaming about cookies again?" I asked.

He nodded. "Cookies are life." It was as good a philosophy as any.

"We're here. Are you coming inside? Or do you want to sleep some more."

Jacoby mumbled something about being my 'prentice and hopped out of the car.

Oscar opened the front door just as we approached.

"You made it in good time! Come in, come in!" he said, waving a hand to usher us inside. He wore a short lab coat and goggles perched above his bushy eyebrows.

"Thanks for seeing us so soon," I said.

"Of course." Oscar nodded to me then to Emil. "I'm always up for research shenanigans. You know that."

Emil's eyes were huge as he took in the workspace. Oscar had stripped the large house down to its struts. Steel beams held up the three story ceiling. The walls were rough brick. In this enormous space, Oscar had set up dozens of workspaces for individual experiments. He led us past traditional alchemical configurations of blazing alembics, glass globes, and retorts. There were more modern setups with thaumagauges attached to computers, plus scanners, cameras, and recorders of all kinds. Oscar described each arrangement as we passed them. Emil looked totally fascinated by it all. I'd lived with two alchemists for long enough to lose that wide-eyed wonder.

Jacoby bounced from one installation to another, prodding every machine. One of these days, he'd stick his business where it didn't belong and lose a finger.

"And this is the heart of my little operation." Oscar stopped at a large glass bulb with a brown substance percolating over a flame.

Emil peered at it and sniffed. "Is that coffee?"

Oscar beamed. "Only the finest beans Montreal's greenhouses can produce, and brewed the old fashioned way."

I rolled my eyes. "Yes, I remember my grandmother brewing coffee over a Bunsen burner like it was yesterday."

"If you're going to snark, you won't get any." Oscar waggled a finger at me.

"No snark here. We ran through our monthly coffee rations in a week."

Oscar poured three mugs of the brew.

I took a sip and let out a little groan.

"Mmm. Dark and solid and a little bitter. Just how I like it."

Emil smirked. "Your coffee or your men?"

I pointed to my chest and then to his. "Kettle. Pot."

Emil's smirk turned into a grin and a little chunk of the icy worry that I carried everywhere with me these days fell off and melted. It was the first time since Gabe's death that Emil had referenced him with anything but anger.

Oscar held out his hand. "If you two are finished romancing the coffee, show me this thorn thingy you're so excited about." I drew the relic from my pack and laid it in his hands. Over the phone, I'd already explained about its origins and the story of Vidar in the journal.

"Hmm. Doesn't look like much." He ran a finger along the wood shaft and over the brass eagle head. "Does it ping your keening at all?"

"No, nothing. It seems perfectly mundane. But look." I tugged at the eagle head and the blade slid from the stake.

Oscar whistled. "Nice. A weapon within a weapon."

"Within a third weapon," I said. "We think the stake was originally part of a longer walking staff."

"Well, let's see if it's anything special." Oscar laid the thorn on a scanner and took some images. He ran various tests with a thaumagauge and swabbed it with multiple substances. Half an hour later he pronounced it magically inert.

"Are you sure this is the same relic described in the journal?" he asked.

"Nesi seemed to think so, and I've never known him to be wrong."

"I guess there's only one test left then." He looked pointedly at Emil.

"You want me to activate it? I don't even know how."

"Of course you do, son." Oscar unsheathed the blade and handed it to Emil.

Emil frowned. "You want me to blood it, don't you."

Oscar nodded. "It's a vampire relic. It's always about the blood."

Emil sighed and took the blade. He was about to stab his finger when Oscar intervened.

"Wait! Let's do this properly. In the name of science." He brought Emil to a machine that looked like a vital signs monitor.

"Take off your shirt," he commanded. Emil handed me the thorn and removed his shirt. He was thin, but not to the point of emaciation. He had the sturdiness of a young colt. Oscar stuck a bunch of electrodes to his chest, neck and head. He turned on the monitor. The flat line bumped in a slower than human beat.

Oscar frowned, bunching up his eyebrows. "I suppose that's a normal heart rate for you." He checked a few more signals and seemed satisfied.

"All right. Have at it."

Emil stabbed the tip of the thorn into the end of his finger. A small dot of blood welled. He smeared it along the flat of the blade.

Immediately, my keening picked up the change. It wasn't a flashy bang of magic. It was a subtle shift, like wind parting the leaves in the forest to let sunlight shine through.

"Wow!" I gripped Emil's arm as if that would confirm what my keening was already telling me.

"Did it work?" Emil asked.

"You're human," I said. "At least, I wouldn't be able to tell the difference."

Oscar studied the vitals monitor. It hadn't changed. Emil's heart beat slow and steady. Then he ran a printout from the thaumagauge and waved it at me.

"Amazing! It reads a purely human signature."

"Will it fool the opji?" Emil asked.

"As long as they don't get close enough to put a stethoscope on your chest." Oscar looked pleased, as if he'd created the thorn's magic himself. "Now we just need to test its range."

I recruited Jacoby for that test and handed him the thorn.

"Take this and run outside as far as the gate. Do you have your widget?"

Jacoby nodded and pulled the device from his belt. He was inordinately proud of his widget. No other class two fae that he knew of had one.

"Keep it open to messages and stop running when I tell you to."

Jacoby scampered away. After a moment we heard the front door open and close.

Oscar monitored Emil closely, but I keened the change before his thaumagauge did.

I texted: *STOP*, then added, *Come back now.*

Jacoby arrived a few minutes later, out of breath.

"How far did you get?" Oscar asked.

"I gots all the ways to the gate."

"So about five hundred meters. That's your range." Oscar took the thorn and handed it back to Emil. Already the thorn's magic had wrapped him in its human glamor again.

"So as long as I stay within five hundred meters of the thing, the opji will think I'm human?"

"Best if I fashion a walking stick for it," Oscar said. "Lean on it. With a good limp, no one will try to take it from you. Hopefully."

"And what about time?" I asked. "Won't the blooding wear off after a while?"

Oscar frowned. "My best guess is yes. I would suggest redoing the blooding every few days. Maybe every day. Without extensive study, there's no way to know how long the glamor will last."

"We don't have time for that. If we're going to do this, he needs to leave yesterday." I turned to Emil. "Are you ready for that? You know what it means right?"

Emil was already pulling off the electrodes. "It means I'm going to let myself get captured by the opji."

I nodded. "Exactly."

"At best, I'll be thrown into their krowa pens. At worst they'll discover I'm an opji traitor and kill me outright."

I didn't say anything that would encourage or discourage him. It was his choice to make.

"Give me a minute. I need to think this through." He pulled on his shirt and headed outside. Jacoby followed him, but I held him back.

"Let him go."

"Mister-Emils is mads?" His eye-fringe quivered.

"Not mad, just…worried. Let him sort out his worry and he'll be back."

Jacoby seemed satisfied with that answer and he started fiddling with the dials on some machine.

"Don't touch," I said automatically.

"It's okay," Oscar said. "That scanner's already broken. He can't do it any harm. More coffee?" He held up the beaker and I nodded.

While we waited, I had one other concern for Oscar.

I pointed to one of his many experimental setups. This project clearly hadn't been touched in a while. A bunch of weapons were strewn over a work table—small blades and spears. One sword stood out from the rest. It was clamped into a vise connected to the edge of the table. It called to me like none of the others.

"What are you planning to do with Gunora's sword?" I asked.

Oscar lowered his brows. "I don't know. I suppose I should give it back to Hub at some point. They don't seem too concerned about it."

They wouldn't be. To Hub, the sword was just a hunk of metal, an interesting historical relic, maybe, but a magic dud. It only came to life in a Valkyrie's hand.

"Do you want it?" Oscar asked.

I shook my head, maybe a little too vigorously. "Keep it. But do me a favor? If I don't...you know...if something happens to me, make sure Holly gets it when the time is right?"

Oscar's frown deepened, but he nodded. He was about to say more, but the door burst open and Emil jogged back to us.

His eyes were a little feverish. "I'm in. Give me that thorn and point me toward Vioska."

CHAPTER

7

Two days later, Emil was ready to leave. If I'd left the planning to him, he'd have run off with nothing but the Thorn of Vidar and a canteen. Maybe not even the canteen. He chafed at waiting, but I wanted Raol to take him as far west as he could.

Raol was the ratatosk guide who'd returned from Asgard with me. In just a few years he already had a reputation as the best Inbetween guide around.

Luckily, Raol had been between jobs and staying in Barrows when I contacted him. He'd agreed to make his way to us this morning.

Oscar had wanted to provide Emil with a motorbike or a flying carpet or some fancy contraption, but we'd both nixed that idea. Emil needed to blend in. He was just another human for the krowa pens. So Raol was bringing Emil a horse, bought in Barrows with funds from Nesi.

It takes a village to plan an invasion.

Emil and I waited by the gatehouse for Raol to arrive. He wore a beat-up backpack slung over one shoulder and gripped a wooden crutch in his right hand. Oscar had reconfigured the Thorn of Vidar into the shaft of the crutch. Even under close scrutiny, I couldn't find the seam where the blade fit inside. The brass eagle head was tucked inside a padded block that fit under Emil's arm.

"You're going to have to lean on that thing more," I said. "Maybe even pretend to limp. Otherwise no one will believe a young, fit man like you would need a stick."

Emil nodded. His gaze was fixed on the driveway where Raol would appear.

"You don't have to do this, you know," I said.

"You don't have to invade Vioska either."

"What's your plan if they find out you're opji?"

Emil shrugged. "Kill as many as I can on my way out."

"If you're not back here by..." I counted the months on my fingers, "by the end of March, we're going in without you."

"Deal."

By the time the snows melted in March, I'd hopefully have shored up enough allies to mount an attack on Vioska. As terrified as I was for Emil, I couldn't deny that knowing the opji's strengths and movements would help us immensely.

"It's going to be a rough road for you. Winter will make travel nearly impossible." I hugged myself, already feeling the cold seeping into my bones. Emil seemed unaffected. He gazed toward the road.

"You once told me that misfits change the world." He finally turned to look at me. "This is my chance. I might not change the whole world, but I can do something to improve this little corner of it."

I bit my lip before I said something to take away from his brave words. I remembered the night I'd said that. He'd been so desperate to kill himself that he sneaked into my apartment and stole my sword, hoping the Valkyrie magic would give him a final death.

I'd denied him that death then. I only wished I could do it again.

A gust of wind blasted us and I hugged my arms to my chest. Snow began to fall. Emil tipped his face to the sky and caught some flakes on his eyelashes.

"Your god does have a sense of humor, doesn't she?"

I could dispute the claim that Terra was my god. I didn't revere her or fear her. It seemed to me that a god demanded one or the other.

The sound of hooves on gravel came a moment before we saw Raol on the drive. He rode his small, specially trained pony and led a taller bay behind him.

"That's my ride." Emil strode toward them, stopped and turned back to me. Then he hugged me.

"I'm sorry I blamed you for Gabe." His voice was muffled against my shoulder.

"I know." I patted his arm.

He stood back and smiled shyly as if the sudden emotion was too much. "I'll see you in March."

"Or before then."

"Or before." He actually saluted.

Raol wasn't one for idle chatter. He gave me a friendly nod. Emil tucked the crutch into a saddle bag. It stuck out awkwardly as Emil mounted up and swung the horse around with a backward wave.

Within minutes, I could no longer hear the clop of hooves on gravel. Operation Bloodsucker was officially underway.

I SPENT THE REST of the morning in the barn with my critters. My stomach churned like a wriggling ball of snakes. I couldn't help feeling like a general who'd sent a soldier on a suicide mission. And how many more soldiers would I send to their deaths before this war was over?

Keeping busy was the only way I could stop my hands from shaking and my thoughts from going to those dark places.

About the same time I'd discovered that my bedazzled snail was actually a female, Bijou outgrew her terrarium again. It wasn't easy to sex a snail, and I was learning that it was just as hard to keep her properly housed. If she didn't stop growing soon, she'd be too big for the barn.

Bijou had a decent outdoor pen for the summer, but winter had come early and I wanted something warm and cozy for her. So I spent the rest of the morning cleaning out the last barn stall to convert it into a snail habitat.

After lugging in wheelbarrows of sand from the pit at the back of the garden for a base, I added a good layer of dark earth, then a layer of leaf litter. I'd found an old wagon at a scrap yard and cut off one end. Lying on its side, it made a nice shelter for Bijou to nest in. I added a few rocks and a pool of water.

Hunter, my pygmy kraken, helped by chucking shrimp shells from his perch in the barn rafters. The little rascal had learned how to open the freezer where we kept the feed. Now he helped himself to treats.

I hung a heat lamp above the stall and positioned it over the sand, raising it and lowering it until I felt Bijou could nest comfortably.

A shrimp shell hit me in the back of the head.

"Quit it!" I turned an annoyed eye on Hunter, but he was completely undaunted and tossed another shell at me.

I sighed.

It wasn't even November yet. Winter was barely upon us and already the critters were bored. Hunter had a lovely summer pond to frolic in, but the cold forced him inside. I'd have to consider a bigger indoor tank for him too, but one critter at a time.

I scooped Bijou from her terrarium. She filled my arms. Her gooey underside clung to my shirt and her eye stalks waggled frantically.

"It's okay, girl. We're not going far."

I dumped her onto the leaf litter in her new pen. The eye stalks bent as she took in the space. Then slowly, slowly, she stretched her foot pad to begin exploring.

I wished she didn't need to be alone. Was there some other critter that could live with her? The horse stall was big enough. The peyochip would have been a good companion, but I'd sent the platypus look-alike south to another rescue farm. They would be able to re-introduce it to the brackish swamps that were its natural habitat.

Maybe if Operation Bloodsucker was a success, I'd look into getting Bijou a roommate. Making plans beyond next spring and the looming war seemed pointless. For now, Bijou had Hunter, who'd squiggled down to the pen and was tossing leaves into the air like confetti.

I know what's missing. Branches.

I shut the stall door to head outside and find a few choice logs and branches for Bijou to climb on.

I didn't make it past the driveway.

A van pulled up and parked. Oscar stepped out from the driver's side just as Mason opened the front door to the house.

I smiled and started toward them. We hadn't been expecting a visit. Then I stopped when the back doors of the van opened and the goblins stepped out.

All of them.

Arriz, head of the family, stood beside Oscar, hands on his hips and staring at Mason. The goblin children ranged behind him. Dekar, looking tall and strong, no longer a child. Then Suzt with her fierce look that told everyone to stay away from her siblings. Then Muzzy, Tak, and Gibus, my former barn hands. And finally the twins, Tums and Tad. Tums shot me a smile and a wave before Suzt pulled him under her mother-hen wing.

By the front door, Mason stood with his arms crossed, brows lowered over dark eyes and lips pressed tight. To anyone else, he would have looked stern, angry even. But I knew that meeting the goblins again terrified him.

When the demon had possessed him, he'd terrorized our homestead and beaten Gibus. And no matter how many times I told Mason that he wasn't responsible for the demon's actions, he could still feel his hands wrenching Gibus's shoulder from its socket.

Oscar cleared his throat. "Arriz has a question he'd like to ask. I told him it was better done face to face."

Mason barely nodded and his eyes flicked to Arriz. The goblin stepped forward.

"There is no work in Montreal. Refugees have taken all the jobs. Barrows and Hedge are full of starving families, cutthroats and thieves. I would not subject my family to that life." He took a deep breath and stood as tall as his stooped shoulders allowed. "I come here to ask for my job back. For both Dekar and me, but I want to be clear. My family will be my own. I know the demon was responsible for hurting Gibus, but the boy cannot be expected to so easily recover from that trauma. And I will not subject him to more." He pointed at Mason. "You will stay away from Gibus and the rest of my family. Those are my terms."

He stepped back. No one thought it odd that this slight goblin would demand terms while asking for his job back.

Mason nodded curtly. "I accept."

My heart was pounding. This was big. So big. I didn't know how we would administer Arriz's rules, but somehow, we'd make it work. For the goblins. For Mason.

Oscar squeezed Arriz's shoulder. "That's settled then."

Gibus broke away from his brothers. He bolted up the stairs toward Mason. He'd grown since I last saw him but he was still short enough that he only came up to Mason's elbow.

I started forward, unsure of his intent, but Gibus threw his arms around Mason and hugged him, crying and babbling, "I'm sorry. I'm sorry," over and over.

Arriz lurched forward, but Oscar held him back. Mason stood frozen, his face white. One hand reached for Gibus and patted his back. Then he pulled the child away and knelt. I knew it took every ounce of strength he had to face the victim of his demon. He brushed a tear from Gibus's cheek.

"You have nothing to be sorry for. I am the one who's sorry. For putting you in danger. It's my fault." Tears flowed down his cheeks. He pulled Gibus into a hug, and they rocked side to side as man and child worked out their fear and grief.

I grinned at Arriz. "I guess you'll be taking over the old cottage then?"

Arriz scowled back at me. "I guess we will."

We could make that work. Ludger was spending more and more time at the refugee camp with our new recruits. He'd be better set up there than in the cottage.

I didn't know what was coming for us, what hardships we'd face in the coming months, but for the first time in nearly a year, my family felt whole again.

CHAPTER

8

Kyra's Personal Journal

October 31, 2084

With Valkyrie Pest Control temporarily shut down, I find I miss writing my blog, so I've taken up a journal, partly as an outlet for the fear and worry I deal with everyday, partly as a sounding board for Operation Bloodsucker (what I've started calling this insane idea to fight the opji). Also it might be a good idea to record my thoughts and the coming events. You know, in case the worst happens.

In case I don't live through the fight.

Maybe my children will survive. Maybe they'll find this in my effects and understand that I did everything I could to make their world safe.

Only time will tell if I succeed.

The battle with the opji is coming. Even if I hadn't promised Terra to intervene, I wouldn't be able to look the other way.

The opji have burned miles and miles of forest. For what purpose? I can't even guess. They are taking captives at an alarming rate. No homesteader is safe. Nici's plot with the shar-lil proved they are planning a greater assault. How long until they turn their attention to Montreal?

We need more information—information that Hub hoards like a miser keeps his gold. Mason believes they know more than they are saying, that there may even be factions among the human and alchemist parties working with the opji.

I cannot believe that would be true. To what end? What benefits could the opji possibly bring to the table? They offer only death and enslavement. Anyone who thinks they can trust these monsters is a fool.

We gather an army to us. So far they are mostly refugees fleeing the fires and the opji. Most of them are more interested in the security and regular meals we provide than in fighting.

The bluecaps are making their way from Grandill. I sent messages to Soolea in Winaskwi and Herne at Annequin lodge. Both have pledged support. Mason and I have other feelers out, other connections that may or may not bring more allies. It's a slow process.

Soon I will begin negotiations with the godlings, though their in-fighting has become critical since Nici's betrayal. I don't know if I can bring them around. Only their pure hatred for the opji keeps them in the talks. We shall see.

Captain Glenda Lowe has been a staunch supporter, but even she seems cautious. How can we fight such an enemy? They have evaded us for fifty years. They are too many and with the influx of refugees, Hub resources are spread too thin. These are her arguments against an all out assault, and I have to admit, they are valid.

The only reliable news Hub has been able to give us is that Ichovidar leads the opji. Until now, the opji mage king was only a myth, a name whispered among frightened homesteaders. But we can now confirm Ichovidar is real and he has been the driving force behind two attacks on Montreal Ward in the past four years.

We have some unfinished business, Ichovidar and I. It's possible that I had a hand in the deaths of two opji in his family—Nici and the un-

named opji prince that attacked Soolea's homestead. I plan to confront him with those deaths and shove them right down his throat.

But I need an army to do that. And even more importantly, I need reliable information. How many wojaks can the opji put in the field? What are Vioska's defenses? And the big question, what is Ichovidar's end game?

I sent a spy into Vioska to find answers to these questions. Emil rode out yesterday. He left during another unseasonably early snowstorm. But the weather won't be the worst thing he faces on his long journey west.

I feel woefully inadequate to this task. I wish Terra's eye had fallen on another. But wishing will not magically make the opji disappear.

And so we plan. We gather. We get ready to fight.

CHAPTER

9

April 9, 2085

On a bright spring morning, I decided to put my nervous energy to good use and turn over my vegetable garden on the far side of the barn. Emil was already a week overdue, and as I jammed the spade into the rich black earth, I tried not to think about what that could mean—both for Emil and our campaign against the opji.

Raven and the goblin twins were playing soccer in the yard. They no longer fought over the ball like a pack of wolf cubs. They'd all matured in the last year. Even Princess seemed less interested in chasing the ball. She lay in the sun on the warm gravel with her muzzle on her paws.

I stretched then leaned on my shovel watching the boys bounce the ball off their heads, knees and ankles, passing it from one to another in a circle.

Princess lifted her nose and howled a greeting and a warning. I turned and shielded my eyes from the sun to see who was arriving. I wasn't too worried about strangers coming up our drive.

Six weeks ago, Errol had returned from his visit to Cece, and in that time we'd completely reinvented our house ward. Errol had increased its size, and it now encompassed the cemetery and a good portion of the forest beyond. Before the redesign, we'd let the ward down during the day or if visitors were expected. It had been a simple thing to do. A ward stone was moved aside to break the flow of sympathetic magic. Putting the stone back in its place reignited the ward.

This new, bigger and stronger ward took much more magic to maintain, and with the growing number of people camped out in our woods, we needed a better system. It was no longer feasible to shut down the wards every time someone came calling.

Errol and I had spent weeks planning and building the new ward. The demon had left thousands of bones on our doorstep after his last attack. Bones were potent magic. After consulting with Joe Mountainclaw in Winaskwi, we used them for the foundation. I'd also learned a neat trick from Herne at Annequin lodge, and we built two gates into the ward—one at the end of the driveway by the old maintenance road and one in the forest, past the cemetery. Family and close friends like Oscar were still keyed to it, but visitors could only access the homestead by one of the gates, which were guarded twenty-four hours a day by carefully selected crews from the refugee camp. They had a curated list of people they would let through without making a call to the house. If someone was heading down our driveway, they were an ally.

Shielding my eyes from the sun, I watched a long line of figures approach. The bluecaps had finally arrived.

Princess ran forward, warning off the intruders with sharp barks. Then she recognized Neva, the bluecap matriarch who'd treated Princess's wounds in Grandill. The hound ran to her and nearly smothered poor Neva with her affection. Raven whistled and Princess bounded back to him, leaving a startled and soggy Neva behind.

The bluecaps continued their forward march.

I joined Raven in the driveway. Jacoby and the goblin twins left the soccer ball for this more exciting adventure and fidgeted with nervous energy.

"Are those real bluecaps?" Tums asked. "I can't wait to tell Suzt. She made us read all about them last week. This is so exciting!" The goblit bounced and Jacoby, infected by his enthusiasm, danced alongside him.

"May you be cursed to live in exciting times," I mumbled. Raven shot me a glance and a frown. I smiled to show him, I didn't really mean it. Except, of course, I did. It was a Chinese curse, considered the worst of a set that began with *may the gods grant you everything you wish for*. I had no doubt that before this year was through, we'd run the gamut of ancient curses.

73

Neva led the band of bluecaps with her husband Cletus. He carried an axe on one shoulder. Behind him came dozens more—men, women and children—along with several donkeys pulling tarp-covered carts.

I turned to Tums. "Go find Dekar and tell him the bluecaps have arrived." The twins ran off to find their brother.

The bluecaps had been living on Grandill Island for over fifty years. They'd made a home there despite the limitations of forced confinement, restricted food, and a proximity to the worst criminals in Montreal's history. They were an industrious people, descendants of old-world dwarves who mined for gold and gems. On the island, they'd built homes, tools, and weapons. They'd farmed and hunted and lacked for little in comfort. Except freedom.

When that freedom had finally been granted, they'd packed up their entire village and moved it off the island. Since then, Mason had been in contact with Cletus who spoke for all the bluecaps. Already, they'd seen firsthand what the opji were doing on the mainland, and they'd agreed to fight with us.

Our army had been slow to build, but seeing the train of bluecaps and their supplies really made it hit home. We were now a force to be reckoned with.

Cletus and Neva stopped beside the gatehouse. The long line of bluecaps halted behind them. Cletus took a moment to scan our little homestead with a critical eye. I had no doubt he was sizing up its fortifications and finding them wanting.

In turn, I inspected his little band like a general sizing up her troops. There were children and some elderly, but the bulk of the group was fit to fight. My eyebrows raised when I spotted a tall young man and woman in the parade. Even in their human forms, I keened their kelpie magic. And that wasn't all. My eyes ran along the group right to the end where four large, shaggy creatures loomed.

"Welcome, Cletus." I nodded at him and then toward his wife. "Neva. We are glad you could make the journey."

The pair stood about as tall as my elbow. They were stout across the shoulders and made more so by the many coats, packs and gear strapped to their backs. Both had blue-black hair, though gray was starting to creep into Neva's. Cletus's dark eyes seemed lost behind a large nose and full black beard. Neva's features were more refined, but she still looked like she'd been roughly cleaved from a block of wood.

"Took us a bit longer to clear out of the island than we expected," Cletus said. He leaned in as if to impart a secret. "We were only a year away from digging out of there, you know. So we collapsed the tunnels. No good letting the real criminals out."

"And yet…"

My eyes shifted to the kelpies waiting awkwardly as if they were afraid to be overlooked but more afraid to be seen. And the second group of creatures. They lagged behind the train, but their immense size made them stand out.

Cletus waved at the pair of kelpies and they trotted over. After giving me shy smiles, they kept their eyes fixed on the ground.

"This is Dennet and Perri," Cletus said. "Formerly of Felix's clan."

I gripped Raven's hand, knowing the horrors that name would conjure for him. I had no idea what crimes these particular kelpies were guilty of, but I'd witnessed their clan's brutality first-hand during my short stay on the island.

The kelpies bowed. I didn't recognize them, but I'd been mostly confined when I visited the kelpie camp on Grandill—confined in a shack and later chained to an altar while my cousin Gunora injected me with a deadly and mystical disease. The battle that ensued was pretty hazy in my memory.

"Why were they released?" I asked.

Cletus unhooked the pack from his shoulders and let it drop. He rolled his shoulders to loosen them after their long march.

"Your husband's inquiries into Grandill's management caused a big kerfuffle."

"Kerfuffle?" Cletus had the vocabulary of a Victorian auntie.

"Aye." His brows lowered. "A big one. Those ministers from the city started poking into everything—safety protocols, human and non-human rights violations. They even did a census and discovered that Dennet and Perri here were never convicted of a crime. They were born on the island, like your boy there." He nodded toward Raven whose expression was shuttered. This was the first time he'd faced some of his mother's clan since we left Grandill over four years ago.

I turned to the young kelpies. Dennet was slim with big-boned features and dull brown hair. He gripped Perri's hand as if she might flee. Her long auburn hair covered one eye and she peered at me from behind this curtain.

Were they siblings? Lovers? Both? It was really none of my business. Life on the island had been a twisted and savage affair. I wouldn't judge them for just surviving it.

Cletus pulled me aside, and I leaned down to hear his words.

"Between you and me, they aren't the sharpest of wits, but they're not criminals either, and they deserve a chance to prove themselves." Bushy eyebrows met over his prominent nose and he held my gaze with a steady, almost daring look.

I considered the problem. Kelpies were formidable opponents. They could run faster than humans and with the rich magic in the Inbetween, they'd shift into their horse forms in an instant. Their teeth were made for rending meat, not chewing hay, and their hooves could stomp a man to death. I wouldn't want to meet one alone on the moors, but we needed every soldier we could muster if we were going to win this war. If Cletus vouched for them, that would have to be good enough.

"And they're willing to fight?" I asked.

"You can ask 'em yourself."

I turned to the kelpies. "Are you ready to fight vampires? That's what we're doing here."

Dennet nodded, then after a moment Perri did too. They were nothing more than scared kids, but I'd seen first hand what kind of fighters kelpies could be.

"Fine." I nodded to Cletus. "They can stay. But I expect you to keep an eye on them."

He waggled his brows. "Both eyes."

I turned my attention to the second group of strangers. Four enormous beings hung out at the end of the bluecap train. They were easily seven-feet tall and covered in shaggy white fur that had a dingy yellow cast to it.

"You brought yetis?"

Cletus shrugged. "They sort of attached themselves to our caravan. I couldn't turn them away, now could I?"

"But they're yetis," I said, as if that fact explained my reluctance.

"Oh, they're not so bad. A little rambunctious after a few dips of the ale mug, if you know what I mean. But that big one, that's Howf. He's the leader as far as I can tell. He's a good sort and keeps the others in line. They want to fight like the rest of us." He scratched his beard. "Now, I don't speak much yeti, but they keep talking about some devastation. It seems the opji have destroyed much of the forest they live in."

"The forest fires." I nodded. "They've been burning the trees for over a year. We're not sure why." It was one of the questions I hoped Emil would answer when he came home. If he came home.

That brought me to the next dilemma. The fae were serious about debts. Leaving one unpaid could bring bad luck of the worst kind for both parties. But Mason and I had discussed this at length. We could not buy loyalty from the bluecaps, and that's what we needed for this fight. We needed people who fought because they had family and homes to lose, people who fought for their very existence. Only that kind of heart would win against heartless vampires.

I was glad to see Mason coming out of the house to back me up in this delicate discussion. He joined us on the driveway and after greeting Cletus and Neva he said, "You know, when I petitioned Parliament for your release, it was not with the intent to have you fight the opji. You are not indebted to us."

Cletus looked at Neva and she nodded. "Oh, aye, there is a debt there my friend, but that's not why we agreed to this fight. Those Hub soldiers came for us in January and let us out the prison gates in a blizzard, no transport, no provisions. And we'd expected none." He pounded a fist on his chest. "Bluecaps look after their own. We set out from that miserable island with everything we could carry. It was slow going and took us nearly three months to get here. And we learned much along the way. We met with homesteaders fleeing opji raids, talking of forest fires destroying their lands," he nodded toward the yetis, "and above all a pure hatred for the opji who stole kinfolk to keep as slaves." He leaned in. Anger made his cheeks red. "The bluecaps will never be prisoners again. If we have to fight to keep our new freedom, we're ready."

Arriz and Dekar arrived from the back garden. Since their return, Dekar had shown a real aptitude for organization and I'd given him the job of settling in newcomers. So far these had included a clan of Cricket's hidebehind cousins, some of my dryad kin sent by Lisobet, a group of goblins that Dekar had befriended in Barrows, plus nearly a hundred refugees.

Knowing that the bluecaps were coming, we'd set aside a large parcel of land for them on the far side of the cemetery.

"Show them where to settle," I said, then held Dekar back before he turned away. "Make sure they have provisions. Nobody goes hungry."

Dekar nodded. Mason and Cletus were deep in discussion as they headed through the hedge to the cemetery path. I left them to settle in and returned to my garden work.

Just before lunch, I heard the sounds of trees falling. The bluecaps were already building shelters. Terra wouldn't like the destruction of more forest, but she could go suck an egg. If she wanted us to prevail, we'd need shelters.

I was leaning on my spade, admiring my hard work and my now seed-ready garden when Gita began to wail from her den inside the barn. I almost shrugged it off. Since the earthquake last fall, Gita had been more weepy than usual, but this time Grim came skidding around the corner of the barn. His tail was puffed up like a brush and his eyes wild.

"Come now! It's Holly!"

CHAPTER

10

Two small words that stopped my heart. *It's Holly.* I threw down my spade and bolted after Grim. He loped up the small hill toward the upper edge of the bank barn. We dashed past the horse paddock where Gallivant pawed the air and Clover ran in circles. I had no time to figure out what had upset them. Only Holly mattered.

Grim leaped nimbly onto the picnic table set up under a giant willow tree in the back garden where Mason had built Holly a sandbox. I skidded to a stop. My keening was screaming at me that something was wrong. Holly's buckets and trucks lay discarded in the sand. A ragged tear in the veil shimmered in the air beside the sandbox.

A dimensional portal.

My mind froze. My heart pounded. I clenched my fists and, irrationally, all I could think about was the dirt crusted under my nails.

Suzt stood beside the portal, her face ashen. Through the tear I saw Holly and Shar sitting on a grassy knoll.

In an alien world.

"I'm so sorry, Kyra." Suzt's voice hitched. "I don't know what happened. I looked away for only a moment. I swear! I don't know how she opened it!"

I ignored her for the moment. Only Holly and Shar mattered now. And I didn't blame Suzt for any baby-sitting transgression. I knew how quickly children could find mischief, but there was a big difference between trying to climb a bookcase and opening a rift to another world.

How had Holly even done it? Was it even Holly? Maybe Shar had opened the rift.

79

The edges of the tear were ragged. This wasn't a stable portal. Fear shot through me like electricity—fear that the door would suddenly slam shut and I'd have no way to get to my babies.

Shar let out a gurgle and hopped on the grassy hill. Holly saw me and shrieked in delight. "Mama!" Then her attention was stolen by something in the distance and she toddled off the hill, away from me.

I jumped through the portal feeling the sting of its magic, knowing that simply crossing the boundary might be the catalyst that broke the rift's magic in our realm, but at least I'd be on the right side of the door with Holly and Shar.

The portal held. I keened its hum behind me as I took a moment to study the landscape.

Holly and Shar had come down the hill to sit on the bank of a slow moving river. Between us lay a hundred yards of rock and bare ground. Other than the mound of grass they'd been sitting on, the entire landscape was either gray stone or gray water.

I recognized the desolation from the brief view Terra had given me on Mount Trembles. This was the barren world that Shar would one day claim. But even as I watched, green shoots burst through the rocks on the river bank. Reeds grew and flowers popped from swaying green stalks all around Shar and Holly. They were blooming for Shar. This was her world.

Holly plunked down in the growing greenery to pluck blossoms. Her blond curls fluttered in the alien breeze. Shar lifted her snout and made little chirping noises.

"Holly, honey. Just stay where you are, okay? Mommy's coming."

My baby girl turned to me with a big smile. Her chubby fingers fiddled with something—a charm on a long leather thong.

Dear All-father. She had the pendant Terra had given me. I'd put it away in a box on my dresser, but my daughter's keening was hypersensitive, and she must have felt it calling to her. And now my carelessness had put us all in danger.

I climbed down the bank. Holly stood up. One hand gripped the pendant. The other held a delicate white flower.

"Fower!" My daughter never spoke when a bellow could do the job just as well.

She took a step toward the water as if to throw the flower into the river.

"Holly! Don't move! Don't go near the water!" I had no idea what lurked in that river. This place looked barren, but looks can be deceiving.

I reached my pair of intergalactic escapees and took the pendant from Holly's hand. She let out a screech, loud enough to stir the primordial soup of this new world. I wasn't in the mood to cajole her out of a temper tantrum. Instead, I scooped her under one arm and Shar under the other and bolted through the portal.

I dumped the screaming, squirming toddler in Suzt's arms and turned back to close the rift by twisting the onyx moon on the pendant. The portal winked out of existence.

Shar squirmed in my grip and I let her down in the sandbox. She snuffled the ground around the closed portal. Holly didn't give me a chance to scold or even to thank the All-father for her safe return. She was a sensitive child in every way. Her keening had picked up on the burst of magic from the closing rift and her emotions reflected the fear and agitation coming off Suzt and me.

She took a deep breath and screamed. And screamed. Her face turned red and sweaty. I sat on the picnic table, held her in my arms and let her cry and thrash it out. I let her feel the feels and keen the keens. Shar climbed onto the bench beside me. Her big eyes looked worried behind the lattice-work shell. I ran a hand along her smooth back in reassurance. She snuffled my leg with her three-pronged nose and settled down to wait out the tantrum. Holly wailed and rubbed her leaky eyes on my shoulder. I patted her back until her cries subsided to hiccups.

Grim, deciding the emergency was over, jumped down from the table and stalked off toward the patio, swishing his silver pantaloons.

"I'm really sorry," Suzt said.

"It's okay, really. My fault. I shouldn't have left the pendant hanging around."

Suzt eyed the silver and onyx pendant on the table.

"That little thing is the cause of all this trouble? I saw it around Holly's neck. I thought you gave it to her."

I closed my fist on the pendant and stuck it in my pocket. "Please don't mention this to anyone, especially not your brothers."

Suzt nodded. "Tums couldn't hold onto a secret if it was sewn into his pocket." Goblins had great aphorisms.

"Exactly. And with all the visitors around here lately, I don't want anyone to get ideas."

"But what's it for? That jewel, I mean. Why would anyone need to open such a door?"

"Terra gave it to me. It's for Shar." We both looked down at the little critter with the big eyes. "One day that world will be her home."

"You can't mean to leave that poor wee one in that…that awful place!"

I closed my eyes and breathed in the scent of my daughter's hair. It was usually as calming as a soporific, but not this time.

Shar's future was something I had tried to put out of my mind. I knew it was coming, but I thought we had years and years before she'd be mature enough to take her place as the great spirit of her own realm.

But what about those flowers and green growing shoots? Did that mean Shar was ready to bring life to the lifeless planet? Should I be opening the portal more often, letting her grow within that world?

I had many questions and no answers. Terra might have helped, but I had no desire to seek her out again.

All I could do was hold my babies close and hope that when the time came I would be wise enough to let them both make their way in whatever world they chose.

CHAPTER

11

'd been sitting in the corner of my daughter's room for over an hour, watching her sleep. I hadn't even bothered with a chair but just slid my back down the wall and tucked my knees under my chin. Shar had played with Jacoby for a while, but now they both slept sprawled across Holly's bed too.

It was late.

I should really go to bed.

It had been three days since Holly and Shar were nearly lost in an alien world. They seemed to have forgotten their adventure already, but I couldn't.

I watched Holly sleep some more. She was so...precious. Not as in sweet and cute, which she could be, but precious as in beyond worth, beyond rare and special. And she'd almost been lost to me in the blink of a closing portal. Both of them.

As a rescuer, I keenly understood wrangling rule number twenty-one: sometimes the right thing to do is let them go. The only critters I kept in cages were those I couldn't let back into the wild because they wouldn't survive. All the others stayed of their own free will.

Shar was different. She was just a baby, but she was growing fast. Or at least her magic was. It seeped off her when she slept, despite the puckwudgie's constant magic training.

One day soon, I'd have to let Holly go out into the world on her own too. That was the unvoiced agreement between parent and child. It didn't mean I didn't worry about her. I did, but they were earthly worries that I could wrap my head around. Would she find someone to love? A good job? A happy life? Could I keep her safe from vampires and other predators long enough to find those things?

My worry for Shar was on a whole other level. She was a world seed, a nucleus of magic so potent it would one day create life on a new planet. How did any parent prepare for that?

I keened Mason's deep thrumming magic in the doorway.

"Come for a walk with me."

I shook my head.

"I'll just sit here a while longer."

I heard him disappear into Raven's room next door. He came back with a sleepy Princess. The hound yawned and bowed and settled across the doorway to Holly's room.

"Raven promised to keep his door open and headphones off. Princess will sleep right here, and Dutch is making bread in the kitchen." Mason held out his hand. "Come walk with me."

I hesitated.

"Mom! Go outside!" Raven yelled from his room. "Your stress is stinking up the whole house!"

Teenagers. Keeping it real since 1960.

I sighed and grabbed Mason's hand. He pulled me up and we stepped over Princess who rolled to show her belly. I paused to give her a quick scratch.

The night air had a lingering chill as if winter didn't want to give up its grasp. Up the hill and past the barn, smoke came from the chimney of the Goblin's cottage. A light burned behind the curtains, but no one stirred. By silent agreement, Mason and I headed up the driveway toward the Guardians' gatehouse. Angus perched on the roof above the front door.

"Evening, Captain." He nodded toward us. "It's a fine night for an amble." Officially, Angus had taken over as Captain of the Guardians when Mason became Prime Minister, but he would always think of Mason as his captain.

"Everyone settled in at the camp?" Mason asked.

"Oh, aye. There was a bit of bad blood between the yetis and the hidebehinds, but old Cletus got that sorted. He doesn't suffer the gowks, you know."

"That's good." I had no idea what a gowk was, but Angus seemed pleased.

Cletus kept his bluecaps in order. I was glad to see his authority was extending to the growing and eclectic group of settlers in the camp.

We left Angus to his watch and headed through the hedge. At the gate, I paused to look back at the house. Golden light shone from the lower windows. It looked idyllic, the perfect refuge in the forest that protected my family, but this week had shown that nowhere was truly safe. Not really. My family could be taken from me in an instant.

Mason saw my uncertainty.

"They'll be fine for a few minutes. Come on." He laced his fingers through mine and we headed down the path that cut through the cemetery.

The snow was mostly melted, but a few patches still clung to the ground on the shady side of gravestones. A black spot blighted the ground where Kester and I had trapped the demon last fall. Nothing would grow there now. Mason's eyes slid over the spot. His grip tightened on mine. This little yard held so many memories for us, some good, some bad.

We passed one of the oldest graves.

"That's where I almost skewered you," I said. "Remember? I thought you were a poacher."

Mason chuckled. "That was the day I learned never to startle a Valkyrie with a sword."

"A solid lesson."

We stopped and he rested his hand on another headstone. "And this is where Ollie dug up the bloodstone. Have you had any news from the dragons?"

"Not yet. I reached out to Herne but he hasn't seen the thunder around Annequin Lodge in months. Avie contacted Carmen too. She promised to have her teams look out for them."

I'd first met Carmen Perez-Malone around Christmas two years ago, when a thunder of dragons had nested on Roden & Hogg's scavenging site. The dragon queen turned out to be Ruby (or Kalindari as I now knew her), the dragon I'd helped in the past, and so she agreed to negotiate with me. The negotiations had proved valuable to R&H and Carmen still remembered us at Christmas with a bag of precious coffee beans.

"The dragons could be anywhere on the continent. Heck, for all I know they can cross the ocean. I'm not relying on their help."

"It was a long shot," Mason said. "But there will be others."

I nodded. So far we'd gained promises from Soolea's people in Winaskwi and a growing faction of displaced homesteaders in the shanty towns north and south of Montreal Ward. The godlings were still being difficult. The Olympians, who hated the vamps with all the passion of their gods, had pledged their support. The Saivites were less forthcoming. Gabe's father hadn't survived Nici's plotting, and the Hindu pantheon was now led by Gabe's sister-in-law, Uma. She didn't like me much.

The other, smaller godling pantheons were led by a former fae minister, Ken Okorafa. I'd dealt with him before and he seemed a fair man. I hoped that he would be sympathetic to our cause, and maybe even drag Merrow Farsigh, the fae Prime Minister, into the fight. We had a meeting booked with him for the end of the week.

I spied a flash of silver fur through the trees. Grim was out patrolling the homestead's perimeter again. Errol would be riding on his shoulder, looking for soft spots in the ward and boosting it when he could.

As we strolled through the forest, we were greeted by a chirp from a hidebehind. One of Cricket's clan was guarding the ward gate tonight.

"All quiet, Soren?" I asked.

"Quiet," he chirped.

The hidebehind bent his trunk-like body in a mimic of a bow. His nearly translucent wings were folded neatly behind him. He had twiggy arms and a crown of sticks, with a flat face textured like bark and deep-set black eyes. He stood under two cedars that had nearly blown over in a storm and whose trunks now bowed together to form a natural arch. Anyone walking through the woods would never suspect it was more than that, but Errol had used this doorway as the marker for the ward gate.

Beyond it I could see flickering campfires where the bluecaps had settled, and more camps further out with refugees from Hedge and Barrows. After that, the Inbetween spread before us in all its magnificent and savage delight.

I keened the ward as we passed under the arch. It was a friendly tickle that reminded me we no longer enjoyed the homestead's protection.

Neva spotted us first as we came into camp.

"Come have a cuppa, dears." Before I could protest, she pushed a horn cup into my hand. I politely took a sip. It was some kind of mulled spirit, like fortified wine—sweet and spicy and packing a punch.

"Come, come. Sit." Neva ushered us toward a communal bonfire. The bluecaps had done a lot in the few days since they'd arrived. Already, sturdy structures were going up. Tents filled in other spaces. It was a comfortable and vibrant community.

The yetis eyed us warily and didn't make a move in greeting. They had their own fire and hadn't built a house yet. I wasn't sure yetis needed shelters. There wasn't much weather that could get through their pelts.

Around another, smaller campfire sat a goblin, two brownies, two wood trolls, and a couple of fae I didn't recognize.

Neva saw my gaze shift to this new group. "They showed up this afternoon." She gave me a calculating look. "There are more coming in every day. Seems like you've got the knack for talking up this war. They're all fired up and ready to fight."

I sipped my drink and considered her words. In the last few months, I'd met with Hub officials, godlings and even a representative from the Knackers, the gang of thugs and thieves that ran cage fights in the shanty towns. By now, everyone in Montreal had probably heard about the crazy Valkyrie with a vendetta against vampires. If I had a talent for rallying troops, we'd have a much bigger army by now.

"Just don't let them near the homestead. The only guards on ward duty are ones I approve." I didn't need brownies running amok on my property.

"Of course." Neva turned me away from the other bluecaps settled around the campfire. "When do you think we'll be, you know, chasing vamps?"

It was a good question, but I didn't have a good answer.

"I'm hoping for support from Hub, but so far they're unconvinced of the urgency of the matter. Mason and I will be meeting with them again this week. I'll have a better answer for you then."

Neva slapped her hands on her thighs. "Good enough. We have work to do here that will keep us busy. Axes to sharpen and spears to harden." There was a twinkle in her eyes as if she were talking about trimming the yule tree.

Mason was deep in conversation with Cletus on the other side of the bonfire. I was suddenly very tired. This week had taken a toll on me, and I wanted to get an early start in the morning. We had several possible new allies to petition.

I was just about to signal to Mason that we should leave when I noticed movement by the yeti camp. The shaggy creatures stood up in such a hurry that one knocked over the stump he'd been sitting on. Then they did the most astonishing thing. They bowed. Not a bend from the waist, but a full prostration with hands outstretched and heads resting on the muddy ground.

A woman hobbled into camp.

She was tall, but thin and slightly stooped. She held a bent stick like a staff and walked slowly with a pronounced limp. Brown hair streaked with gray was caught in a rag tie at her nape and the ponytail fell to her waist. She wasn't dressed warm enough for the weather and her hand on the staff was red with swollen knuckles.

Bluecaps emerged from tents and half-built shacks. A murmur rippled through them, then one by one, they also bowed. Behind me a hidebehind gasped. "Terra!" Then he also bent in prostration.

Terra smiled and raised a thin hand as if in benediction. She looked frail and worn down, except for her eyes. When she turned them on me, they blazed with dark fire.

I nudged Mason. "You can see her, right?"

"Uh-huh."

"Good." That meant I wasn't lying in a coma somewhere dreaming that the god had come for a visit. Even so, when I reached out to take her arm, I more than half expected Terra to vanish in a cloud of smoke.

Instead, my hand closed over a very solid elbow—solid but much too thin. Her clothes were ragged and too big for her, as if she'd stolen them off a clothesline. Bones jutted through the thin jacket. I glanced down at her feet. She wore open-toed sandals in April, when the snow was still clinging to patches of forest. Her feet, like her hands, were red and raw from the cold.

Her gaze caught mine and held it.

"Hello, Kyra. How's my war coming?"

Then the god of all Earth collapsed.

caught Terra as her legs gave out. It was like catching a bag of bones.

"Don't make a fuss." She wheezed and I could hear phlegm in her lungs. I nodded to Mason and he scooped her into his arms. Terra mewled in protest and we both ignored her.

The bluecaps waited with heads bowed as we moved through the camp. At the ward gate, Soren touched the divine toe dangling over Mason's arm and made a trilling sound that could have been a curse or a prayer. From his wide-eyed look of wonder, I was betting on prayer.

Perfect. That's all I needed—a bunch of pilgrims banging down our door for a glimpse of the divine.

I glanced at Terra. With her head flopped on Mason's arm and long hair hanging in dirty mats, she didn't look divine. So how had the yetis recognized her? And the hidebehinds? Did that mean she'd been visiting them in their dreams too? Or she'd sent her mountain devil after them? I had a brief image of the fiery mountain devil coming up against the yetis and laughed.

"You okay back there?" Mason said over his shoulder.

"I'm fine. Just contemplating the insanity that is my life."

Mason grunted and stepped over a grave. We were halfway through the cemetery.

I had so many questions that would have to wait. My first priority was taking care of the god, not in the sense of prayers, but in the very real sense of tending to her broken body. Mason jogged toward our yard as if he didn't carry a burden.

Gita, who had recently taken to prowling restlessly at night, met us at the barn. She peered at the god in Mason's arms, let out one huge wail that sounded very much like an expletive, then shut herself inside the barn.

Terra didn't seem to notice. She was barely conscious.

Inside, Mason carried her up the stairs and set her down on a chair in the spare bedroom while I drew the bath. When I came back, Terra was already snoring with her chin fallen toward her shoulder. Her breath was an unhealthy rattle in her chest.

"I already called Nori," Mason said. "She's stuck in Barrows at the hospital without transport. I'll have to go pick her up."

"Could you?" I wasn't sure a god could actually die, but if so, I really didn't want her to expire in my spare bedroom.

"Of course. I'm going right now."

"Before you leave, can you wake up Jacoby? Ask him to find Terra some clothes to wear from my dresser. Something comfortable with warm socks. Then get Dutch up and ask him to make tea."

"I will." He kissed me, then held my cheek in the palm of his hand. "Be careful. We don't know what any of this means."

I nodded. Terra might seem like a frail old lady but the sudden appearance of a god on your doorstep was never the opening act of a happily-ever-after story.

"Terra?" I shook her gently. She snorted and came awake. "Let's get you in the bath." She seemed dazed, but she didn't resist me as I helped her into the bathroom and pulled off her grimy clothes. They were beyond cleaning or repairing, and I threw them right in the trash. Her body was painfully thin. I could count the ribs on her back as I helped her into the tub.

She cried out when her raw feet sank into the water. Even tepid water can feel like it burns on frostbitten skin. I lifted her feet and propped them on the end of the tub, tucking a rolled towel under her ankles for support.

Terra closed her eyes and I examined her feet. They looked like someone had taken a cheese grater to them. Blisters had formed and burst on top of other blisters. Skin peeled. Joints were swollen and red. How had she walked on these? And for how long?

I let her soak but sat on the toilet seat and watched. I didn't trust her not to fall asleep and drown, which brought me back to that question. Could you kill a god? Someone had certainly given it a good try.

And how was she even walking in our world? The last time I'd met her, across the veil, she'd explained to me how gods germinated life in a new world—the way Shar would, one day. Eventually, their magic grew too great to interact with the life they created. When Terra's magic reached its apex, she'd moved into a different plane and watched the world she'd nurtured from afar. She'd assured me that a true god couldn't manifest in our world, not without breaking the laws of reality.

And yet. Here she was.

The warm water seemed to rouse her. She moaned and turned her head to lay it against the porcelain.

"I'm going to wash your hair. Is that okay?" I lifted a hank of hair. The last time I'd seen her, it had been a lustrous brown. Now it was streaked with gray and matted with twigs and dirt.

Terra mumbled something that I took as an affirmative. I did the best I could, lathering and rinsing her hair, but she was barely responsive and offered little help. The bath water was murky after the first rinsing and I washed it a second time.

Once out of the bath, she trembled in the cool air. I dried her quickly and wrapped her in a fluffy robe. Then I sat her back in the chair in the spare room and tucked a blanket over her knees while I tried to comb out her hair.

Jacoby arrived with clothes and fussed with the socks. His tongue jutted from the corner of his mouth as he slid them on Terra's swollen and inflexible feet.

Dutch appeared in the doorway, took one look at our wasted visitor and sucked in a sharp breath. Our eyes met over her head, and I nodded. Mason had obviously filled him in about our illustrious guest.

He left without another word, but by the time I had her combed out, Dutch re-appeared with a steaming mug.

"Bone broth." He handed it to me. "More fortifying than tea. I'll put some biscuits in the oven, in case she's feeling up to something solid later."

I took the mug and thanked him. "Help me move her to the bed."

We tucked pillows behind her and Terra roused enough to take a few sips before I set the mug on the side table. Then I sat and listened to the death rattle of a god.

NORI ARRIVED LOOKING HAGGARD. Because of the opji raids, the shanty towns were bursting with refugees. All those people crammed into close quarters proved the perfect breeding ground for an epidemic, and last year the flu had ravaged the population. The virus was wearing itself out, but the hospitals were still past capacity and Nori had been in the thick of it for months. It showed on her face. Her skin was so pale it was almost luminous. She'd cut off most of her glossy black hair and pulled it back into a short ponytail. Dark circles ringed her eyes and new lines had appeared at their edges. In those creases, I saw the shadow of her lost Grandfather, Yuki. He'd been a great sorcerer, and his wisdom was reflected in Nori's eyes.

She put one hand on Terra's chest and listened to her heart and lungs. Terra didn't wake up.

"Pneumonia." She felt for the pulse on her wrist, then examined the red, swollen knuckles and said, "Pernio." When she saw my confusion, she added. "Chilblains."

"Are you sure?" I wished I could pull those words back as soon as I said them. I didn't want to insult Nori's medical skill. "I'm sorry."

She waved my apology away.

"I've seen a lot of this in the last few months. Hundreds of people with no shelter from the cold." She held Terra's hand in hers. "It will pass, but hurts like hell."

"Her feet are worse."

Nori lifted the blanket to expose the blistered feet.

Nori just shook her head. "She's been walking for weeks, maybe months. We call it refugee foot. Nothing for it but to keep them clean and dry. I'll give you some antibiotics for the pneumonia. I'm sorry I can't do more, but I'm all tapped out." She patted her chest. I knew what a toll healing took out of Nori. She gave a little bit of her magic—her essence—every time she healed. It was no wonder she seemed to have aged ten years in a few months.

"She needs bed rest," Nori said, "lots of fluid and good food. She's too thin. Who is she anyway?"

"A friend." That wasn't exactly true. One did not presume friendship with the gods, but it was the only answer I could give. "Is there anything…unusual about her?"

"You mean like is she fae?" Nori cocked her head and studied Terra. "Not that I can tell. She's the most human one in this room, anyway."

I nodded. That's what I thought too. Ever since Terra arrived, I'd been periodically scanning her with my keening but she registered completely human and magic free.

Nori leaned back and stretched her back. "If you don't mind, I'll grab some sleep at the gatehouse. Haven't had a decent night's rest in months. Then tomorrow morning I can try to do something about those blistered feet before I head back."

"Of course. Whatever you need."

Nori considered the patient once more. "Does she have anything to do with this fight against the opji?"

"I think so. She might be pivotal even."

"Well, I hope she recovers then. And you know, I'll be ready when you call. Me and a few other doctors at the hospital. We're tired of all this death. We're ready to take the head off the snake whenever you are."

"Good to know. Thanks."

TWO DAYS LATER, TERRA was already whining to get out of bed.

"No way." I tucked the blankets firmly around her waist. "You stay put or I'll shackle you to the headboard."

She grumbled, but not for long since she had a hard time staying awake. I let her sleep.

When she woke again, she enjoyed a short visit with Holly and Shar. She found them delightful, but I knew how exhausting their exuberance could be, and I limited their visits to no more than a few minutes.

As I shooed them out the door, Terra was already slipping back into sleep.

So far, she'd given no explanation for her astonishing appearance.

On the third day, I found her sitting in the chair by the window. Her eyes seemed less sunken but her complexion was still an unhealthy gray. Before returning to the hospital in Barrows, Nori had used what little reserves she had to heal Terra's feet. The blisters were gone, but under the fuzzy socks, her feet were still red and swollen. I couldn't imagine the pain she'd experienced even hobbling from bed to chair.

I set a tray on the side table and served her a mug of tea with honey. The tray also held a plate of Dutch's famous Welsh cakes and a bowl of fresh fruit.

She sipped the tea, added more honey and sipped again. Then she bit into a cake and closed her eyes as she savored it. She put the scone down after only one bite. Her sad smile brought out the wrinkles around her lips.

"I'd forgotten how amazing food is. Amazing and shocking too. It sets your mouth abuzz. I can feel it all the way down." She patted her thin chest and grinned at me. "Warm and spicy."

I pulled a second chair to the window, then leaned over and pinched her arm gently.

"What was that for?"

"Just checking to see that you're real and not the product of my fevered imagination."

"Oh Kyra, don't be obtuse." Terra pursed her lips, reminding me of Gita. "And stop fussing over me. I'm really here and I'm solid flesh and bone. Let's move on to more important matters."

I sipped my tea, studying her. "I just don't get it. You made a big deal about the whole 'My magic is too big to manifest in this world' thing. You invaded my dreams. You had that mountain devil after me for months." My voice rose as I numbered her transgressions. "You dragged me all the way up Mount Trembles to your shrine because you couldn't step foot in our world. And now?" I waved a hand at her very corporeal self.

"That was before." Terra's brows lowered.

"Before what?"

"Before the opji scourge stole my pith." Her lips were pressed thin, accentuating the lines around her mouth.

"What exactly does that mean?"

Instead of answering, she picked up an orange from the bowl and started to peel it. It was painful to watch her stiff hands pull back the skin of the orange. I reached out to help, but she swatted me away. Her gnarled fingers dug into the peel. Juice squelched over her nails. She pulled away the orange skin and held it out, white side toward me.

"The pith. Neither the flesh nor the heart, but the substance that connects the two."

"This isn't going to be one of those conversations where I end up with more questions than answers, is it?"

"Only if you don't keep quiet and listen." She pursed her lips, then relaxed. "The pith separates the flesh from the skin. Without it, neither would hold its shape. The juice of the flesh would leak through the skin, yes?"

I nodded.

"The pith protects the flesh. It also supports the peel which protects the heart from the outside world. It is an interstitial substance and necessary to the essence of both spirit and body. That is what the opji stole from me."

I had a crazy moment imagining the vamps peeling back layers of Terra, like that silly old joke my mother used to tell me. How do you make shepherd's pie? First you peel two shepherds...

Terra saw my expression and said, "You find this amusing?"

I reined in my hysterics and shook my head. "No. I'm just confused. The opji stole your pith? How?"

"They set a thousand poor souls on fire along with even more trees. It gave them enough power to enact the Gadzic, an unholy rite that separated my pith from my body and my spirit."

By the All-father. I knew things were bad in Vioska, but now they were burning people alive? I tried to focus on the rest of her words.

"So the opji have some inter-spacial substance you call pith—"

"Interstitial," Terra corrected.

"Whatever. And this," I waved a hand at the frail body seated before me, "is your flesh. Where is your spirit."

Terra sighed. "My spirit is where it always was, in the heart of the Earth."

"And you can live like this, as three entities?"

"It's complicated, but yes. We may be separate but we are always connected. A bit of my spirit resides in the flesh. A bit of the flesh in the pith, and so on. We can never truly be torn asunder."

I was having difficulty wrapping my head around the logic.

"If you're here, does that mean there is no one left in control of things?"

"Whatever do you mean, child? Speak plainly."

"All right. Over the years that I've been blessed with your favor—and I use that term loosely—I've pieced together a few ideas about how the great spirits and The Great Spirit work."

"Oh, please, do enlighten me." Terra crossed her arms and settled more deeply into the chair. I ignored her sarcasm. I needed to hash out the ideas that had been clouding my thoughts for months.

"Minor great spirits, what the Algonquins called manitous, are the essence of a thing. The first idea of a mountain. Or a bear. They embody the very spirit that first allowed that thing to manifest in our world. These spiritual ideas grow and change over time. Am I right, so far?"

Terra's mouth was pinched in disapproval, but she nodded for me to go on.

"But the world also had a manitou. It was once just an idea that grew and took on power. Like a seed taking root and putting forth leaves. Shar is one such manitou seedling. You were one too, once upon a time."

Terra nodded again, her expression softer now.

"Eventually this spirit seedling grows in power—becomes so great, it can no longer stay in the world it created for fear of breaking the natural laws. How am I doing?"

Terra nodded for me to keep going.

"So when you left Earth, its spirit remained at its heart, here with us. And yet somehow you are that spirit. I don't get it."

"What's not to get. Humans have been giving their gods dual or even triple personalities for millennia. It's like the Christians' God the Father, God the Son and God the Holy Spirit. They exist together and apart. It's one of those theological ideas that doesn't bear close examination. It has to be taken on faith."

"Okay. I can accept that. But my worry is that if you are here in this corporeal form, does that mean Earth's manitou is dead? Or have you been severed from it?"

I didn't know which idea frightened me most. A dead planet sounded like a recipe for apocalypse. On the other hand, a Great Spirit without reins could be catastrophic too.

Terra considered me for a long time, as if deciding how much truth she could tell me, or rather how much truth I could bear. Finally, she sighed and leaned her head against the chair. I thought she'd drift off to sleep, leaving me with no answers again, but she finally spoke.

"The opji spell woke me on Mount Trembles over six months ago. You might have felt the Earth quaking at my return."

Oh, my gods. The earthquake last fall. That had been Terra's re-entry into our world.

"You walked from the summit of Mount Trembles here? In the middle of winter?"

She nodded without opening her eyes. "When I first woke, I didn't understand what they had done. All I knew was that I was alone. Truly alone. I could no longer feel the Great Spirit inside me. As I lay there in the cold, my senses returned and I felt the power, not in me, but all around me. We were together but separated. That's when I understood. They'd taken my pith."

"But for what purpose? What is the point in stealing your pith?"

She opened her eyes and fixed her gaze on me. "They locked me in this weak body, so they can kill me." She ran a hand down her chest and stomach. Her knuckles were still red. Some of the blisters had popped and left ragged, oozing skin.

"Is that possible?" The thought of killing a Great Spirit nearly undid me. The repercussions were unimaginable, but they would make the Flood Wars look like a tea party.

Terra took my hand. "Don't worry, dear. They can kill this body, but not my spirit. Not the Earth's spirit. It is eternal. But as long as they hold my pith, I can't fight them either. I have no power without it, no way to connect my will to my spirit."

She sank back into her chair again. I could see she was worn out. I had so many more questions, but they'd have to wait.

I sighed and tucked the blanket around her legs.

I'd waited five months for Emil to return with information about the opji's forces, and now, it seemed, we were out of time.

"If only we knew what the opji wanted. All this would make more sense."

"Oh, I know what they want," Terra mumbled, half asleep. "They want chaos."

studied my grapefruit, thinking about Terra's explanation of pith. I didn't quite grasp her meaning. I could see it on the edges of my vision, but if I turned to look it full in the face, the meaning ghosted away. I stared at the pink, juicy flesh that was the heart of the grapefruit. Heart. Pith. Flesh. All one, but separate.

I sighed and stirred the fruit wedges aimlessly. I wasn't hungry.

Terra had slept most of the day yesterday, and when I peeked in her room this morning, she was still sleeping. Mason had been out the night before, trying to garner support from the few contacts he had left in parliament after fire-bombing his short-lived career in politics. I hadn't heard him come home, and I'd left him snoring quietly when I got up.

That was half an hour ago. Now he walked into the kitchen looking fresher than I felt.

He quirked an eyebrow when he saw me in rapt contemplation of my citrus.

"Thinking deep thoughts?"

I sighed and pushed the bowl away.

"I'm thinking about pith."

Mason managed to grin and scowl at the same time. He poured a mug of coffee. Rations meant we had one each in the morning and I'd almost drunk his too. He sat beside me at the table, cradling his mug.

"Pith?" He took a sip of coffee, frowned and pushed the mug at me. I sipped. It was over-cooked and tasted like burned ass. I drank it anyway.

"Yesterday, Terra tried to explain the difference between spirit and pith, and how they can be separated from the body." I waved a hand in the air. "It's all just crazy talk, I think. But now I'm trying to imagine how one might store something like pith."

Mason chose a blueberry scone from the basket in the center of the table, as I knew he would. "Ah. That would be a pith jar."

I gave him the stink eye. "You're just making that up."

"I'm not." He held a hand to his heart as if to swear it. "Alchemists use pith jars all the time. A blazing alembic separates a substance into its elements. A pith jar stores them. Witches call them spirit jars."

"So a spirit jar is like a bloodstone?" We'd encountered our fair share of bloodstones, magically inert vessels that could store vast amounts of magic, including spirits.

"Not exactly." Mason chewed and swallowed before continuing. "A bloodstone holds an entire spirit and discards the body. There is no coming back from that separation. Except by divine intervention, of course." He smiled wanly.

"Of course."

Terra had brought Mason back whole and uninjured from his imprisonment in a bloodstone. The only other bloodstone I had known to be cracked had been Polina's, but the spirits in that one didn't return as flesh and bone.

"It's a bit of a misnomer," Mason said. "A spirit jar holds only a portion of the spirit."

"What Terra called the pith."

"Exactly. If pith is taken from a mundane, they will continue to live for a while at least, but they'll be weakened and eventually die. From a fae or another magic user, they'd lose their magic entirely until pith, body and spirit are re-united."

"And pith taken from a god?"

Mason tilted his head and frowned. "You mean from Terra? Is this what happened?"

I nodded. "She says the opji stole it from her."

"*Ciboire!*" Mason smashed his fist on the crumbs of his scone, mashing them into the table, then continued with a lengthier catalogue of French curses. Was it wrong that I found him sexy when he ranted in French?

I let him wear out his stockpile of swear words before continuing.

"She says we have to get her spirit jar back, but I'm not even sure what we're looking for."

"The jar will probably be made of crystal. That's the most inert substance. It could be shaped like anything. A pendant, a bottle or a vial. Anything hollow with a lid that can be sealed by magic. The pith will be a gas-like substance inside. Terra must ingest it, in order to restore herself."

I had suspected as much. "So we have to get her to Vioska."

He nodded. "And soon. If the opji have taken her out of play, it's because they plan to move quickly."

"I was thinking the same thing. It may already be too late. I wish she hadn't taken so long getting to us."

Terra appeared in the doorway like a wraith. "I'm sorry that Mount Trembles is so far away. And I didn't show up in this world with a widget or I would have called you sooner." Her voice was stern with only a hint of mockery.

Mason stood so quickly, his chair tipped backward. He caught it without taking his eyes off Terra.

"My lady, I haven't had the chance to thank you properly." He went down on one knee and took her red, swollen hand in his. "I was lost and you found me. You were the light that led me through the darkness. I will never forget. And you will always have the force of my prayers, no matter what body you wear."

Wow, and…wow! Mason had never spoken of his time inside the bloodstone. In the first weeks after his return, he'd struggled with the memory of the demon's many crimes. I hadn't pushed him to talk about being trapped with the demon, first in his own body, then in the bloodstone.

And what it must have been like to be freed by Terra.

He still knelt in front of the frail, old god with his head bowed over their clasped hands.

"Don't make such a fuss." Terra pulled on his hand, forcing his eyes to meet hers. "You've lived a long life. You should know by now that the gods never do anything without reason."

Mason nodded. "And what is your reason?"

Terra pulled her hand away, and sighed. "Pour me some tea and sit. Then I'll tell you."

After dropping three large dollops of honey into it, Terra sipped her tea. Her body might look frail, but her eyes were sharp as she studied us.

Finally, she said, "You wondered what would happen to a god with no pith?"

How long had she been standing outside the kitchen, listening to our conversation?

"She becomes human. More or less." Terra pressed a hand to her chest. "This body will die like any mortal's. And while it lives, I am cut off from the Earth, from the source of my spirit, my magic. My power."

"And if you get your pith back?" I asked.

Terra smiled. It was a terrible expression, full of the awesome weight of divine knowledge. Outside, the sun dipped behind a cloud, and I had the irrational feeling that she'd made that happen.

"With my pith comes my connection to my power. The opji have made a crucial mistake. Separated from this world by the veil, I could only manipulate from afar, use my agents to do my bidding." She nodded toward Mason and I, not seeming to care that we might take offense at being called her minions.

"But they brought me here. And if I recover my pith, I will have power beyond all reckoning. Power enough to obliterate even the memory of the opji from this world."

"So they'll be guarding that spirit jar like it means their lives because it does," I said.

Terra nodded.

"And we need to recover it."

Terra nodded again. "You were always meant to be my generals in this war. But now I will march with you."

I rose to make more coffee. To hell with rations. If we were going to war, there was no point in saving the few luxuries we still had.

Terra stopped me with a hand on my arm.

"There's something else you need to know. It's about the shar-lil."

I sat, all thoughts of coffee vanishing.

14

fter breakfast, I helped Terra back to her room. She leaned heavily on me and closed her eyes as soon as I tucked her into bed. She was asleep before I shut the door.

Mason had Holly's breakfast in hand, so I headed out to the kitchen garden. It was a little early for planting, but this garden was mostly herbs, and many were perennials. They didn't really need my fussing to grow. I was the one who needed to fuss. I needed to put my hands to work on something to distract my brain from Terra's revelations. So I clipped old growth and pulled weeds. And I worried.

Terra had confirmed my worst fear. Shar was pivotal to Ichovidar's plans and he would come after her.

Of course, I'd known that the vamps coveted the shar-lil. That's where I found her in the first place. Nici had most certainly been sent by Ichovidar to break Shar's magic. She'd anointed the little critter with gallons of godling blood in hopes of breaking her. What had Nici hoped to achieve by this breaking?

Chaos, Terra had said. If Shar grew to her full potential here on Earth, that's exactly what we'd have. Chaos. Not the sterile action-movie kind of chaos. True chaos. A rending of time and space.

I pulled winter debris from the garden fountain—handfuls of mushy leaves and muck that I dumped in a bucket destined for the compost. While I worked, I thought about Terra's last admonishment before exhaustion had taken her.

"Shar is a baby only in your eyes. She masks her magic well, thanks to Mr. Ludger's teaching, but she's grown in power since I last saw her. Soon you will have to make the decision to let her go."

I hauled a fistful of gunk from the fountain and threw it into the bucket with more force than was necessary. It splashed back, flecking my cheeks with sludge.

Great. I wiped my face with the back of my wrist. That made things worse as I smeared muck with dirt from my gloves.

Mason came out of the kitchen door, carrying Holly. Shar and Jacoby hopped around his feet. He put Holly down and she immediately made for the fountain.

"You've got something on your face." He pointed to my chin.

"Here?" I wiped at it.

Mason grinned and made a swirling motion that encompassed my whole face. "Looks like you've been finger-painting with mud." He tried to wipe some of it off with his sleeve, but Holly was already flinging more muck around, so I told him to leave it.

"You okay?" He frowned and tucked my braid behind my ear.

I looked down at Shar, who was stretching her front paws to the rim of the fountain and snuffling the muck too.

"It just seems unfair. I can't worry about Shar and be expected to mount an invasion on Vioska at the same time. It's too much." My chest felt tight and I knew I was close to losing it.

Mason took my hands in his. "No one ever said anything about fair."

Oh, that was a big help. I rolled my eyes.

He squeezed my fingers. "We'll take this one step at a time, yes? Vioska first. Then Shar."

"But what if Terra's right? What if I'm blind to her growing power? You should have seen her in that other world through the portal. She was already making it her own."

Mason shook my hands as if he could shake sense into me.

"Vioska first. Then Shar."

I met his eyes and saw the unspoken rest of that thought. If we didn't stop the opji, the rest didn't matter.

I nodded.

"I'm going into town today," he said. "To meet with Ramona and go over her presentation to Parliament."

I nodded. If Terra was right, we had to move soon. And to do that, we needed Hub's resources—soldiers, vehicles and weapons. In three days, Ramona was introducing a bill in the house, asking for that aid.

Mason kissed my cheek despite the muck. He planted another kiss on top of Holly's curls and left.

Grim slunk out the door as Mason went inside. He stalked along the retaining wall, then sat in a patch of sun with his tail swishing the stones. Jacoby hopped onto the wall and lay on his back in the sun too. He was learning to appreciate his days off from apprentice work.

The kitchen garden was a tiny patio nestled between the house and barn. The slope of the hill that led to the bank barn was kept at bay by a stone retaining wall. At the bottom of this hill, a pretty wooden gate separated the garden from the driveway. The only other way into this garden was through the kitchen.

During the summer, Gita grew all manner of herbs and medicinal plants here, but she was getting too old for the heavy labor of spring. It was time to teach a new generation the green skills.

I turned Holly's attention away from the fountain before she got too soaked.

"Come help me with the herbs." I gave her a gardening fork and showed her how to clear the dead leaves away. The tool was too big for her and she abandoned it, preferring to dig in the dirt with bare fingers. She patted last year's oregano plant and it immediately perked up like a soldier standing at attention in front of a beloved general. She poked at the creeping thyme and the brown vines stirred.

My widget buzzed on the stone bistro table next to the fountain.

"Gentle with the thyme baby," I said, as I pulled off my garden gloves. Holly cupped tiny stalks and cooed at them. In truth, thyme was pretty hardy and she could have pulled half of it out without doing much damage, but when you had a child that could call forth the vines and make them explode all in one breath, you taught her to respect the green.

I left her babbling to baby shoots and picked up my widget. There was a message from Carmen Perez-Malone. The opji incursion west of the city had affected her business too. Roden & Hogg scavenged bullas, the little time-capsules that sometimes erupted from Earth's core. With opji running rampant and burning half the northern forest, R&H had severely limited their reclamation business.

I scanned her message:

Shareholders agree. It's time to take the fight to Vioska. R&H has your back. Give me three days notice and we're ready to go.

This was great news. R&H had military-grade vehicles and weapons at their disposal. So far, the government of Montreal hadn't stepped up to provide anything in the way of arms or manpower, and I didn't hold out much hope for Ramona's plea. It was good to know we had other allies and resources.

As I texted back my thanks to Carmen, a commotion on the driveway made me look up. I heard a vehicle park, a car door closing and footsteps coming toward the garden before I saw anyone.

That was odd. The dryads were on guard duty by the gate today. They wouldn't let anyone through without my permission, except for…

"Hello, Kyra."

My grandmother, Lisobet, Ranger to the dryads who lived near the Pocono Mountains, had come for a visit.

Holly froze with her fingers stuck deep in the wet earth. Every dormant herb in the garden suddenly bristled.

For months, while I hunted the demon, Lisobet and Gita had been the only mothers Holly had known, but that had been half a year ago, a long time to a toddler. I had no idea how she'd react to seeing her great-grandmother again.

Lisobet opened the gate, then crouched with arms wide. "Hello Holly."

Holly paused, then from somewhere in her toddler brain the memory of love and comfort came back to her.

"Nana!" She flung herself into Lisobet's arms. Lisobet hugged her, mud and all. I saw actual tears in my grandmother's eyes. Who knew? I thought she was made of wood. She'd certainly never shown such emotion with me. Toddlers are powerful magic.

I LET LISOBET TAKE Holly inside and get her cleaned up while I swept last year's leaves from the back patio and cleaned the table and chairs, getting them ready for what would be the oddest tea party I'd ever hosted.

Jacoby showed up with Terra leaning on his fuzzy shoulder. I settled her into one of the chairs with a blanket over her lap. I'd sent Gita a text and she arrived a few minutes later, blinking into the afternoon sun.

"My lady." She nodded tearfully at Terra and took a seat.

Lisobet and Kester, my grandmother's half-demon boyfriend, joined us too. Kester held Holly in his arms. He was a fierce-looking man who used his looks to intimidate in the boardroom and the Senate. But Holly didn't notice. She clung to him like he was her favorite grandpa. And I supposed he was. It helped that he fed her toffees when he thought I wasn't looking.

I'd already warned them about our divine guest. I wasn't sure how Lisobet was going to act when faced with the god she revered. I didn't expect her to go all fan-girl on me.

"My lady." Lisobet bent one knee to the ground in front of Terra, bowed her head and waited there until the god placed the hand of benediction on her. If it wasn't already the end of the world, this gesture of supplication from my haughty grandmother would have shaken my world view.

"Do you come to join the fight?" Terra asked.

Lisobet rose, her face flushed. "You know the dryads do not seek out aggression, my lady. But we will defend to the death." A small smile lit her eyes. "And we know the right end of an arrow." She turned to me. "We will defend your home and your family. Seek out your battle and know they will be safe, no matter what happens."

No matter what. Three small words that could change my daughter's life. If we lost this fight, Holly would grow up among the tree-houses of Bosk. Would that be such a bad thing? Only if I wasn't there to see it.

Kester stepped forward and bowed to Terra. "I have no problem with killing a few vamps." His grin made him look a little maniacal.

Lisobet sat and took Holly on her knee. She shooed Kester away like a fly. "Battle talk later. Go make yourself useful in the camp and let us womenfolk chat." Far from being insulted at her dismissal, Kester kissed the top of her head and murmured something in her ear that made Lisobet turn a little red and press her lips together in disapproval. Then he nodded to Terra and to me in turn and left.

"Jacoby, go with him, please," I said. "Make sure the bluecaps know he's a friend."

Jacoby snatched a scone from the table and trotted after Kester.

Five women sat around the patio table—a banshee, a dryad ranger, a god, a toddler and me. The three elderly ladies eyed each other over the rims of their cups. Holly mashed a scone to pulp on the table.

Terra's hand shook as she lifted the teacup to her lips, sipped and placed it back on the table. The redness was fading from her knuckles, but she didn't seem to be getting stronger. I worried that if she continued to be separated from her pith, she'd only get weaker.

She patted her lips with a napkin and said, "With your grandmother here to defend the homestead, you have no more excuses. We must leave for Vioska before it's too late."

I shook my head "We still have allies to persuade to our cause. We meet with the godlings tomorrow and Ramona speaks to Parliament on Monday. We'll have a better estimate of our fighting force then."

Terra had lifted her cup again and she let it drop to the table with a crash. It might have been her weak grasp, but it startled me. I reached for her hand, and she swatted me away.

"Stupid girl! Stalling will lose this war for you. For all of us!"

She put a lot of venom in those words, and they hit me like a slap to the face.

Lisobet's eyes were narrowed. She was a Terran devotee, but she was also fiercely proud, and family meant more to her than any religion. The crashing teacup had startled a cry from Holly, and Lisobet jiggled her, making soothing noises until she settled.

Gita wept openly, of course. I didn't take that as support or abandonment. I sat back and crossed my arms.

"Running to Vioska without enough information or resources won't win this war either. You're in the real world now. We have real world problems like getting enough weapons and feeding that army." I pointed toward the camp outside our ward. "These meetings in the next two days will determine what kind of force we can expect when we reach Vioska."

Terra opened her mouth to rebuke me again, but I held up a hand. "I promised you a fight and I will deliver. I swear it. Just give me a few more days. On Monday we will make plans to leave, one way or another."

Whether or not we had support from Hub, the godlings and the fae, we'd go to war. I had three days to convince our allies to join us.

Terra watched me with lips pinched tight. She sighed.

"I can see I will not dissuade you from this folly. You will do something for me at least. I need paper and pen."

"Paper?" We didn't keep paper in the house. "Just a minute." I used the patio door that led directly to my bedroom and found the box of Nesi's journals beside my bed. I ripped out a blank page and found an old pen at the bottom of the box.

I laid both on the table before Terra like an offering.

"I hope the pen works. It's been in storage for a while."

Terra gripped it in her stiff fingers. I could see the effort and pain writing cost her. Beads of sweat broke out on her forehead. Finally, she folded the letter and handed it to me.

"Give this to my priest."

"Almarick?"

"Yes."

I took the letter. "Will he believe? I mean, how will he know it's really from you?"

"Tell him I came through the red door."

CHAPTER

15

The next day, Mason and I drove into the city. We had a meeting scheduled with the godlings. I watched the remains of Montreal's ill-fated rapid transit rail system pass us by and brooded about the future.

"Penny for those dark thoughts?" Mason had one hand on the steering wheel as always, but the traffic was light and he let the autopilot drive.

I sighed and leaned my head back against the seat. I had so many thoughts, all of them dark. I went with the least harmful.

"I'm just wondering how we're going to keep certain people out of this fight. Like Raven."

"Order him to help with the wounded. Joe will keep him in line."

"Yes. I thought of that." But we both knew ordering Raven and ordering Thunderbird weren't the same. "What about Jacoby and Grim?"

That concerned wrinkle appeared between Mason's brows, but he was also smiling. "Grim can take care of himself. And Jacoby would follow you into hell if you asked him."

"Exactly. But the one thing he won't do is stay home." I jerked a thumb toward the back seat where Jacoby was asleep. Or so I thought.

"'Prentices don't stays home!" came the protest.

"See?" I said.

"We'll just have to find a suitable apprentice-sized job for him." Mason grinned. He might find it funny, but I was feeling the stress of planning a war. If I started counting my concerns, it would lead to hysterics. He reached over the console and gripped my hand. His touch was warm and solid. He didn't let go until we parked at a rundown community center in Lachine.

I remembered this place from the one year I'd joined the swim team as a kid. Back then it had been a state-of-the-art facility with pool, library and gymnasium all combined in one building that looked over Lake St. Louis. The Flood Wars had taken a chunk out of this shoreline, collapsing the pool and gym. When the waters receded only the old library was left standing. No one used it anymore, which made it a perfect spot for clandestine meetings.

Not that the godlings were hiding their activities anymore. Nici had killed most of their leaders, leaving their pantheons without focus or purpose.

Ken Okorafa, an Anansi godling, had stepped into this void. He'd resigned from the fae party and begun the slow process of uniting the godling clans. From what I saw as we entered the old library, he hadn't been too successful. The room was clearly divided into factions. Ken's Anansis were arrayed behind him at the head table. To his left sat the remains of the Olympians. I didn't recognize the man who'd taken over from Dimitrios. The Saivites, now led by Gabe's sister-in-law Uma, sat on Ken's right. Even with Gabe gone, she saw me as a rival, not an ally. I didn't expect her to follow me into any battle. She sat up straighter and glared as we took our seats at the table, then pointed at me.

"That women is a siren who leads good men to their deaths. I refuse to engage with her, and I want my protest of this meeting noted for the record." Uma crossed her arms over her chest.

I turned away from her and spoke only to Ken Okorafa. "And I refuse to negotiate with someone who molests teenage boys."

Ken's eyebrows rose. Uma made a strangled noise.

That's right, bitch. I know your secrets.

The rest of the meeting went much as I expected. The Olympians were all for cutting off some vamp heads. They'd been targeted by Nici's recent schemes, and they hadn't enjoyed their loss of power when she enthralled them. They would have been good allies if they weren't so hot-headed. A group of Olympians had already gone off hunting opji. They hadn't returned.

Okorafa was the only voice of sanity on this council. He listened without interrupting as Mason laid out our evidence that an attack from the opji was imminent. Uma fumed through it, interrupting with rude questions and snide remarks. When we were done, Ken thanked us and said they would discuss our proposal.

Outside, I walked much too quickly as if I could outrun my anger—anger that was pointed mostly at myself for letting Uma get under my skin. I hopped into the passenger side of the van and slammed the door. Jacoby had been playing on his widget in the back seat while he waited for us. He saw me sitting with arms crossed and lips pressed tight against a scream.

"Is Kyra-lady mads?"

"Yes."

He poked his head into the front seat. "Is Kyra-lady mads at me?"

I looked at his fuzzy face all full of concern and couldn't help but smile.

"No. I'm not mad at you." I scratched him behind the ear.

"Can I helps?"

"You already have."

"Well, that went well," Mason said as he got in the van.

I turned away from him. "I'm sorry. I don't know what came over me."

"It was the memory of Gabe…what he did for you. For all of us."

Even Mason couldn't bring himself to say it. Gabe had sacrificed himself instead of following through on Nici's order to kill me—a sacrifice that let us finally take her down.

"But you can hardly blame Uma for her feelings," he said.

I grunted. "I still don't like her."

"Me neither. But we need the godlings in this fight."

"Do you think they'll join us?" I asked as Mason started the van.

"I think so. Okorafa has always done the right thing, but only after he carefully weeds out all the wrong things."

"Are we goings for ice creams now?" Jacoby piped up from the back seat.

Oh, how I wished I could be the apprentice and only have to worry about the logistics of snacks.

"Soon, buddy," I said. "We have one more stop to make."

WE PARKED ON LEVESQUE Boulevard, as close to the old cathedral-turned-temple as we could, then hiked up the fifty-one stairs (yes, I counted them) to reach the grand facade of the church. A set of massive oak doors trimmed in solid iron met us. Two steeples flanked the doors, pointing the way to heaven. A round stained glass window sat between them like the eye of a god.

111

The Catholic cathedral had been abandoned during the Flood Wars, when so many people lost faith in their gods as the bombs fell. Afterward, the Terran priests claimed it and Terra's magic bolstered the forest around it, hiding the church from the busy city just a few feet from its doorstep.

I ignored the giant doors—they probably didn't even open—and headed through a smaller door on the left corner of the building. Mason let out a low whistle when he saw the interior.

"I can't believe this exists in the city and no one knows about it."

"Not no one. The priests know. And Terran pilgrims, I guess." But I had to agree. It was a spectacular sight. The church had been gutted to leave one massive room filled with soft light from windows high up on the walls. The entire space was filled with life—trees, flowers, birds and small creatures. It was a microcosm of the world Terra aspired to, all carefully tended by the priests.

One of those priests was sitting under a willow tree, asleep with a book on his lap. His head was bowed, but I recognized Almarick by his wild mane of curly hair. The remains of a sandwich lay on a plate beside him. While his chest rose and fell in the smooth motion of sleep, a chipmunk hopped over his lap and stole a crumble of bread off the plate.

"This is the mighty warrior Terra calls to her aid?" Mason's eyebrows rose.

"Less of a warrior and more of a steward, I think."

The chipmunk bolted as we approached. Jacoby ran after it and was soon lost in the foliage. I let him go. He couldn't truly get lost inside the temple.

I cleared my throat and nudged the priest's foot with my toe.

"Almarick?"

He came awake with a snort. The book toppled off his lap and spilled the mug of water beside the plate. He jumped up, grabbed the precious book and tried to blot its pages on his smock.

"Look what you've done!" he snapped. Then he turned to me and his expression softened.

"Kyra!" He dropped the book and embraced me. "I've often wondered what became of you!"

I endured the embrace stiffly.

"I'm sorry. I promised to return with news of the demon, but things have been…busy."

Mason watched our exchange with open curiosity.

"Almarick, this is my husband, Henry Mason."

Mason held out a hand. Almarick took it with wide eyes and a mouth hanging open. "But you! You were…I mean the demon was…" The good priest was at a loss for words.

"It's all right. You can say the words. I was possessed by a demon. I have your god to thank for my release."

"So it worked! I must hear all about it! Come, come. Let's take tea in my study. This is huge!"

He was already turning away before I could catch him. We followed along the winding path through the forest until we came to a wall—how odd it felt to find a wall in the forest!—and a door through which we found Almarick's office. The desk, shelves and chairs were piled high with books and scrolls. He moved some of these aside, making room for us to sit before turning on a hotplate to boil the kettle.

Then he sat on the desk, beaming at us. "Now you must tell me absolutely everything."

"We will but first you have to read this." I held out Terra's letter, then pulled it back. "Promise to keep this secret. Tell the temple priests but no one else." I didn't need my home becoming a shrine for pilgrims because it had once been the resting place of the god.

Almarick nodded with eagerness plain on his face. He took the paper, unfolded it and studied the cramped handwriting. As he read, his expression went from curious, to surprised, to shocked.

I knew the gist of the letter's contents. Terra was telling him about her recent incarnation on Earth. She was calling her acolytes to join her in the war against the opji.

Almarick read it at least three times.

"Is this true? How can it be?"

"She gave me a code word, so you'd know it comes from her. She said to tell you she came through the red door. Does that mean anything to you?"

Almarick sat heavily in his chair.

"The red door is where I see her in my dreams. Always through the red door. It opens and she speaks to me, but she never comes through."

He pinched the letter between thumb and forefinger, holding it like it was a holy relic.

"If this is true, if the opji have done this to my Lady, we will avenge her." He turned his gaze on me. "The priests of Terra are at your disposal."

I laid my hand over his.

"Will your priests fight?" Almarick started to nod, but I cut him off. "With guns and swords, not pens." He hesitated, then shook his head.

"But we can still help. We are healers. If nothing else we can roll bandages and fetch water." He stood up straighter. "We will do whatever our lady requires of us."

I could see resolution in his bearing. "Fine. The lady wants you to meet her at these coordinates." I showed him my widget and he scribbled down the directions to camp Dorion.

16

The next morning, we got ready to drive back into town to hear Ramona's plea in Parliament. Jacoby, after learning that we'd be in more boring meetings all day, opted to stay home.

"You're still on duty," I said with fake sternness. Jacoby prided himself on being the perfect apprentice and I wouldn't take that away from him.

"I ams?"

"Yes. Weapons aren't allowed inside the Parliament buildings. I need you to look after my sword while I'm gone."

Jacoby stuck a finger in his ear and considered.

"Will it screams?" He was familiar with my blade's separation issues, and his keening was sensitive enough to hear the blade's anxious calls for me.

"I don't think so. Look."

I pricked my finger with a pin and ran the blood along the flat of the blade.

"Call it a test," I said. "You keep the sword with you. If it cries, bring it to me. Don't teleport. Get Dutch to drive you. Understood?"

"Understoods." Jacoby hefted the sword. It was wider than his skinny arm and when he dropped it, the tip dragged on the ground. But it was quiet. I didn't anticipate any problems while I was gone. The blade had matured during the last battles with the opji, as if the bloodings gave it more confidence to be alone.

After sorting out Jacoby and my sword, we turned to the next problem.

Terra wanted to testify before Parliament. She had knowledge of opji strengths and movements, but with no way to prove it. I thought of her standing up in front of a full court of ministers, announcing she was the god of all Earth and that she'd had omniscient sight until the opji forced her into a mortal form. I could just imagine the looks on the ministers' faces.

When I put Terra's suggestion to Mason he said, "They will think we all have spiders in our minds." He made a twirling finger motion to go along with his old French idiom—they'd think we were all crazy.

He was right. The ministers would dismiss us out of hand. Some people would believe, of course—the fanatical Terran supporters for one, but they'd spent the last several years sabotaging public works and being a general nuisance. Their voice was meaningless in Parliament. And did we really want them following us, only so they could touch the hem of their god? No. We needed soldiers, not apostles.

I convinced Terra to stay home, using the excuse that Almarick and his priests would be arriving that morning. She conceded. Really, I thought she was too weak to make the trip anyway. I hoped that Almarick would step up to the task of caring for her, because soon my attention would be needed elsewhere.

Two hours later, Mason and I sat in the balcony reserved for public spectators and listened to Ramona as she tried to convince the ministers to invade Vioska.

Ramona Becker was a seventy-five-year-old alchemist who'd been a member of the Alchemy Party since its inception, some fifty years ago. She knew every player and which buttons to push. She spoke to the three ministers sitting at the bench. None were Prime Ministers. The humans and fae had sent deputy ministers for this court. And since Ramona was the acting Prime Minister of the alchemists, a lower ranking minister sat in for her on the bench. Behind her were row upon row of ministers and aids for the various parties. Most looked bored. Some focused on their widgets, typing messages even while Ramona spoke about Montreal's inevitable invasion by opji forces. One elderly minister slept with her head fallen forward.

I wanted to scream at them from the balcony. *Pay attention!* Mason could feel my agitation. He laced his fingers with mine, pulling my hand into his lap and gripping it fiercely.

Ramona spoke for fifteen minutes without interruption, outlining the latest information from Hub about opji movements and the number of displaced homesteaders.

"We estimate that the opji have murdered over a thousand homesteaders and taken five thousand more captive. They are building an army of wojaks, and they're going to let them loose soon."

From the bench, the human minister leaned forward to speak into his microphone.

"Are you suggesting that the might of Montreal Ward cannot stand against a few wojaks?" He didn't let Ramona answer before he went on. "They will break against our ward like waves crashing on a sea wall. And the ward will hold, just as it has held for over fifty years."

Ramona countered with even more stats about the rising death toll and the cost to Montreal's food production, but it was obvious she was losing the battle. It was nearly lunch and in their thoughts, the ministers were already sitting in one of the cafes that lined the street outside the Parliament building.

Mason motioned me to follow him. We rose and pushed along the row of spectators with whispered apologies. We left the session room for the brightly lit main hall. Mason didn't stop there. His dark expression told me he'd had enough of politics for one day, and his quick pace urged me to follow him toward the front doors.

We nearly ran into Captain Lowe as she came out of an office. Glenda had been a detective with Hub for many years, and was recently promoted to Hub logistics. She still wore her hair short, but not in a military style. The softer cut emphasized her big eyes.

"Just the people I wanted to see." She beckoned with one crooked finger and turned for the office she'd just vacated. Mason and I followed.

The office was little more than an interrogation room. She closed the door and sat on the single desk. Her long legs were covered in silky pants and she wore three inch heels. I considered high heels in the same category as thumb screws, and women who wore them always impressed me. That someone would willingly strap those things to their feet and walk around all day in them! It was bravery of a caliber I couldn't muster.

"Did you see their faces?" Glenda asked. "You'd think Ramona was making them listen to the quartermaster's laundry bill." She slammed her hand on the table, then rose and paced the room. Her heels clicked on the tile floor.

"I knew we wouldn't persuade anyone with the facts," Mason said. "They need to feel threatened or they won't move."

"But you're still going, aren't you?"

Mason glanced at me. When he didn't answer, Glenda prodded. "I know all about that little army you've been amassing in Dorion Park."

Mason opened his mouth to protest, but Glenda held up her hand. "Don't lie to me, Mason. You haven't exactly been subtle in your inquiries." She frowned. "People are watching you."

"Is that a threat?" Mason's voice was just above a growl.

Glenda smiled. "Not from me. Just a warning. And a promise. Parliament might not sanction your war, but there are many in Hub who agree with you. Many who would even follow you." She opened the tablet and held it out to Mason. He didn't look at it, preferring to lock onto her gaze instead, as if trying to read her for lies.

"That sounds like civil war to me."

"Nonsense. It's only civil war if we fight on Montreal soil. At best, it's desertion. And there are many who feel that is worth the risk. Take it." She nudged the tablet toward him. Mason glanced at the screen and flicked through a series of images, then handed it to me.

I also scrolled through image after image of wojak soldiers huddled in snowy pens, marching through burned out trees and…the last image made me stop. Breath hitched in my chest.

"What the hell is that?" The image was blurry, but the scale of the beast was clear. It stood head and shoulders above the wojaks that circled it. Black hair covered chest and forearms that bulged with muscle. Its face was indistinct but I got an impression of sharp teeth. Lots of teeth. Shackles circled its wrists, ankles and neck with heavy chains attached. Two opji held each chain as the beast strained against them, like a massive dog pulling its leash to go after a squirrel.

"We're not sure what it is, but we think it came through the veil. Possibly a lesser demon."

She let that idea sink in. A lesser demon wasn't the same as the thing that had possessed Mason. That kind of demon was the yang to a god's yin. Their power was too great to manifest on this plane, so they invaded hosts.

Lesser demons were more like magically potent beasts—strong, smart and powerful, but small enough in magic that a strong mage could pull them through the veil. Rivaling factions had used them to devastating effect during the Flood wars.

"We think they've been conjuring more than just this," Glenda continued. "For months, maybe. Remember that earthquake last year? What if it wasn't an earthquake? What if the opji caused it when they pulled this…this beast through the veil."

It was a good hypothesis, even if I knew it was false. Terra had come through the veil that day, but that didn't mean the opji hadn't conjured worse things too.

"Does this deter you in any way?" she asked.

"No." I handed her back the tablet.

"Good. Then you have my support when you need it."

"Thank you."

We left the Parliament building with mixed feelings. Officially, the government of Montreal wasn't going to give us squat. Unofficially, if Glenda could be trusted, we had a fighting chance. So the question became, did I believe Glenda?

By the time we arrived at the Winter Palace for our next meeting I had the answer. I did believe Glenda was sincere. I just hoped that was enough.

MERROW WAS HER USUAL sunny self. She sat in her chair with a straight back and a dark expression. She'd let her glamor fall, the one that usually hid her long wings, and they jutted above her shoulders, somehow looking like weapons.

We sat before her desk and she was silhouetted by the sun streaming through the window. Her black eyes scrutinized first me, then Mason, then back to me again. I couldn't help feeling like we'd been sent to the principal. Her gaze finally came to rest on Mason.

"You abandoned me." Her voice was low and her body posture rigid, like she was a coiled spring ready to pop.

"I did not." Mason's pose was oddly relaxed, as if he were denying Merrow her right to be angry. "They were going to vote me out. You know that. I resigned to save the party a scandal. Ramona is better at governing than I was anyway."

"She's a pit bull."

That was actually a great description of Ramona. Pit bulls could be fierce, but they were also smart, loyal and kind of sweet. I'd seen Ramona display all those traits.

"Yes, but she could be your pit bull," Mason said, "if you'd only reach out to her. You have more in common than you know."

Merrow dismissed that idea with a slight curl of her upper lip. Her chair was low-backed to accommodate her wings, and they suddenly fluttered behind her. It was a small movement that showed her agitation, like ruffling papers on her desk.

"And will Ramona be backing this foolish fairy tale war you've concocted?"

When the leader of the fae calls your aspirations a fairy tale, it's probably time to re-evaluate your life choices.

I hadn't really expected help from the fae. Merrow was entrenched in her paranoia. No matter what stats we threw at her, she wouldn't budge from her stance that war with the opji was both unnecessary and unwarranted.

By the time we left, I felt like I'd run a marathon.

Pushing open the door of the Winter Palace, I sucked in cool air, then stomped through the parking lot. It was four in the afternoon and the palace guards were changing shifts, so there was a lot of activity around the grounds. Two imps jumped aside so the crazy human who was mumbling curse words could stalk by.

I finally stopped in the garden by a massive willow tree just coming into spring buds. Picnic tables were set up for employees to enjoy the gardens on their breaks. I threw myself onto a bench and laid my head on my arms.

A moment later, I felt the bench rock as Mason sat down.

"We have our answer now." He stroked my back. "We have some support. It will have to be enough."

I turned my head without lifting it from my arms. "Is it though? How can we say it's enough?"

"It's enough because it has to be."

I made a face at his logic.

"I know why you're really stalling," he said. "You're waiting for Emil."

Ugh. How could I love that he knew me so well, and also hate that he knew me so well?

"He said he'd come back." I couldn't hide the petulance in my voice. We both knew that if Emil could have come home, he would have.

120

"He's already two weeks overdue. We have to assume he's not coming."

I sat up. "So that's it? Emil is the first casualty and we haven't even gone to war yet?"

Mason nodded. "Maybe. But Emil wouldn't want us to stop because of him."

Heat prickled my eyes. "But I sent him there."

"You're the general. That's your job."

"Why can't you be the general? You could lead better that me."

He was silent for a moment. "I see. You're feeling inadequate to the task. You're the only one who feels that way. And to answer your question, why you? Terra chose you because you're capable, and because you have an army that will follow you. You didn't know it, but you've been building that army for years. Every act of kindness, every small battle you fought and won, every life you saved, they're all coming back to you now."

He fell silent. That was a lot for Mason, the man of few words, but he wasn't finished. "Carmen's scavengers are coming because of their debt to you. Even Glenda knows she owes you for saving the city from more than one disaster. They fight for you." He tapped my shoulder. "Do you think those bluecaps, dryads and hidebehinds would follow me? Non. They follow you because you had their backs. And now they have yours. And so do I. And so will Hub, you'll see. Everything will turn out all right."

"You really believe that?"

"I do. The powers that be wouldn't have freed me from a demon only to toss me away to a blood sucker. So I have to believe we will come through this."

"The powers that be." I snorted. The powers that be were currently nesting in my spare room, reading one of Gita's old paperbacks and eating apple scones as fast as Dutch could bake them.

I filled my lungs with air and let it out slowly, releasing some of the anxiety that had been dogging me all day.

"You're right. No more excuses."

Mason nodded, his expression grim. "No more excuses."

I'd been putting off the inevitable, hoping we'd garner more support. Hoping that Emil would make it home. But neither of those things were going to happen. It was time to face the piper. The undead, bloodsucking piper.

"Let's go home and tell Terra the good news." I rose from the bench and my widget buzzed with an alert.

All travel restricted. Bridges closed until further notice.

Mason read the same message on his widget. Suddenly the Winter Palace was buzzing with activity as people rushed from the lot toward the building.

"What the hells?" I asked, but Mason was already dialing his office.

I scrolled to the news channels, but even they were having a hard time catching up. The reports stated only that a fight in Barrows had escalated to the point that Hub soldiers had been brought in.

That seemed sketchy. There were always fights in the shanty towns. Jam too many desperate refugees into one space and that was bound to happen. But those fights rarely made the news.

Something else was going on.

Mason ended his call. He rubbed the back of his neck, making his hair stick up.

"It's bad isn't it?"

He nodded. "Opji attacked the Hub barracks."

CHAPTER

17

I was already digging through the trunk, when I remembered that I'd left my sword at home. Distance made our connection faint, but I keened its agitation in reaction to my own.

I grabbed whatever other weapons I had on hand—a knife and a homemade dart gun with enough tranquilizer loaded to take down a werebear.

Mason grabbed my arm, forcing me to look at him.

"What are you doing?"

"We're going to Barrows." It was a knee-jerk reaction, but if there were vampires, I wanted to be in on the fight.

"No, we have to go home."

That stopped me. He was right, of course. If the opji were that close to Montreal, we needed to protect our family.

I pulled my widget from my pocket and dialed Dutch's number. It rang and rang, then went to voicemail. I stared at Mason, fear streaming from my every pore. He hit a button on his speed dial.

In seconds, Dutch's voice came over the speaker. "What's up. I was just getting out of the shower."

"Is everything okay?" Mason asked.

"Yes, of course."

"Good. Lock everything down. No one leaves the house until we get there. Except for Grim. Ask him to alert Cletus."

"Sure, but alert him about what?"

"Turn on the news. The opji have attacked Barrows."

I could already hear the sound of the vid screen in the background, then came Dutch's muffled, "Oh, shit."

"We'll be home in an hour." Mason ended the call.

The Winter Palace was on the east end of town. We were at least an hour from the Gallop Bridge. Without traffic.

"You drive." Mason got into the passenger seat and dialed his office. I started the engine and tore out of the parking lot. Mason asked to speak to Ramona and was put on hold.

I navigated rush hour traffic with my knuckles squeezing the steering wheel. Why were there so many cars? My rational mind told me there were always cars at five in the afternoon, but that did nothing to soothe my nerves.

Holly was at home. Raven too. And Shar, Princess, Jacoby…my entire family was vulnerable. I tried to reassure myself that our ward was solid.

"How are we going to get off the island? They said all the bridges are closed."

Mason still had the widget pressed to his ear. He held up a finger as someone came back on the line.

"I don't care if she's in a meeting. Get Ramona on the phone or I'll have you fired." His voice was pure, calm menace. I'd forgotten how scary he could be when he put his mind to it.

He lowered the widget slightly and said, "Don't worry. I'll get us across that bridge."

We were passing through Sayntanne by the time Mason sorted things out with Ramona.

"She's going to contact the guards at the ward gate," he said as he hung up the phone. "They'll let us through."

But when we got to the bridge, we realized it wasn't going to be that easy. A long line of cars had stopped along the old highway. I pulled the van to the side and drove slowly along the shoulder. Cars honked at us and I gave them nervous waves as we passed. I parked in front of the fence that blocked access to the bridge.

Six armed guards stood with their eyes fixed on the line of cars. Mason got out and spoke to one. His curt hand gestures said the guard needed some convincing. Finally, a senior officer came out of the guardhouse and waved us through to a chorus of angry honks from waiting cars.

I shuddered as we passed under the great ward of Montreal. Then pain shot through me. I let go of the steering wheel and grabbed my head in both hands.

"Whoa!" Mason took the wheel and put the van on auto. "What happened?"

"I...I don't know." My vision was already clearing. "It was some kind of a backlash. Like...a ward breaking."

All the color drained from Mason's face. He dialed Dutch again. The call went straight to voicemail. He dropped his hand to his lap still clutching the widget. I knew we were both willing it to ring, but it remained silent.

I took control of the van again and drove the dirt roads of Dorion Park like I had all the demons of hell on our tail. As the van skidded around a bend, I smelled smoke.

My heart pounded. Something was very wrong. The van couldn't go fast enough. The setting sun blinded me as we drove west along the last access road before turning into our driveway.

The dryads waved to me as we zoomed through the ward gate, and I slammed on the brakes at the guard house. Dozens of bluecaps milled around the yard.

"What are they doing here?" I jumped out of the van.

Cletus pushed through the other bluecaps to meet us.

"Bloody bastards! They took us by surprise but we gave as good as we got, I tell you! Drove them right off!"

My mind was numb. Mason pressed him for details, but their voices were faint and far away. I gazed around the yard. Bluecaps, goblins, dryads, humans and hidebehinds all mingled together. Some were bleeding. Gallivant had flown his pen and he pawed the ground by the front door. I could hear Clover screaming in his paddock, desperate not to be left out. Smoke shrouded the forest behind the house.

Then Terra fell out the front door, one hand pressed to her chest. Almarick followed her, looking distressed. Lisobet came next, holding a screaming Holly, and I forgot everything else. I ran to my daughter. Her face was red from tears. She held out stiff arms and cried, "Mama!"

Lisobet handed her over and I gathered my baby into my arms. Terra leaned heavily on me. She seemed out of breath, and one frail hand clawed at my sleeve.

"He was here," she wheezed.

At first, her words didn't register with me. Holly pressed her tear-stained face against my shoulder and all my thoughts were for her.

"He's the one. The mage from my dreams! Ichovidar!"

Her words finally broke through my shock. The opji had been here in my yard, my house. They could have killed my family.

Ludger staggered out the front door, let out a wail to rival Gita's and collapsed on the front steps. Terra stared at him in a daze. I grabbed her sleeve and shook her.

"Ichovidar? He was here? What did he want?"

Terra's fingers grasped my arm, their grip pinching. Then she pointed into the trees just as I realized who was missing.

"Shar." Her voice was barely above a croak. "They took Shar."

stayed long enough to get the gist of things. The opji had attacked the bluecaps' camp, but only as a decoy. They sent wojaks in to keep the bluecaps and others busy while Ichovidar set the forest on fire behind the house and broke through our ward. The amount of magic needed to break the ward was staggering. That was the backlash I'd felt on the bridge.

He'd come in alone and taken only one thing. Shar.

By the time the bluecaps realized the ward had been breached, he was already gone.

"Someone check on Errol," I said over my shoulder. The ward's backlash had probably laid him flat. But I had no time to find him. I had vamps to catch.

I left Mason to deal with the aftermath of the attack and jumped onto Gallivant's back, wrapping my fingers in his mane. The scent of blood and smoke agitated him and the pegasus was ready to fly.

We launched into the sky and circled the house. Mason called up to me, but I just shook my head, not wanting to hear whatever warning or reprimand he had to give.

Gallivant soared above the trees. I urged him onward, north and slightly west, and scanned the canopy below, looking for any trace of opji movement. Wind pulled tears from my eyes and they mingled with rain, which stung like icy pellets.

Within minutes, I was soaked through and realizing the futility of this hunt. The Inbetween was vast and dense. Even in April when the trees were only beginning to bud, it was nearly impossible to track anything from above.

Then Thunderbird appeared on my wing. He let out a piercing caw and banked left, dropping low over the trees.

"Aroooooo!" A black and white body zipped by me, did a loop-de-loop and took the lead. I should have known. Princess was never far behind Raven. Now I felt guilty about my rash decision to hunt opji. I had no qualms about putting myself in danger, but I hadn't meant for others to follow.

Still, I wouldn't turn back now. Not without Shar.

Gallivant's tail lashed with every beat of his mighty wings. The black clouds offered little light for a search, and I leaned precariously over Gallivant's shoulder squinting into the gloom.

Another call had me turning in my seat. There, coming out of the shadows from the east, coming fast. First just specks on the horizon, then growing into multi-hued shapes—dragons!

Carmen and Herne had promised to do their best in contacting Ollie's thunder, but I'd held out little hope of success. Even if they'd managed to find them, the great queen was under no obligation to help us.

But here she was. Even in the dim light, Kalindari's ruby scales seemed to glow. A battalion of jewel-toned warriors were arrayed behind her. The dragons surged forward until we flew in a loose formation. Kalindari kept her distance, but her presence on my wing was reassuring.

Princess zipped around Gallivant as if trying to shield me from all the dragons at once. She snarled as a great blue dragon dove from above. Gallivant reared, nearly unseating me. Thunderbird screamed and dropped from sight. I thought he'd fallen back until I saw him flying below us.

My kid was trying to protect me, in case I fell.

I put that thought away, not sure how much control Raven really had over Thunderbird. Princess settled when she realized the dragons meant me no harm, but I could still feel Gallivant's agitation.

I focused on Ollie, who flew with ease off our left wing.

An image of burning forests popped into my head, then a gathering of wojaks.

Your enemy is our enemy. We will burn them just as they burned our forest.

Ollie's mind-speech was strong and clear.

Thank you. But my child is with them. She rides with a sorcerer, the one who looks like this. I projected an image of the blond opji I'd killed near Winaskwi, hoping he looked enough like Ichovidar that Ollie would recognize him.

Ollie dipped his head slightly.

We will leave the sorcerer alive if we can.

He pulled up and circled around his thunder, letting out a long, wailing roar like a battle cry. The dragons dropped low to fly just above the tree tops. Thunderbird and I took our positions on the right flank.

With methodical precision we swept the forest, back and forth for an hour. By then, I was nearly frozen. My rage had cooled too, leaving only fear in its place.

Fear for Shar.

Ichovidar had targeted her. The fight with the bluecaps had been a diversion. I'd go so far as to say the attack on Hub barracks had also been a diversion, meant to keep Mason and me on the island long enough for Ichovidar to sneak in, take his prize then melt into the forest.

Through the veil of rain, the sun was a deep red ball on the horizon. The thick layer of clouds hanging above it were lit with ghoulish reds and purples.

I was just about to turn back for the homestead when Kalindari roared and let out a plume of fire that hit the ground in a clearing. Opji and wojaks ran for the trees like bugs scuttling across a floor.

I wiped rain from my eyes and urged Gallivant lower. The opji had turned to fight, flinging arrows into the darkening sky. Gallivant screamed and joined the dragons even though he had no weapon of his own.

I strained to see through the rising smoke. None of the opji had white-blond hair. I swung Gallivant away and let the dragons vaporize the vamps with fire. Trees ignited along with shrieking vamps, but they quickly turned into steaming husks under the driving rain.

My hands were freezing and I could barely hang onto Gallivant's mane, but I urged him higher so I could get a lay of the land.

The sun had dipped below the western horizon, giving just enough light for me to see the edge of the wastelands where the opji had burned thousands of hectares of forest.

We were too close to Vioska. If we met a full battalion of wojaks and opji, the dragons wouldn't stand a chance. And Gallivant was tiring. I listed to one side as his left wing dipped. Only then did I realize that one of the opji arrows had struck him on the rear flank only inches from my thigh. The arrow hadn't pierced deep. I yanked it out and blood flecked the wind. I pressed my bandana to the wound and called to Ollie.

Turn back. We will meet them in battle soon.

He dipped his head.

When you call. We will come.

The dragons circled and flew off, their colors glistening in the fading light. I turned Gallivant. The cloth was already soaked through with blood.

Should I put down in the forest and walk him home? The sun was only a fading glow now. I didn't relish the idea of trekking through the dark Inbetween. And walking would be no better for the pegasus than flying.

Thunderbird cawed and led the way home with the hell hound close behind. I gripped my pegasus with determination, and pushed soothing thoughts at him.

Ichovidar had escaped us this time, but I wouldn't rest until I had Shar back.

CHAPTER

19

My bandana was soaked in Gallivant's blood by the time we reached home. He struggled to keep us in the air. Every beat of his wings must have aggravated the wound. I put him down on the service road about a kilometer from our driveway and we walked the rest of the way.

Horses are such a contrast of temperaments. The same creature that balked at a stick in the road hadn't been afraid of dragons or vampires.

"Such a silly pony." I patted his heaving neck and told him over and over what a good boy he was.

Thunderbird landed beside us. His great talons raked the gravel road, but before the dirt even settled, Raven was standing before me, fully dressed and not even wind-ruffled. His expression was full of concern.

"Is he okay?"

I lifted the bandana and looked at the oozing wound. "I think so. Can you run ahead and get Gita to start making a poultice? I'll need Muzzy and Tak to help too."

Raven nodded, shifted into a pony and galloped off with Princess loping behind him. My kid was amazing.

Gallivant and I walked on. Now that the urgency had passed he thought we were out for a leisurely stroll and kept trying to veer off the road to eat spring shoots.

By the time I got him into the stall beside his paddock, I was dead on my feet, but I wouldn't leave my horse unattended. Muzzy brought a bucket of fresh water and Tak distracted Gallivant with treats while we cleaned the wound. Clover was no help. He sensed danger and the scent of blood on the air and galloped around the paddock like a show champion, which kept Gallivant on high alert.

Gita arrived, weeping profusely into a bowl of green goo. Banshee tears are full of healing properties. After a minute she shut off the waterworks like turning off a faucet and stirred the concoction. Gallivant—the same horse who'd just faced down a horde of armed vampires—whinnied and danced away when he smelled the foul brew in Gita's bowl.

"Easy." I patted his neck and turned to Muzzy. "Go put a halter on Clover and take him out to the pasture." Muzzy's eyes were wide and round. He nodded and dashed off.

I turned my attention back to the agitated pegasus. At least in the small stall, he knew enough not to flex his wings. Tak tried to soothe him, while I took the bowl from Gita and slathered green goo onto the wound. Gita handed me a fresh towel and some vet wrap so I could secure it in place. Gallivant was tired after his adventure. I took the feed bucket from Tak and sent the others away.

"I'll watch him for a few minutes, make sure he doesn't tear off the bandage." It wouldn't hold all night, but I wanted to give it enough time for the herbs and banshee tears to seep into the wound.

After they left, the quiet of the night settled into me. The horse paddock, like the barn, was one of my safe places where I usually came to think, but I didn't want to think right now. That way led to fear and pain. I wanted only to coast, to pet my horse's velvety nose and let everything else drift into darkness.

While Gallivant finished his grain, I took a curry comb from his brush basket and rubbed down his sweaty flanks. The repetitive motion soothed my frayed nerves.

Hunter dropped from the rafters onto Gallivant's back. The pegasus didn't even blink. With the warmer weather, Hunter had been enjoying his outdoor pool. He could stay out of the water for nearly an hour, and he had the run of the barn and horse paddock. It didn't surprise me that the pegasus and kraken had bonded. Hunter's little tentacles crept over the bandage, touching it the way a hound sniffed a trail.

"Don't pull that off," I said. "It's medicine."

Hunter watched me with those massively evocative eyes. The tip of one tentacle tapped the bandage again, then he crawled along Gallivant's back in that peculiar cephalopod gait that was something between a stretch and an ooze. He settled into the crook where Gallivant's wing met his shoulder.

Mason brought me a steaming mug of coffee laced with Dutch's homemade Irish Cream. I could have kissed him, and I did—after taking a long sip of coffee-creamy goodness.

His eyes were hidden in shadow, but he gazed into the trees as if looking for a fresh attack.

"Raven says you didn't find Ichovidar."

And just like that the weight of our troubles came crashing down on my shoulders again. I felt myself crumple inside. Mason caught my mug in one hand and my shoulder in the other.

"Come inside. Oscar's here. It's time to make plans."

I nodded and put away the brush.

As we headed toward the house all my inner calm left me.

Shar was gone. Taken.

"They're going to kill her," I whispered. "No. Worse. They're going to drown her in blood and use her for some hideous rite."

Mason stopped me on the front porch. His left hand crept around my lower back while the right brushed hair from my face then cupped my cheek. I wanted to lean into the touch, but I was shaking too hard.

"She's stronger than they know." Mason pulled me against him. "Shar's inner light shone through their dark rites once before, remember?"

I nodded and sniffled back tears. "I know, but she's just a baby. They're going to hurt her."

"We won't let that happen."

I felt the low rumble of his voice against my chest. His eyes were dark and bottomless. I latched onto his gaze like a lifeline. He kissed me. There was no heat in it, no invitation to sneak away to our bedroom. It was so much better than that. It was a kiss that united us. A seal that recognized the hard-won battles we'd already fought and promised more.

I leaned my head against his chest, taking one selfish moment to listen to the tolling of his magic. Then I smiled. There might have been tears in my eyes, but Mason chose to acknowledge the smile instead. He kissed me again on the tip of my nose and we went inside to plan a war.

My clothes were still damp and covered in blood. Mason wrapped me in a blanket and sat me on the chair closest to the fire. He knew I wouldn't rest until we hashed out what had happened. Jacoby sat beside me. He kept patting my leg. I wasn't sure if that was meant to reassure him or me.

Inside the circle of firelight, anxious eyes watched me—Lisobet, Terra, Gita, Angus and Mason. Almarick fluttered at Terra's shoulder, not sure how to help his lady. Even Kester and Dutch stood by the kitchen watching silently. Grim perched on the table beside Errol's bonsai tree. The bodach sat beside his ceramic house, digging his walking twig into the dirt. Raven pulled a chair from the dining room and hung over it with Princess at his feet. The whole gang was here, except for the puckwudgie. Ludger had taken Shar's kidnapping as a personal failing. Terra was worried he would hurt himself, and had ordered Dutch to give him one of Gita's sedative teas. He was sleeping in the gatehouse now. I knew he was a terrific teacher for Shar and Holly, but I hadn't realized how attached he'd become.

Suzt had offered to take Holly for the evening, but I needed my baby close to me. I'd already lost one today. The excitement had been too much for her. Dutch had made her a sippy cup of warm milk and now she was sprawled across Mason's chest fast asleep.

The crackle of the fire competed with the rain battering the windows to create a lulling, shushing noise. Along with the warmth from the fire, I could feel myself drifting. But I couldn't rest. Not yet.

"Tell me what happened."

Terra spoke up. Her voice was raspy, like she'd breathed in too much smoke.

"He came in alone. From the back. We were all on the front porch, listening to the fight in the camp. Stupid." She shook her head. "We should have known it was a diversion. Then the hound started barking and the cat said he smelled fire."

Lisobet took over the narration at this point. "I rushed to the edge of the garden and saw smoke. But I'd sent the dryads to help the bluecaps. By the time I called them back, the opji was already retreating into the trees with Shar tucked under his arm." She bowed her head. "I'm sorry, Kyra. This is my fault."

I shook my head. "It's not. I put too much faith in our wards."

"Gttyhvb," Errol said.

"No. Not your fault either. We know so little about the opji and even less about Ichovidar's capabilities." The fact that our ward had been so easily breached was only one alarming thing among many.

"And you're sure it was Ichovidar?" I asked.

Lisobet looked at Terra, and she nodded.

"I've been watching him for years, from my mountaintop. I'd know the taint of that monster anywhere. If I'd had my magic, I would have sensed him coming. But then he would have known me too."

I sighed and felt deflated.

Terra was a victim in this just like the rest of us, maybe even more so. I'd lost loved ones, and would maybe even lose my life, but she'd lost everything that made her a god. She'd once seemed ageless, now she just looked old. And tired.

Mason stood up with Holly draped over his shoulder. "I'm going to put her to bed. I suggest we all get some rest. Kyra and I already discussed this. It's time to take the fight to Vioska. And now…" He paused and looked at me. I nodded. "Now, we need to move fast. We'll be leaving Wednesday at first light."

It was Monday. That gave us about thirty-six hours to prepare. No one protested. Kester pushed away from the wall he'd been leaning on.

"I'll go tell Cletus and the others."

Mason headed toward Holly's room.

I showered and dressed in comfort clothes—sweatpants and a soft t-shirt. I planned to go to sleep, but my legs were restless, and some kernel of worry was nagging at me, like a stone in my shoe that I could no longer ignore.

I slipped into Terra's room. The god was tucked into bed, but her eyes were wide open. Almarick had made himself a sleeping pad of blankets on the floor.

"Can you leave us alone for a moment?" I asked. He opened his mouth to protest, then looked at Terra.

"Go on," she urged. The priest rose and slipped out the door.

When he was gone, I sat on the edge of Terra's bed, and studied her face. She seemed to be shrinking. In the forest by the bluecap camp, she'd seemed formidable, even with her swollen hands and feet. Now she was diminishing, like a sponge that was slowly drying out.

"You haven't told me the truth."

Terra huffed and raised her chin. "I told you the truth as you needed to know it, but truth shrinks and expands according to circumstance."

"So what aren't you telling me? Why were you pushing for us to go to Vioska so quickly?"

She squinted and I wanted to shake the truth from her.

"You got your way. We're going. But I need to know. Did you have something to do with Shar being taken?" There was no point sugar-coating my worst fear, that I'd let her into my life, I'd let her into my family, and she'd betrayed me.

She sat straight up. "Of course not! How can you say that?"

"Because I wasn't moving fast enough for you. You said that a dozen times. Maybe you didn't steal Shar but maybe you saw an opportunity to force me into action."

"Never!" She sagged against the pillows. "I would never do anything to hurt Shar. Or you."

I examined her words with my heart and my keening and decided they were true.

"So tell me then. There is something you're hiding. You're not Hub and I'm not a civilian on a need-to-know basis. Tell me everything."

"Fine." She laid her head back and closed her eyes. "Getting to my spirit jar isn't just about returning my magic. It's more than that. I'm fading. Dying." She opened her eyes. If she thought that knowledge would shock me, she was wrong.

"If I die, if this mortal body fails, my spirit will rejoin with the Earth. We will become one again, but…"

I waited for her to finish. It was a long wait over a steep cliff with a nasty jolt at the end.

"But the body, the spirit and the ghost are not one right now. If I die without my pith, my own sentience—the consciousness that sets me apart from the Earth will be lost. At least for a while."

"You mean you won't be able to meddle in the affairs of humankind? Not even by sending in that pain-in-the-ass mountain devil?"

Terra shook her head.

"For how long?"

"For me, it will be no more than a long nap. For you, it will be lifetimes. Your dreams will be free from my intrusions. But don't worry, the Earth will go on much as it has for eons. As it did before I decided to intervene."

"But what about the wards? And magic? And the fae and the creatures who've made Earth home since the Flood Wars?"

Even though the resurgence of magic had caused cataclysmic destruction, I didn't want to return to a world without it, a world of hard tech and no wonder. Despite the hardships of living within Terra's strictures, I liked our world full of magic.

She patted my hand again. How could a gesture that was meant to reassure be so unreassuring?

"Don't worry. Earth does things in her own time. Magic will fade one day, but your descendants will be dust long before that happens."

Shockingly, thinking of my family as dust did little to settle my nerves.

AFTER TERRA'S REVELATION, I couldn't sleep. Mason, Kester and Dutch were conferring quietly in the kitchen.

"I'm just going to check on Gallivant," I said as I let myself out the patio door.

The rain had stopped, and the air hung like a wet carpet. I slipped and skidded across the muddy ground to the horse paddock. The sun wouldn't be up for hours yet, but even the nocturnal critters had worn themselves out and the night was silent.

Clover had calmed down. I gave him a good scratch behind the ears as I passed through the paddock. Gallivant let out a sleepy whuffle when I stepped into his stall. I checked the bandage by the light of my widget. The wound had stopped bleeding and Gita's magic was already healing it.

As I filled his water bucket, a shadow broke away from the corner of the barn. Raven stepped into the pool of light that fell from one window.

"You should be asleep," I said.

"So should you."

He was taller than me now but still thin and wiry. He'd never be a large man, but his shoulders were starting to fill out. He wasn't a kid anymore.

"That was pretty intense today." His hands were jammed deep into his pants pockets.

"It was. Were you scared?"

"No." Then he grinned. "Yes. You?"

"Terrified."

"Does that ever go away?"

"No. And you don't want it to. If you're not afraid going into a fight, then you're just dead inside."

Raven nodded. "Joe said something like that."

Joe Mountainclaw had done wonders for Raven. Last year, his Thunderbird heritage had so terrified him that he'd been on the brink of denying his own magic. Now he could switch between pony, human and eagle forms with an ease that would make most shifters jealous.

Raven shuddered and looked out at the night. "I feel like there's a giant shadow hanging over us. Thunderbird feels it too. It makes me itchy, like he's ready to burst out of me."

I squeezed his arm. "Tell Thunderbird to hang in there. We might need him again before this…whatever this is, is over."

"It's war, Mom." His eyes were huge and dark.

I sighed. "It is war. And I wish you didn't have to be part of it."

But we'd already had that argument. I wouldn't stop him from joining the fight. One didn't forbid Thunderbird anything.

He patted Gallivant on the neck. "Do you think he'll be ready to fly again soon?"

"I don't know. I wanted him to come so I could scout from the air, get a lay of the land before we attack Vioska. But it's not fair to ask that of him when he's wounded. I think I'll have to leave him behind."

"I can do it."

"No."

"I can!" His face was so earnest. "I can fly just as high as Gallivant. The opji arrows won't touch me. I can be your scout."

"No. We discussed this. Joe and Nori will need you to stay back and help with the wounded."

"And I will. I promise. But let me scout first, please. I love Shar too. I want to be useful. You would do it, if you could."

By the All-father. At what age did kids learn to push all your buttons?

"We'll see. Let's talk it over with Mason first."

Raven grinned. In kid logic, "We'll see" was already better than "No."

Mason appeared in the doorway of the barn. Raven opened his mouth to ask about scouting, but Mason held up a hand.

"I heard. We'll talk about it later." A widget was in his other hand. He held it out to me. "It's Avie. Trevor was at the barracks when they were attacked. The opji took him."

All the blood drained from me. Raven grabbed my arm as my knees buckled. I put the widget to my ear to hear my best friend sobbing.

CHAPTER

20

Kyra's Personal Journal

April 17, 2085

It's been a year since I thought I'd lost everything to the opji. Last spring, the vampires started their push eastward, burning homesteads and taking hostages for their krowa pens. It feels selfish to say these attacks caused me to lose everything, when so many others truly lost their homes, their families and their lives. But I lost my heart in that fight. They took my husband from me as surely as if they'd killed him. He came back, but we are forever changed, as Montreal will be if we don't do something about this opji incursion.

I've spent the past six months begging, cajoling and bribing different factions in Montreal to join our fight. And now we're out of time. I can only hope that people will do the right thing and honor their commitments.

Because the call goes out now.

Tomorrow we leave for Vioska. The opji have a weapon that cannot stay in their hands. With it, they will tear apart the very fabric of our reality and replace it with a monstrous version of their making, a world devoid of green life, a world where humans and fae will be nothing more than feed bags for the insatiable opji bloodlust.

I leave my family, I leave my job and my city for a fight that seems un-winnable but must be won at all costs.

I can only hope that one day, my daughter will forgive me and understand why her mama had to go away.

I paused my typing and stared across the yard. I sat in the morning sun on our patio. New buds on the maple trees glistened like emeralds. The goblits were playing soccer in the yard. Princess barked as she chased the ball. Holly was stacking stones at the end of the patio with Grim as chaperone. His tail twitched. He was holding in his cat urge to topple her tower.

It was a perfect spring day, just the way I wanted to remember my home.

Mason joined me on the patio, bringing a steaming mug. Our coffee rations were nearly depleted, but we'd silently agreed that on this day we wouldn't skimp on any luxury.

Tomorrow we would leave for Vioska and the battle that had been brewing for over five years.

Mason sat and angled my computer to read the last words of my journal. I had no secrets from him. Holly toddled over and started building a new tower of rocks on his knee. She sang "Cockles and Mussels," an old sea shanty that she'd no doubt learned from Gita, but she garbled the words and it came out as *Cockas and Musses.*

My chest constricted as I watched her easy innocence.

Not today. No sorrow. Let's enjoy one more day as a normal family.

I breathed in and out, not releasing the tension—that was impossible—but taking some of the wind from its sails.

Mason finished reading. "It's very good. You should publish it."

"Publish? Why?" The thought of putting my very private thoughts and feelings online made me all squishy inside, and not in the good way.

"Because we begged the fae and the godlings. We tried to convince the human ministers that they were in danger. We even sent the Guardians into the shanty towns to recruit. Few people seem convinced there is a war on the horizon. Or if they do, they figure someone else will take care of the opji." He smiled at Holly as she hummed and placed another stone on top of her tower.

"Some will come. And there may be others," I said.

"There are definitely others. And we need to reach them. Publish it."
I read over my words again and added another few sentences:

I'm not sure if I believe in the great benevolence of gods, but I have glimpsed the opposing ferocity of evil. Its power lies not in strength of arms but in the willful ignorance of its target. Those who turn away from this fight will only feel opji fangs on the back of their necks. There will be no escape.

Every homesteader outside of Montreal Ward lives in fear of the opji—of being killed…or worse. I can think of no greater horror than watching my children grow up inside a krowa pen, knowing they will one day feed the opji bloodlust or become a mindless wojak killing machine.

Since the Flood Wars ended, the opji have sought a way to break the gods' hold on this world. And now I fear they have found it.

If we do not stop them, the krowa pens will soon be full of Montreal's children.

Tomorrow I go to war. I go because I love my family and my city. I go because there is no one else to stop the evil that is coming. I go knowing the odds are stacked against us. We are woefully few against so many.

This is not a drill, and this may be my last blog. In three days we muster at Vioska. I beg you, if you have any love for your family and friends, join us. For if we fail, the opji are coming for your families next.

Mason read the words and nodded a silent agreement. Before I could second-guess myself, I shot a zing of magic to my fingertip and hit *enter* to send my plea out into the world. I could only hope it wouldn't fall on deaf ears.

Holly let out a screech and slapped her tower sending stones crashing to the ground.

CHAPTER

21

For two days, we traveled toward Vioska—a caravan of humans mounted on horseback, carts carrying bluecaps and priests, yetis lumbering alongside and gargoyles flying overhead when they could. Voices were hushed. Only the squeak of saddles and the crunch of cartwheels marked our train.

Jacoby rode on his special seat behind me. His fingers dug into my waist so hard, I would be bruised. He knew the things that could run in those trees. So did I and my eyes never stopped scanning left and right. The forest seemed to be watching our passing, watching but not interfering.

Near dawn on the third morning, Mason headed back to the end of the train to make sure the Guardians were secure for the daylight hours. He caught up to me just as the sun glimmered through the trees behind us.

"Every one's keeping up with our pace," he said. "How long until rendezvous?"

"According to the map, we're almost there. Another couple of kilometers."

Mason nodded but didn't comment. There was really nothing left to say. We'd said it all already. We dared not dream past tomorrow. Instead, we hoped the sun would rise in a clear sky. We hoped that around the next bend, we'd find an army of allies waiting for us, people who'd honored their promises to join us in this fight.

Only half those wishes came true.

The sun rose behind us in a brilliant pink splash, but when the trees parted on the clearing ahead, it lit up only a small group of waiting allies.

Where were Carmen and the Roden & Hogg soldiers? Where was Oscar? And the alchemists? I hadn't held out much hope for Captain Lowe and Hub, but this collection of a few dozen people was much worse than I'd expected.

A man rode forward on a huge reindeer. A young woman followed him on a brindled goat that was bigger than my quarter horse. I knew those mounts. The goat was Lucille and the reindeer had the unlikely name of Norma Jean. They were the Wild Hunt beasts from Annequin Lodge.

"Greetings, Kyra." Herne nodded to me, then bowed low over his mount when he saw Terra in the cart behind me. "My lady. You bless us with your presence."

I wasn't surprised that Herne, godling of The Hunt would recognize Terra. He turned his attention back to me. "You remember my daughter, Charlotte?"

I smiled. "Yes. She saved my life. Not something I would forget."

Charlotte reddened just a bit. She *had* saved me after my very first opji bite all those years ago. She was older now, more woman than girl. Her blond hair was tucked under a wool cap, and she sat on her saddle with confidence.

"I am glad you're here," I said. Soon, we'd need all the healers we could get.

Lucille sidled forward and snuffled my leg. Aw. She remembered me too. Spencer gave her a side-eye but didn't balk.

"I'd hoped for more reinforcements," I said to Herne.

"It's early yet." He scratched the hair around the nubby horn protruding from his head. "We only just arrived last night. The Inbetween is not an easy road. You may find others have been waylaid too."

I nodded.

"Have you seen any opji in the area?"

Herne grinned. "Vioska is only few kilometers that way." He pointed westward. "But you must see for yourself. It's a sight you won't easily forget."

"I believe it." I had a feeling this whole adventure would be indelibly inked on my psyche.

I gave orders for the others to make camp, but I wanted to see the enemy first hand.

"Cletus, I want you to come with us. Can you ride?"

The bluecap pulled at his beard considering. "Dwarves aren't meant for horseback. The stirrups never reach my feet, you see."

Herne watched him with amusement, then said a quiet word to Charlotte. She dismounted and brought the goat toward Cletus.

"Here, take Lucille. There are no stirrups that will guide her anyway. But she won't toss you, and she'll get you where you're going, I promise."

Cletus came up to Lucille's shoulder. He suffered through a thorough examination by her snout, then heaved a great sigh.

"Someone find me a mounting block."

While Cletus struggled onto his mount, I thanked Charlotte.

"Our friend, Nori is a healer too. She's in charge of setting up a mobile hospital. Will you help? I'm afraid there will be many casualties before this war is done."

Charlotte smiled. "I will give my service wherever it's needed."

Terra insisted on coming along while we scouted the opji. Almarick helped her into the saddle behind me. Jacoby wasn't happy about being displaced, and I told him to help Nori set up the hospital tent. Almarick protested about letting his mistress go on alone.

"Don't fret like an old man," Terra snapped. "We're just going to have a look-see. Help the others set up camp while I'm gone."

Almarick bowed to his mistress, though his hands were twisted in his robe. It wasn't easy being the acolyte to a stubborn god.

Herne led the way through the dense woods. Mason joined us and Raven ran in his pony form with Princess at his side. The hound bounded up and down our line, but Raven had lost his childish exuberance for running. That both pleased me and saddened me.

"When we get there, I want you to fly up and take a look at the lay of the land," I said. "See how far we are from Vioska, mark any possible hazards, and give us an estimate of how many wojaks they have in reserve."

Raven tossed his head, shaking his black mane.

I wished I hadn't been so impulsive about going after those opji with Gallivant. It terrified me to put Raven in danger, but Mason and I had discussed it. We hoped that if we let him have this little taste of responsibility and excitement, he would keep his promise to stay out of the rest of the fight.

The trees ended abruptly and we stopped to gaze at a massive field of blackened tree trunks that ringed Vioska. The rooftops of the opji city were like inkblots on the horizon, though one domed building towered above the others. The red haze of a blood ward shielded the whole city. Smoke rose from dozens of smoldering fires on the outer edge of the ring of devastation. Closer to the city, nothing grew in the ash between stumps. It was an apocalyptic vista of gray and black…and ghosts. Hundreds of them. Thousands. Their ethereal bodies milled about the open field, looking lost and confused.

Dear All-father, so many souls taken in violence by the opji.

Behind me Terra swore. You might wonder how the god of all things curses? The answer is like a sailor, only worse.

"I felt every one of those trees die," she said, "like the cells of my own body were being eaten by cancer."

Of course. Leave it to Terra to ignore the ghosts and mourn the trees.

The morning was bright. Wind turned smoke in the field into little cyclones.

Terra pointed west and I followed the line of her finger. I could just make out row upon row of wojaks gathered in front of Vioska, outside the red ward. They filled the plains from one edge to another. From that distance, the black mass of bodies looked like writhing beetles. I only wished I had a can of bug fogger big enough to wipe them out.

"We're calling it the Devastation," Herne swung an arm to encompass the field of death. His voice seemed oddly flat as if the gray was seeping into us too. "It goes on for miles. They've been burning the forest for months, creating this no-man's land to protect their town. No way we can attack them without being mowed down by their arrows."

Cletus urged Lucille forward. The massive goat trampled through ash. Charcoal snapped under his hooves. He urged the mount about a hundred yards into the Devastation, stopped to examine the land, then turned back to join us again.

He tugged on his beard as he considered. "We could dig under it."

I gazed at the shimmering red haze. I wasn't sure the others could see it.

"There's a ward around the city," I said. "It's a blood ward too. It won't be easy to break."

"Well, aye. Wards are a problem," Cletus said. "Can't promise to be able to go under that. Depends on how deep it's set in the ground. But we could bring our army right to their door without being shot at in the open."

It was something to consider.

146

I sent Cletus back to camp to start working on that problem, then faced the Devastation again. We needed more information.

Raven had already transformed back to human. He stood by Spencer's side, waiting for permission to fly. I gave into one last motherly urge and brushed the unruly white lock of hair from his eyes.

"No heroics, right? You go up high enough that they can't hit you, even if that means you don't get exact numbers."

"Got it." Raven had a dare-devil gleam in his eye that I didn't like. Then he crouched, and in the time it took him to jump, he transformed from boy into Thunderbird. It was a beautiful sight.

The hound leaped into the air after him.

"Princess, no! *Hael!*" I called after her, but it was too late. I should have had her on a magical tether. Now, instead of just worrying about Raven, I had to watch both of them fly toward the enemy.

Mason rode up beside me and held my hand. When Raven was halfway across the no-man's land, a barrage of arrows flew up from behind the line of wojaks. They filled the sky.

Wojaks are killing machines—teeth, claws, and strength all add to their viciousness. What they didn't have was dexterity or intelligence enough to use a weapon like a bow. That meant behind the army of wojaks was a second army of opji.

"Dear All-father," I whispered, then remembered that the god of all things was sitting in the saddle behind me. "Sorry," I mumbled, but Terra didn't seem to take offense at my invocation of a foreign deity.

"We'll need all the help we can get," she said.

A second volley of arrows darkened the sky. While Thunderbird's wings were ponderous, Princess zipped around him like a rocket. They flew high enough that the arrows peaked and fell before reaching them, but it was still heart-stopping to watch.

Mason had been observing through an alchemical scope. He lowered it now and said, "That's an impressive range. Three hundred meters at least. They must be using longbows." He raised the scope again and made a calculation. "They're about half a kilometer out. That means we're out of range."

"Then we muster here tomorrow, unless they attack before then."

"They haven't moved since we arrived," Herne said. "I don't think they're planning to attack. Only to defend whatever is behind those lines."

Mason handed me the scope. I brought the city into focus. It was bigger than I had assumed. The domed building looming in the background had pretensions of a palace. From Glenda's reports, I knew it was the Hall of Mages, Ichovidar's lair.

I tilted the scope down and focused on the rows of wojaks—pathetic, filthy creatures with almost no resemblance to the humans they'd once been. They were in constant motion, snapping at one another, snarling, pacing. Most had hunched shoulders, matted hair and desiccated skin stretched over their bones, but a few were freshly turned. These were the most horrifying because their faces retained enough flesh to show expressions of hate and madness.

I lowered the scope. I'd seen enough.

"Ichovidar is back there," Terra said. "My spirit pulls on me, like he is dangling it just out of my reach. I must get there." Her fingers crabbed at my arm. "Kyra you must take me there!"

"I will. I promise. But we have to get through those wojaks first. And the ward."

The king of the opji held more than Terra's spirit. He also kept hundreds of captive humans, maybe thousands. And my baby Shar.

I wanted to storm across the Devastation right now and take her back, but seeing that line of wojaks and the hail of arrows made me realize we were woefully outnumbered.

Thunderbird let out a tremendous caw that shook the morning, and he dove into a hail of arrows.

Oh, gods! No!

He screeched as he fell on the undead army. What in the hells was he playing at?

His massive wings beat once and a concussion, louder than thunder, filled the air. It shook the ground. Wojaks toppled. Giant talons grabbed something from behind their line and Thunderbird flew away. Arrows pierced his side, his wing, his tail. He screamed in rage or pain and flew straight up, carrying away his booty. Princess zoomed around and through the arrows, somehow missing the strikes.

They flew out of range, winging back across the apocalyptic field.

Thunderbird dropped his captive with a bone cracking thud not a hundred yards ahead of us.

It was huge, much bigger than any wojak, and impossibly it was already starting to rise. Its bare shoulders were massive and covered in scars. Red-ringed eyes flashed with crazed hate. I knew that look. It was a wojak, but it wasn't human.

Mason jumped off his horse, dashed out and decapitated the creature as it rose to its knees.

"It's an ogre!" he called back. "Undead!"

Was that even possible? I didn't understand the rite that created wojaks, but I'd never seen another undead creature other than ghouls. I'd assumed only humans could be turned.

Now we had ogre wojaks. In life, ogres were nearly unkillable. They weighed twice what a normal human male weighed, had skin like elephant hide and the muscle of a grizzly bear. Add to that the insatiable bloodlust of the undead and total disregard for its own safety, and you had a nearly undefeatable enemy.

How many ogres were in that wojak army? Thunderbird wouldn't be able to snatch them all away, even if I granted him permission, which I wouldn't.

Despair threatened to choke me. My ears registered the scolding tone of Terra's voice, but my brain couldn't grasp the words. The reins slipped from my frozen fingers. I felt myself teetering sideways, but before I slipped from the saddle, Mason was there. I hadn't even seen him run across the burned out ground to catch me.

Thunderbird let out another caw and he shifted. Raven landed beside the dead ogre. If the arrows had wounded him, he showed no signs. He prodded the dead creature with a toe and a huge, childish grin lit his face. Princess landed beside him, panting heavily. Her tongue lolled like this was all a terrific game.

Rage is a powerful emotion. It's a harsh taskmaster and fuel for a desperate soul. Rage brings clarity. It's sharp and cold like a blade made from ice. Long after love and hate wear out, rage continues. And when it's finally gone it leaves a giant hole—a damp, dark breeding ground for fear and despair.

I'd lived for years with the aspect of a demon stoking my rage and coloring my entire world, so now I was suspect of the raw emotion whenever I felt it creeping back inside me.

I jumped down from horseback and marched into the Devastation. While I kicked aimlessly at broken and burned branches, I examined the rage coursing through me. Was it a taint from the dead demon? No. I recognized the fuel behind the rage. It was…fear. I acknowledged it, then I leaned into the breathing exercises my mother had taught me long ago, and finally, I let it go.

When I had my emotions under control, I stalked over to Raven. He was braced for my wrath, but I just grabbed him in a hug so fierce that he let out a puff of air. He wasn't a child. I couldn't punish him or ground him. I couldn't even scold him.

I shoved him away a little too roughly. Tears were leaking down my face. "Don't ever do that again."

"Aww, I'm alright."

"You promised to stay out of the fight."

"I know, but I wanted to hurt them. Just once. And when I saw those ogres I also saw my chance. I promise I'll stay back with Nori now."

Mason joined us on the field. "What else did you find out?"

The opji army still hadn't moved, and we all turned to gaze across the Devastation.

"I can't be sure how many wojaks there are. Hundreds, at least. There's a whole bunch more of those ogres too. At least a dozen. And they have something in a huge metal cage. I couldn't get close enough to see what it was."

"That's okay," I said. We'd find out what other little surprises the opji had in store for us soon enough.

Raven was still hyped up from his brush with death. He shifted to his pony form and ran off toward camp with Princess barking at his hooves.

I turned to Mason. "Can you see the ghosts?"

He gazed across the field. "Yes. They're everywhere."

I nodded. In the Nether, I'd given Mason a piece of my ki, which imbued him with my ability to see ghosts.

"What about bones. Can you…you know." I didn't really want to say it.

"You want to know if my aspect of the demon is entirely gone? Or if I can still call the dead?"

"Yes."

Mason rubbed at the back of his neck. "It's gone. If there are bones of the dead buried here, I can't sense them."

I took his hand and squeezed it. "That's good. I'd rather face a thousand wojaks than lose you to the demon again."

He nodded toward the waiting army. "Looks like you'll have your wish."

Another volley of arrows darkened the sky.

What were they shooting at?

A figure zig-zagged through the smoke, coming straight at us. Mason glanced through the scope then handed them to me with a grin.

I took a second to focus, then I recognized him.

Emil!

He bolted across the field. An arrow slammed into his back and he fell, but he was up in an instant, staggering, half crawling, half loping the final distance as he outran the arrows and they struck the ground behind him. He swerved around the dead ogre and dropped at my feet. A huge grin broke through the ash smeared on his face.

"I thought you'd never come." Then he passed out.

"Kill it before it wakes up!" Herne shouted. His arrow was already knocked in his bow. I jumped in front of Emil's prone body.

"No! He's a friend."

"He's a vampire!"

"Put down your weapon, Hunstman!" Terra snapped. "The girl knows what she's doing."

Herne looked from me to Terra, then grumbled. "Fine. I'll leave you to it. But if you're not back by sunrise, we're taking the fight to the vamps without you." He turned his great reindeer and rode into the trees.

Vampires don't stay unconscious for long, not even with an arrow in their back. Before Emil woke, Mason put a foot on his hip and yanked out the arrow. Emil jerked and let out a hiss. A few minutes later, his eyes opened. I reached out a hand and he took it, pulling himself to sit upright, then even farther so he could stand and hug me.

I squeezed him back.

"I'm so glad—" I stopped. Emil's magic was all wrong. His heart didn't beat. I pulled away, but he hung on. A manic grin appeared through the mess of dirt and blood on his face.

"Don't look so stricken, Kyra."

"But your heart…you…"

"You can say it. I'm a card-carrying opji."

Mason pulled me away from Emil and edged between us.

Emil shook his head. "I would have thought you'd be happy for me. No more bloodlust."

"I am. I mean, I will be, I think."

"Just as soon as you decide if I've gone all evil, right? Well, I'm here to prove that being opji doesn't make you any more evil than being human does. Or fae. Or shifter. In fact, there are many opji inside Vioska who abhor what Ichovidar has done. They will fight with us as soon as we give the signal. Fight from within Vioska."

Emil was thin to the point of emaciation. His cheek bones jutted like blades, making his eyes look sunken. The dark curls he'd so loved had been cropped short in a military style. He would have looked like crap except for the zeal that lit his eyes.

I glanced at Terra who still sat on Spencer's back. She shook her head. She had no idea what to do here either. Emil saw the look and gave a bitter laugh.

"Is that how it is then? There's no trust left between us?"

I made a split second decision that I hoped I wouldn't regret and pushed past Mason to take Emil's hand.

"Of course not. I just want to be sure you're safe and healthy."

He took a deep breath that expanded his chest and let it out. "Never better. I never knew what I was missing."

"So they gave you the zycha?"

He nodded. "Against my will, but yes. It wasn't a pretty sight. I went into it kicking and screaming, convinced that their death rite would change me forever, like some kind of brainwashing. They thought so too because as soon as it was done, they let me roam free around the city."

"And did it? Change you?"

"Hells, yeah." He crouched and jumped straight up, rising at least six feet in the air before landing like a nimble cat. "I'm stronger and faster. And I heal even more quickly than before." He flexed his shoulder to show that the arrow hit was already healed. "But the best part is that my bloodlust is under control. I barely need to feed more than once a week now."

A muscle twitched on his eyebrow. There was more he wasn't telling me, but standing in a burning field with an army of vamps across the way, wasn't the place for catching up.

"Come on." I tugged on his arm. "Meet the others. I'm sure they all want to hear anything you can tell us about their defenses." I paused, and made him meet my eye. "That is, of course, assuming you're willing to tell us."

His gaze hardened. I couldn't read this new Emil. Was he angry? Hurt? Hiding something?

"I'll tell you everything you need to know to wipe out those bastards."

He left the field and hopped into the saddle in front of Terra. The god didn't seem perturbed to have one of her enemy so close. She wrapped her arms around his waist and they trotted off.

Mason mounted into his saddle, then helped me up to ride behind him. I pressed my head against his shoulder.

"We should watch him." As soon as the words left my lips I regretted them, but Mason nodded.

"I'll put Cricket on him. Nothing escapes the hidebehind."

CHAPTER

22

When we arrived back at camp, we found that Nori and the Terran priests had erected the make-shift hospital tent. They were busy organizing supplies and barely looked up when we arrived. I couldn't help looking at the hospital and wondering how many of our people would need its services in the coming days.

I also found that our numbers had swelled.

"Kyra!" A male voice boomed. I knew that voice, and I swiveled in my saddle, looking for the blond giant who stood a head above everyone else. I jumped off the horse and ran for Huyn. He ignored the hand I extended and swept me into a bear hug instead.

"You came!"

"Wouldn't have missed the chance to stake a few vamps!" Huyn laughed with that gut-shaking mirth I remembered. "And I brought some of your cousins."

Dozens of Aesir warriors and Valkyries milled about looking bored. One Valkyrie smiled shyly and nodded to me. I crossed the space between us and took both her hands in mine.

"Anni. Thank you for coming." The One-eyed Father knew the current Freya of the Valkyries had no love for me.

"I bring greetings from King Frode." She leaned in and lowered her voice. "You saved us from our biggest folly. Now I come to aid in the fight against your greatest enemy."

"Thank you." It was woefully inadequate, but that's all I had. My thanks.

I turned back to Huyn. He was shaking Mason's hand, a little too vigorously. Mason had an unhinged gleam in his eye.

"Come on you two," I grabbed both their elbows. "Save the testosterone battles for the opji. We have a war to plan."

"Uh, Kyra?" Huyn jerked a thumb over his shoulder. "I brought a few of my fight buddies to the party too. I hope that's okay."

I glanced at the group standing nearby. Unlike the fit-looking Aesir, these men and women were a shamble of brutish faces, scarred from knife wounds and tattooed with gang tags. It was the kind of crowd you didn't want to meet alone at night on any street.

"Fight buddies? You mean Knackers?" A couple of years ago, I'd met Huyn after his winning fight in the Knackers' club. They pitted humans against fae and beasts just for shits and giggles. I'd reached out to the Knackers weeks ago, but never heard from them.

"Does Mr. Gaffer know you're here?" I wasn't supposed to know the name of the shadowy figure who led the Knackers. Nobody was.

Huyn turned me away and whispered, "You shouldn't use that name so lightly. Just speaking it aloud is a death sentence in certain circles."

I whispered right back. "I'm about to face an army of vampires. I don't care."

"Fair enough." Huyn leaned back with a grin. "Where do you want us?"

I called Herne over and asked him to settle the newcomers, but stopped him before he strode off again.

"Give me some time to settle in, but then we have plans to make."

Herne nodded. "That's your command tent there." He pointed to the largest tent in the clearing. "Get comfortable. I have a pot of stew going. I'll bring it along in about an hour."

I watched him leave with the others and thanked the One-eyed God for innkeepers. They were the most practical and efficient people.

Emil stood in the middle of the busy camp with a faint smile on his face as he watched the bustle around him. He wore the distinct black pants and jacket of the opji. It was an old-fashioned style that hinted at a military cut. People gave him a wide berth. Herne had probably warned them about this opji who was—impossibly—a friend, but they weren't ready to trust him yet. Poor Emil. It was the story of his life.

"Come on." I beckoned him toward the command tent. Before we made it two steps, I heard raised voices and the sound of engines. I turned back to the road, hoping beyond hope that Captain Lowe had come through with the Hub cavalry.

A line of six armored trucks drove into camp. They had gun turrets on the roof, mounted with something that looked like small canons. The lead car stopped and a tall, elegant woman stepped out.

It wasn't Hub, but the next best thing. Roden & Hogg mercenaries had arrived.

Carmen came forward with her hand outstretched. "Kyra! So good to see you again." Everything about Carmen was big and bold, including her mane of corkscrew curls that I'd always envied and her grip as she shook my hand.

"I'm so glad you decided to come," I said.

"Wouldn't miss killing some opji. Their attacks have brought the scavenging business to a standstill, so you're doing us a favor."

The passenger side of the truck opened and another figure emerged.

Avalon Moodie.

The ghosts on Vioska field had more color than her complexion. She squinted into the pale sunlight, looking lost and confused.

"Avie! You were supposed to stay out of this!" I ran over and put an arm around her. Avie had nine kids at home. With Trevor captured, they'd already lost one parent to the opji. I didn't want them to lose another.

"I brought supplies. Healing stuff. From Cece."

"You could have sent those. You didn't have to come."

"I know." She shook her head even as she agreed with me. "I couldn't stay away. I just…" Her breath hitched and she pressed a fist to her mouth. "I just couldn't stand by and do nothing." Her pleading eyes met mine. "The not-knowing, it's going to kill me."

No, I thought. It won't. But a vampire bite just might do the trick.

"I understand. Come on. Let's get you settled. Nori is here. You can help at the first aid tent."

She gripped my hand fiercely. "You haven't seen…I mean, there's no news about the captives yet?"

I thought about the army of wojaks waiting to face us in the morning. They'd all been human captives before being turned into undead monsters. Had Trevor been among them?

I shook my head. "No news yet."

Avie nodded and let me lead her away.

I'D STARTED THINKING ABOUT certain people as my captains—Herne, Carmen, Cletus, Huyn, Anni and, of course, Mason. These were the people who led others and expected me to command them, ridiculous as that idea was.

As the sun started its decline, I made the rounds of the camp, quietly asking these captains to meet me in the command tent in half an hour.

Huyn declined. "I'm a fighter, not a planner," he said. "Just point me toward the vamps when you're ready." So I left him at his campfire with the Knackers.

I found Neva in the bluecap camp, but Cletus was already excavating under the Devastation. I asked her to send one of the bluecaps with a report on their progress by the end of the evening.

The rest of us met in the command tent. We had only one rickety table and camp chairs around it. Mason had projected a map of the area on the table.

As the afternoon wore on the others arrived and took their seats. The inside of the tent was dark and hot. I studied the faces around the table. To anyone else, Mason's expression would have been broody, but I knew it hid his deep worry. Emil still looked amused. Kester had come with Mason and lurked by the open tent flap. Carmen was all business and sat with a tablet on her knee, ready to take notes. Herne and Anni filled out the rest of the group.

I don't know how Terra heard about the meeting, but she arrived too, leaning heavily on Almarick's arm. Jacoby came in with them and sat at my knee. I appreciated the weight of his small body leaning against me.

I looked to Mason, making a plea with my eyes for him to take over, but he just nodded at me to continue.

Fine. I could do this. What was the first step to running a war? A sudden panic sent my mind spinning off the rails. Everyone was looking at me, and my mind was blank.

From outside, the low murmurs of our soldiers filled the background.

Emil cleared his throat. "If you don't mind, I'd like to start."

I nodded toward Emil as if that had been my intention all along. His lips did a weird half smirk, half smile thing. Sweat pooled in my palms and in the small of my back. I took a deep breath and pretended to be the general they all expected.

"Thank you, Emil. For those of you who don't know, Emil is an opji." I spoke above the sudden grumbling that produced. "Who was raised in Montreal. He has been spying on the opji for us since November." I waved a hand at Emil so he could continue.

"First, I'd like to state for the record that I may be opji, but I'm not on their side of this conflict."

"How are we supposed to believe that?" Herne asked. His arms were crossed over his broad chest.

"Emil has been my friend for years," I said. "He's no more opji than I am."

Herne let out a noncommittal grunt.

"Thank you," Emil said. "But that's not entirely true. I was born to the opji, but my upbringing has proven that their zycha rite is nothing more than indoctrination. At least as far as believing in their…fanaticism. Taking the zycha rite doesn't automatically make someone evil. I am proof of that. My moral compass remains the same, despite their attempts to convert me." He turned to meet Herne's eye. "I will be glad to discuss that in more detail with anyone who wants to know more, but right now, I believe we have more pressing matters. Please let me outline what I know about the opji defenses."

Wow. Emil sounded so…mature. Whatever he'd undergone in the months since I last saw him, it had affected him on some deep level.

"Please go on," I said.

Emil smiled. "The opji have several lines of defense. You saw the wojak army already. And the opji archers."

"What are their numbers?" Mason asked.

"I estimate the wojaks to be nearly a thousand head. The opji archers, about two hundred. There are other opji in reserve too. Say, another four-hundred foot soldiers and two dozen sorcerers."

"And those ogre abominations?" Mason asked.

"About a dozen. But there's something worse. They have a demon."

That had everyone sitting up straighter.

"A demon working on their side?" Mason asked. I knew what he was thinking. Any general that trusted a demon was as good as dead. Demons had their own agendas. Always. And that agenda usually meant consuming as much human and fae flesh as possible.

Emil nodded. "On their side, but not willingly. It's caged for now, both physically and spiritually. The sorcerers believe they have it under control. But if it gets out of that cage…" He lifted his hands in a shrug. "Killing it might not be possible."

"Just one demon?" I asked.

"They had more." Emil paused and his glance rested on Terra. "I heard they sacrificed them in some great magic last fall. Only one remains."

One was enough. Glenda's report had been right after all. The opji had already pulled the lesser demons through the veil. There was no telling what other magical monstrosity Ichovidar was capable of.

"Fools," Herne said. "If their damn bloodlust doesn't kill us all, that demon will do it."

I turned to Kester, who'd been silent as a wraith up to this point. "Can you and Mason work with Emil on that? Find out everything you can about this demon?"

"Of course. But it might make no bit of difference. Demons are near impossible to kill, as you know."

"We'll figure something out." I met Mason's eye. He smiled encouragingly, but others shifted uncomfortably in their seats. Those weren't the words you wanted to hear from your general.

"You must get me to that sorcerer, and I will end this war for you," Terra said. I waited for her to elaborate, but she didn't, and it wasn't my place to reveal to the others that she was a god who'd lost her magic. Her voice was weak and cracking, and after that proclamation, she seemed to fade. Herne looked away as if embarrassed to see the god so frail.

"And where is Ichovidar in all this?" I asked. "Is he commanding his troops on the front line?"

Emil shook his head. "Ichovidar is holed up in the Hall of Mages. He won't be joining the fight. He has other things to do."

Those other things included sacrificing Shar. Emil and I would have a discussion about that later in private.

"What about the city itself? Vioska is protected by a blood ward. Is that right?" I wanted Emil to confirm it for the others.

"Yes, and it's a good one," he said. "Sunk deep into the ground and fortified every week with blood." No one had to ask whose blood.

Emil smiled. It wasn't a happy smile, more like the grin of an evil mastermind. "But the good news is that Ichovidar has put his army outside the ward."

"Why would he do that?" Herne asked. "Sounds like a trap."

"It is. He wants you to fight the wojaks in the open because he has every confidence that they'll decimate you. That burned out field extends all the way around the city. There's no way to approach without being seen. They'll shoot you down long before you get to it."

"We're already working on that," I said. "The bluecaps are digging under the plains. We hope to be able to come up right in their faces here." I tapped the map projected on the table. "Carmen will bring her tanks in beside the tunnel and we'll strike at the army from both sides." I looked to Carmen for confirmation and she nodded.

It was the barest whiff of a plan, but given enough luck, I thought we might even pull this off.

"Is that all you can tell us?" Herne said gruffly.

Emil smiled and shook his head.

"There are two more things you need to know." He held up one finger. "First, there are opji who would defy Ichovidar if they thought they could get away with it. I was in close contact with a group of dissenters. They call themselves the Bunters. If they think there's a chance he will fail, they might come to our aid."

"If and might," Mason said. "Doesn't sound promising."

Emil shrugged. "It's a chance. But we should look for their signal."

"And what will that be?" I asked.

"Fire. Lots of it."

"And the second thing you wanted us to know?"

Emil looked right at me. "It's about Shar. Maybe we should speak in private."

I sucked in a breath. "No. They need to hear it too."

Emil nodded slowly. "Ichovidar has great plans for your little shar-lil. I'm not exactly sure what, but the elder opji have been talking about it for weeks. It's something that will require great power and sacrifice. Something that will swing this war in their favor. And the heavens must be aligned for it to work. He needs a full moon for the rite to succeed."

I looked at him blankly. I wasn't a werewolf. I had no idea when the next full moon was.

"Tomorrow," he said. "The rite will take place tomorrow night."

That brought silence around the table. I was still hoping Hub would join us, but we couldn't wait.

I put on my best general's voice and spoke with conviction I didn't feel.

"Then we attack tomorrow morning. The sun will rise right in their sensitive eyes and with any luck they won't see us coming."

The meeting broke up. My captains returned to camp to ready their troops.

Terra rose and opened her mouth to speak. I stopped her with a raised hand.

"I know. I'm doing everything I can to get you inside that city."

She clamped her jaw shut and shook her head. Was my god losing hope? She shuffled out, leaning heavily on Almarick.

Only Mason, Emil and I remained in the command tent. Except for Jacoby, who'd fallen asleep under the table. Gods, I wished I had his knack for sleeping anywhere.

"Do you think we have any chance of succeeding?" I asked Emil.

"There's always a chance." He reached under his jacket. "I brought you a gift, just in case you get your wish and come face to face with Ichovidar." He pulled out the Thorn of Vidar and handed it to me. I ran my hand along the wood spike, then gripped it, twisted and pulled out the wickedly sharp blade.

"He's going to be really mad when he finds it gone again." Emil grinned that evil grin again. "Really mad. Use it."

I hung the stake on my belt and nodded. Tomorrow I might get my chance.

CHAPTER

23

knew I should get an early night, but I was restless. I walked through the camp with Jacoby following sleepily at my side. As we drifted around parked vehicles, tents and makeshift horse pens, I silently counted campfires and estimated the fighters gathered around them.

Not enough. Not nearly enough.

Conversations were hushed and the night was filled with nervous energy that tempered the expectancy one would expect before a battle.

We were a rag-tag group—humans, fae, beasts. I estimated we had about three hundred fighters to put in the field. Three hundred against a thousand wojaks and as many opji. We had some fire-power. The addition of Carmen's tanks would even the odds a bit, but we were seriously outnumbered. We all knew it. And yet, what other options did we have?

The yetis and the hidebehinds seemed to have bonded and they were camping together near the bluecaps. Grim had taken to the yetis too and he sat upright at their fire, his tail swishing back and forth. As I approached, the sweet, haunting music of a hidebehind filled the night. It was similar to a violin, but higher in pitch and more pure, like a violin played by an angel.

Cricket nodded as I stopped to enjoy his little concert. The music tugged at me, even on a normal day, and it brought emotions to the surface. Today it made me want to weep. I hardened my heart against its magic. There would be time to weep later.

I spied furtive movement behind a nearby tent. Someone was trying to sneak away from the firelight. I'd left my sword in my tent, but I unsheathed my hunting knife and crept around the other side of the tent to find two goblins crouched in the shadows.

Dekar rose with a sheepish grin. Muzzy tried to hide behind his brother.

"What are you doing here?"

Dekar shrugged. "I'm old enough to fight."

I pressed my fingers to my temple, wishing away the headache that nagged at me. I could only imagine Suzt's shrill scream when she learned about her brothers' disappearance. There was nothing I could do about Dekar. He was an adult. But I pointed to Muzzy. "You will report to the infirmary and help out there. I will check with Nori and if I find out you left for any reason, I will have you shackled to a cot. Understood?"

Muzzy gaped at me with huge eyes. "Y…yes, ma'am."

I gripped Dekar's arm. "You better stay alive. I can't be the one to tell your father you died."

Dekar nodded, but I could see the relief in his eyes.

Next I checked in at the hospital and warned Nori that she would have a new goblin attendant. Nori had everything in hand. Avie nodded to me from across the tent where she was organizing bandages. I nodded back, wishing she hadn't been drawn into this fight.

When we'd made the whole camp circuit, I returned to the campfire in front of the command tent where Mason brooded over a mug of tea. Terra was packed into a camp chair with blankets tucked around her. The other Terran priests had made camp near the hospital, but Almarick stayed by Terra's side. He'd become her valet, her porter, her nurse and even her legs at times.

Jacoby sprawled in the dirt too close to the fire for a human. I thought about telling him to go to bed, but like Almarick with Terra, he'd become my shadow and wouldn't retire until I did.

Mason patted the seat beside him and poured me a mug of tea from the pot warming beside the fire.

"Terra has an unusual idea for tomorrow," he said.

I sipped the tea and glanced at her. I'd thought she was asleep, but her eyes were half open and reflecting the firelight.

"Well, the gods know we can use any help we can get." As soon as the words were out of my mouth, I shook my head. Would I ever lose the habit of calling on the gods?

"Sorry. What's the idea?"

"Recruit the ghosts," Terra said.

I glanced at Mason. Was she serious? He nodded.

"I guess I could. I mean, they'd be drawn to my sword. But then I'd have to fend them off while they beg me to send them on to the afterlife. And without their human remains, I won't be able to do that. So what's the point? It's not like they could interact on this plane to fight for us."

"You leave that to me," Terra said. "Ichovidar might have stolen my spirit, but I have a little something in reserve. When the time comes, I will use it."

"My lady, no!" Almarick dropped to his knees before her chair. The outburst roused Jacoby. He babbled something about pookas and rolled over in his sleep to bake his other side against the fire.

Almarick didn't quite touch Terra, but he laced his hands together as if in prayer only inches from her legs. "My lady, you cannot do this. You don't have the strength. It will…"

Terra fixed him with a stern stare. "It will what? Kill me?" Almarick swallowed hard and froze under the weight of his lady's gaze. "I will not be kept out of this fight," she said. "I will do my part, and you will help me."

Almarick bowed his head. "Yes, my lady."

Satisfied, Terra turned back to me. "You won't need to use your sword as bait. Mason knows how to call the ghosts. He was once one with their light and can use that knowledge to his favor."

I twisted in my chair to look at Mason. "Is this true?"

His eyes were lost in shadow, but he nodded. "We were just getting to this when you arrived. Terra was about to explain what she did to me."

"What she did?" I glanced at Terra. "You mean the bloodstone. I did that to you." I was the one who'd locked him inside the stone with a demon.

"But Terra brought me out. And that changed me."

"Why didn't you tell me?"

"I wasn't sure until we saw those ghosts. For a moment, standing in that field, I felt the demon's power to call dead things again."

I gripped his hand. "I'm so sorry. I didn't know." I turned to Terra. "Does this mean part of the demon is still in him?"

Terra waved a bony finger side to side. "No. The demon is dead. Or trapped, which is much the same. Do you remember being inside the bloodstone?"

Mason nodded once, a sharp cut of agreement.

"Do you remember the light?"

Another nod. His teeth were clenched so tight, his jaw bulged.

"You walked through the light."

"You pulled me through."

"What was that like?"

"It was…painful."

Oh, gods. Terra was going to drag those horrible memories from him like a blood letting.

She nodded thoughtfully. "Not unlike birth, only this time you were aware of the pain. I pulled you through a veil of life to return you to your rightful place. That's what you felt. The pain of life. All of it at once. Excruciating."

Mason didn't answer. I squeezed his arm, and the muscles were tensed for fight or flight.

Terra continued in her frail voice. "Some of that life—that light—stuck to you. It was unavoidable. But if you speak to them, those spirits will recognize you as one of their own."

"What does that mean?" I asked. "Are you saying he can command the dead?"

"Not command. Asking nicely would work much better, I think. But they won't take much persuasion to fight the monsters that killed them. You must go back to the field tonight and ask them to fight for you."

"And you can make that happen? Make them corporeal enough to hurt the opji?" I asked.

"Yes." Her voice might have been frail, but her confidence wasn't. Almarick bowed his head. I could see his shoulders shuddering.

I turned to Mason. "What do you think?"

He rose from the chair and held out his hand to me. "Let's go talk to some ghosts."

WHEN WE REACHED THE Devastation, we dismounted and tied up the horses. A couple of bluecaps were standing guard beside a hole in the ground. One of them raised her axe as she saw us approach.

"How are the excavations?" I asked.

The bluecap looked young. She wore a helmet that didn't fit properly and drooped over one eye. "Cletus says we're nearly a hundred meters in."

She seemed pleased by this news, so I nodded, but a hundred meters wasn't enough. The tunnel wouldn't be ready by morning. We'd have to fight without that advantage of surprise. I wasn't willing to give up on the plan though. We had no idea what the day would bring.

"Do you have everything you need to keep going?" I asked. "Food, water?"

The guard nodded vigorously and her helmet fell over her eyes. She tipped it back and grinned. "Yes, ma'am. Neva has the kitchen going all night."

We left them to their duty and continued into the burned out plains. It wasn't easy going. The ground was uneven, with lumps of charred wood, stumps and rocks to climb over.

"This will be hell to navigate in a fight," Mason said. I'd been thinking the same thing. Only a few feet in, and my boots were already covered in black sludge from the ash.

We stopped just short of the opji's firing range. The night was cloudy, hiding what I knew was a nearly full moon.

I looked across the open field. The waiting wojaks were hidden in shadow, but between us lay the third army in this battle. The ghosts.

They were more easily seen in the gloom than the morning light. They seemed to mill around aimlessly.

"How do you want to do this?" I'd brought my sword, just in case, but left it sheathed in the saddle bag. I really didn't want to use it unless we had no other choice.

"Let me try something." Mason took a deep breath, squaring himself. He looked over the barren field. Ghosts trundled across the open ground. The spirit lights weren't fast, but neither did they ever stand still. They shifted and blended in a mesmerizing dance.

The dance suddenly changed course, and the lights drifted our way until a crowd of specters stood before us.

"Is there one who would speak for you?" Mason didn't raise his voice. He didn't need to. The spirits heard him on a different plane. The lights shuffled and a figure stepped forward. It was hard to tell her age. The suffusing light smoothed her skin. She seemed young, with longish curling hair. A hardness in her eyes suggested her life, if short, hadn't been easy.

"What do you want?" Her voice was sharp with a faint echo.

"Your help," Mason said.

"Why should we give it? No one came to help us."

Mason bowed his head. "We came too late to help you, and I am sorry for that. But there are others in those krowa pens." He pointed toward Vioska. "We would free them. Tell me your name."

The ghost floated forward to peer into Mason's eyes as if looking for the truth in their depths. There was something familiar about her. Spirits were monochrome, a pale uniform blue, but for some reason, I imagined her with blond hair.

"Janey." Her eyes slitted as if she dared him to do something with that knowledge.

"Janey, I can't command you, but I ask. Will you stand with us in this fight?"

He held out a hand to the ghost. She cocked her head to the side then reached for him. When they touched, a bit of her light infused him.

It was beautiful. After months of witnessing darkness ooze from him like an oil spill, this ethereal light seemed like a true blessing. And then I realized it was. Terra's blessing. When she'd pulled him from the bloodstone, she told me that darkness could only be fought with light. She'd pulled him through her light to bring him home to me. And that divine benediction still clung to him.

Mason had lost his aspect of the demon and gained the glow of an angel.

Janey pulled away and bowed. "We would follow you if we could. We would revenge ourselves and free our families from the opji monsters." Her expression turned sad. "But we have no power in this world."

"We can help with that," Mason said. "When the time comes we will have Terra's intercession. Will you tell the others?"

"Yessssss." Janey's answer came out like a rush of wind. She drifted away, drawing the other ghosts with her.

Mason pulled me to him. His arms wrapped around me, and I laid my head on his chest, listening to the slow tolling of his heart. The wind picked up, howling across the open plain.

And then it started to rain.

I slept for only a couple of hours and rose well before dawn. A few more homesteaders had straggled in during the early hours of the morning, including Soolea, Joe Mountainclaw and another dozen from Winaskwi.

Raven was excited to see his mentor. Joe clapped him in a hug, then Raven led him to the hospital tent. Joe looked like he could bend rebar with his bare hands, but he was a gentle soul and a skilled healer. Nori would welcome his help.

I hugged Soolea. I'd seen others in her village fight the opji, and I had no doubt she would be an asset in the fight.

"I didn't expect you to come," I said.

"I came for Jeremy and Father Hewitt."

Soolea had been pregnant with her first child when opji raiders decimated her homestead and took her husband and father-in-law captive. A horrible, terrible, sickening thought occurred to me, and I gripped her hands tightly. "You might find them in the fight. I mean you might face them…as wojaks."

Soolea nodded and stood taller. Her long black hair was held back with a beaded band and she looked every inch a warrior.

"I thought of that. I'm not afraid. They're already dead. I want their spirits to find peace. If that means I have to kill them again, I will."

In that moment, I thought she was the bravest person I knew.

I sent her away to get fed before the sun rose.

Neva had set up an unofficial mess tent beside the hospital. As I walked by, she thrust a scone into my hand and had another one for Jacoby, who was never far from my side.

"Eat," she said. "You'll need it."

I thanked her and kept going, munching on my scone, as I headed to the horse pens.

I'd found a way to keep Jacoby out of the fight. He would be my official messenger, and carry news from the front lines back to the hospital tent when needed. It wasn't a perfect solution, but a compromise that let him keep the apprentice status that he so coveted.

I turned to him now. "Go to Cletus. Get a status report on the tunnel and come right back. And hurry. We leave soon."

Jacoby loped away.

Mason joined me by the horses. Angus was with him. The sky was just starting to lighten in the east.

Angus took my hands in his brambly grip. "I wish I could be wit' ye, lass." His brogue thickened with emotion.

"I know. But we can't wait any longer."

"I know that too, but I'd have your back if I could."

I hugged him, and his twiggy hair poked me.

"I'll be the first one on the field when that blasted sun goes down."

I nodded through a tear-blurred gaze.

I glanced at the dark sky. The sun would be up by the time we reached Vioska field.

"It's time." As I rose, I heard a raucous call from above. My first thought was that Raven had disobeyed again and Thunderbird was flying, but I spied him standing next to Joe by the hospital tent.

A shadow covered us as a great beast glided over camp. Then another. And another. Kalindari and her thunder of dragons circled in the sky. Two broke away from the others—the massive red queen and Ollie. They landed in the clearing. Ollie's tail swished and took out a tent. Thankfully our little army was already out of bed and mustering. Dozens of people came running to see the new arrivals.

I stepped forward and bowed to Ruby. "Greetings Kalindarixatlajitaxama." Then I turned and grinned at the blue dragon. "And Ollivicenzanhe-axl." I stumbled over their names, but I'd been practicing the pronunciations since our last encounter. My effort didn't go unnoticed.

Kalindari nodded and her voice sounded amused in my head. *We come to do our duty as promised, as ones who live in this world.*

"I thank you. We all thank you."

The great red queen launched into the sky. Ollie tramped toward me. His long body made walking on land awkward. The wings that had once been stunted little flaps now stretched behind him like sails on a ship. He was gloriously beautiful. Standing before him, my head barely reached his chin.

His brilliant copper eyes rested on Mason, then me, then Angus. The gargoyle lifted one hand as if to pet Ollie, then froze. Ollie dipped his snout and let out a breath of hot air in Angus's face.

Aw. A dragon kiss.

Angus stroked the glossy blue scales on his cheek. Ollie tilted his head to lean into the touch and closed his eyes.

From above, Kalindari chirped out a call. Ollie straightened. His powerful legs flexed and he jumped into the sky, following his queen.

Angus whistled. "Look at that. The apple of my eye has come home to roost." A huge grin lit his face. "Just seeing that wee tyke all grown up and full of power...well, that was worth the price of the ride, wasn't it?"

Behind the clouds, the sun rose and Angus turned to stone. I patted his shoulder and gazed up at the beauty of the dragons in the morning light.

"Looks like the gang's all here."

WHAT HAPPENED IN THE next hours, I can only recount as my frail memory recalls it. I saw murder and heard lungs take their last breaths. I saw bravery and terror and evil on a scale that may seem impossible to someone who hasn't lived through extraordinary times. I relate it to you as one cohesive tale, but in truth it was a jumbled torment of pain, fear and anger. Hours passed in a numb blur, and yet certain details stick to me like burrs, scratching away at my memory and impossible to dislodge.

We all knew our jobs. We'd gone over the fight plans a dozen times. Carmen's tanks were going to take out as many wojaks as they could, providing cover for the rest of us. The dragons would back them up, though their firepower was limited. I'd urged Kalindari not to risk her dragons beyond that point. Huyn and the Knackers would go after the wojak ogres. The Knackers had experience fighting unusually large and vicious beasts, and it didn't get more vicious or unusual than undead ogres. Mason, Kester and I were going after whatever was in that giant cage.

Emil had a deadly look in his eye and he wanted opji blood. If he got through the wojaks, his one task was to incite the opji rebels to turn their coats. Finally, a small group of Aesir were going to strike into the heart of those opji archers.

If we got through all those vamps, we still had the ward to deal with, but that was my problem. If it came down to it—if we survived the fight with a thousand wojaks—I would cut a hole in the damn ward and pull Ichovidar out by one ear.

It all looked good on paper, but the One-eyed God knew that battles didn't follow rules. Things could change with the stroke of a blade.

I glanced at the sky. The only indication of sunrise was that the clouds shifted from black to angry gray. I'd hoped for a brilliant sun to cripple the wojaks with their sensitive eyes.

I glowered at Terra who stood beside me. "Can't you do something about those?" I jabbed a finger at the clouds.

"Get me to my spirit jar and I'll change a whole lot more than the weather."

And there was the crux of it. Get inside Vioska and change the world, but we needed to change the world to get inside Vioska.

"Just stay here with Almarick," I said. "I'll come get you when we have a clear path forward."

Terra pursed her lips like she had more to say, but then nodded. She looked old. She was old, ancient really, but now she looked it. The skin around her eyes had shrunken like her skeleton was getting ready to claim her, and she was weaker than she let on. The hand gripping her wooden staff shook.

I turned to Almarick. "Keep her out of the fight, even if you have to sit on her."

The priest looked shocked that I would suggest such a defiling, but he nodded.

I left them to join Carmen and Mason near the single tent set up on the edge of the Devastation. My little army was lined up. Thunder rumbled in the distance. Across the way, the wojaks waited, an impenetrable wall of fangs and claws.

I turned my back on the enemy.

All eyes were locked on me. My friends. My family. My allies. They waited for words of encouragement from their general. That scared me almost as much as the impending fight. What could I say to change the inevitable course of this day?

I looked along the rows of faces. Some were determined. Others scared. I caught Mason's eye. The crease between his brows needed smoothing out, and my fingers itched to do it. He gave me a small nod. It was all I needed. We'd been through so much together, I could hear his thoughts. You can do this.

I sucked in a deep breath.

"Some of you are here because your families were taken. Some of you came because you know that your families are next. We are the only thing standing between them and those killers." I turned slightly to point across the field of ash and smoke. "And make no mistake. Those vampires mean to crush your homes and take your children, your mothers and fathers. We won't let them!"

Shouts of "We won't let them!" echoed right back at me.

"The opji want blood? We're going to show them blood!"

My army erupted in cheers. Carmen signaled her soldiers to go and jumped into her vehicle. The tanks rolled out, flattening paths through the burned out landscape. The rest of us followed at a distance. The ground was uneven and slippery with ash. When we reached the two-hundred meter mark, I called a halt.

Arrows studded the ground only meters away. We were just outside their range.

The tanks rolled on.

Thunder crackled. Dragons echoed this roar from the heavens with one of their own, and Kalindari's entire clan winged by. When the tanks were still a hundred meters from the wojaks, the dragons dove, spitting fire into the vampire ranks. Opji archers launched an assault of arrows. Most bounced harmlessly off dragon scales, but two dragons had their wings pierced. Their cries were terrible. One fell on the edge of the burning field. The others banked and managed to fly away.

Kalindari let out a screech that called her clan to her as she circled high. Into this lull, Carmen's brigade opened fire. The entire horizon was lit up with exploding magic.

In the distance, something roared. The caged demon. Carmen's fireworks enraged it. Or possibly delighted it. One could never be sure with demons.

The dragons came in for a second round of fire. Wojaks swarmed the tanks like ants. The armored vehicles drove over any who got in their way.

For a while, it seemed like the fight would be quick—that superior fire-power would win the day.

But blasters and fire don't kill wojaks so easily.

The fallen rose. Wojaks missing arms, eyes and even half their faces lumbered up from the mud. Some were still on fire. The tanks continued on but now they were in the middle of the fight, overwhelmed by crazed wojaks on all sides.

"Now!" I shouted. Humans, fae and beasts ran. We were armed with blades, axes and spears, and pure raging determination. Dragon fire kept the opji archers busy while we gave Carmen's tanks backup.

The sky opened up, just to remind us how fragile we were. Rain fell in blinding sheets as I tackled my first wojak. He fell and I toppled over him. Teeth clamped onto my boot, I kicked upward, snapping his neck, then swiped my blade across his throat.

I jumped up and faced the next fiend. My sword sang its lust for blood. It seemed to have a mind of its own, slashing, deflecting, and killing wojaks I didn't even see coming. I won't lie, it felt good to finally engage with the enemy that had shadowed me for so long.

Rain turned the ash to soup. The pounding feet and wrestling bodies churned it into a stew of muck and blood.

Cut. Cut. Parry. Cut. My arm never stopped. The wojaks never stopped. Every time I downed one, another took its place. One enraged undead face was much like another. My field of vision was filled with fangs and fury.

Behind all the screams, the roar of dragons, and the pounding of guns came a primal scream of pure alien rage. The demon. It shuddered along my keening, pulling magic in its wake.

I cut down two more wojaks and found myself in a vacuum of death. A dozen decapitated bodies lay at my feet. I took a moment to catch my breath and wipe rain from my eyes. Around me the fighting was going on hand to claw.

The night jaguar pounced on a wojak, tore out its throat and leaped away. Huyn and a Knacker sliced parts off an ogre. Mason was holding his own against an opji. The kelpies were trampling a body into the mud with their hooves. Other soldiers, men and women who'd answered my call, died in the mud.

Soolea whirled like a ballerina. Her long hair flung water with every slash of her blade. Her death-dealing was beautiful and terrifying. She lashed out at another wojak but her reach was too far, and her foot slipped in the mud. She took precious seconds to right herself, seconds that the wojak used to grab her by the throat and lift her into the air. Soolea's eyes bulged. She dropped her blade and clawed at the fist that was squeezing out her life.

I dove across the ground separating us, sliding on the mud. My arms flailed as I tried to find my feet, but my sword knew what to do, and it lopped off the wojak's arm. Soolea dropped to the ground, sucking in air.

The momentum of my slide took me right past them. I landed face-first and came up sputtering mud. The one-armed wojak hadn't even slowed down. It pinned Soolea to the ground. Her hands gripped its neck as she tried to keep fangs from her throat.

And that's when I got a good look at him. The wojak was John Hewitt, Soolea's father-in-law.

In life, John had been a big, jovial man with a head of white hair that always seemed ready to blow away like dandelion fluff. Now he was emaciated, hair plastered to his head, and jaw prominent. His reddened eyes were locked on Soolea's throat.

I pulled the Thorn of Vidar, discarded the wood sheath, and stabbed him through the neck. Gore spattered Soolea's face. The vamp wilted. His grip on her shoulders slackened. She let go and he fell into the mud. He gaped at her, jaws flapping for the blood he was denied.

Soolea rolled over and vomited. Her sword lay in the mud. She picked it up and rose on one knee, then to her feet. She swayed as she raised the blade, but it fell with enough strength to cut off the head of her baby's grandfather.

She turned to me, her face blank with shock. We had no time to mourn. Wojaks scrambled over the dead to claw at the living.

Cut. Turn. Cut.

An undead ogre burst from the wojak ranks, roaring its fury. It had no weapon and needed none. Fists like hammers pounded human flesh. A man fell under that onslaught. One of the Aesir. My heart clenched and I tried to get to him, but an opji blocked my way. He held a bow, but was out of arrows and used the weapon like a club. I ducked under it, sliding in the mud. He lunged after me and my blade pierced his thigh.

His eyes goggled as the Valkyrie magic broke the curse that kept him alive. He choked as his heart began to beat again. His hands gripped the edge of the blade still stuck in his leg. A look of wonder lighted on his face, then morphed to disgust and finally to fear.

That's right, buddy. Mommy never told you about girls like me.

I twisted the blade, shredding the bones in his leg, then jerked it free. I plunged it through his heart and ended his unnatural life.

I put my foot on his chest and yanked out the sword. Another wojak slammed into me. We sprawled in the muck, and I dropped my sword. The wojak's claws raked my shoulder. I screamed more in rage than pain or fear and kneed her in the groin, rolled and pinned her. She wriggled and tried to bite. Her fangs were black with mud. My left hand still gripped the thorn. I stabbed downward, pinning her to the ground like a bug.

I didn't wait to watch the life leave her eyes. I rose on one wobbly knee and scrabbled in the mud for my sword. Standing on shaking legs, I swayed and took a moment to drag breath into my lungs.

A moment was all the rest I got.

CHAPTER

25

could no longer see Carmen's tanks. They were covered in broken, writhing bodies as wojaks hammered on metal roofs and tore off passenger doors. Nearby, nearly lost in the haze of rain, Cricket and two more hidebehinds fought a single wojak.

The dragons roared past with another onslaught of fire. They could only aim for the rear opji guard now for fear of setting our fighters on fire. There were three fewer dragons on the wing, and Kalindari's fire was stunted, more smoke than flame. She didn't have much left. They'd done their job and given us a chance in this fight. I hoped she called her family away before she lost them all.

That alien roar reverberated through the day again. My keening was overwrought and I sagged to one knee, desperate to keep up my wards.

A hand grabbed my shoulder and I jerked backward, ready to lop off another head, but it was Mason. He looked battered. My heart pounded. My arms shook. I let him haul me upright and we clung together. The fighting had moved off, leaving us this small space of respite.

"We're going after the demon." Mason grinned and his teeth shone white against his mud-encrusted face.

I nodded. "Have you seen Emil?"

"No. He was right behind the tanks."

I glanced that way. The tanks were lost now, and there was no sign of Emil.

A shadow crossed us as a dragon flew overhead.

Mason shielded his eyes from the rain as he gazed upward and said, "They're leaving."

"Good. They did all they could."

"Come on. Kester's waiting."

We skidded more than ran across the field. The rain had put out even the most stubborn fires, but the ground was churned up and treacherous. We leaped over bodies, most of them too sunken in mud to recognize.

Something exploded ahead of us. Magic lashed me like a concussion. We flattened to the ground.

Kester landed beside me. Mason covered me with his body as wave after wave of magic battered at my psychic wards.

When the onslaught passed, I squirmed out from under Mason's arm. Kester rose, looking dazed. Mason groaned and held his head.

"What the hells was that?" he growled.

Kester pointed. "Those scavenger people in the tanks. They blasted the demon."

Dear All-father, that would only excite the creature.

We scrambled to our feet and ran.

We'd had the barest of plans to fight the demon. I would bind it with my green magic while Kester attacked it with shadows, and Mason would slit its throat. We could only hope that Emil's intel was correct and the opji had it bound inside that cage. We'd never win against an unfettered demon.

We skidded to a halt. All thoughts of fighting it vanished. The cage was gone. Only blacked metal stumps remained. Dozens of bodies lay in a ring around it as if they'd been blasted off their feet, along with a burning husk of an armored truck.

Carmen's truck.

It was flipped on its side, crushed and on fire. No one was escaping that mess.

Magic streamed from the blast site. The demon stood ten feet tall in the middle of this ruin. She had the build of a gorilla with arms that hung to the ground and a body covered in black hair that did little to mask the slabs of muscle on her shoulders or the breasts hanging ponderously from her chest. Her face and scalp were oddly hair-free and the prominent brow shadowed deep-set black eyes. A broad mouth was stretched in a grin, and she flung her arms wide as if to embrace the sky.

The rush of magic in the air reversed as she drank it all in. I lurched toward her before digging my feet into the mud to stop myself.

The thing about demons is that no two are the same. Their magic is always based in darkness. It could be the ability to call shadows like Kester or to raise the dead like the demon that had possessed Mason. But what all demons wanted was power—power in the form of magic. They craved it the way an addict craved their next fix.

And Carmen's blaster cannon had just given this demon an all-you-can-eat smorgasbord of power.

The demon screamed in triumph. She was free from whatever shackles the opji had put on her.

I grabbed Kester's arm. "When she's finished with this magic, she'll look for more." My voice sounded tinny and I wondered if my hearing was damaged.

Kester nodded. "We have to stop her now."

I tucked the thorn into my belt and gripped my sword with both hands. I stabbed it into the ground, anchoring myself to the deep earth magic. Then I called. Only life could best death. Light against darkness.

I flung my magic out as far as I could. The Devastation had killed off everything alive for miles around, but deep in the earth, life remembered. It was there, waiting for the fires to burn out, ready to burst forth and fill the void with green again. It needed only a little nudge from me.

Green shoots poked through the mud. Roots and vines twined around the demon's hairy ankles and grew up her legs, until they encased her to the waist. She broke off her maniacal laugh to peer down at them, more in curiosity than fear. She struggled against the bonds. Then she strained and let off a burst of magic. The vines withered and blackened.

Kester joined my attack with his own brand of magic. Inky shadows crept across the ground, blending with the mud. I strained to keep the green shoots coming as shadow engulfed them, closing over the demon's head. Behind me I heard the clash of a sword. Mason was fighting an opji.

Emil slid to a halt at my side.

"Run!" I panted. Emil shook his head. He didn't understand. I wasn't telling him to go away. I was still calling the green, and simple words were a strain.

"Go…get…Terra."

Emil's eyes widened. He said something, I couldn't hear over the pounding of blood in my ears, then dashed off.

I pushed more magic into my calling, but the demon had so much power. She blighted my green shoots faster than I could call them.

I sank to the ground. My well was precariously dry. If I pushed any further, the depletion of my magic would kill me. Even my sword was quiet, its magic dimmed.

Kester kept up his onslaught of shadow. From within the darkness, the demon raged, fighting the ephemeral magic with pure fury.

Mason dispatched the opji with a slash of his blade. He whirled around, looking for more, but for the moment we were alone. Even the wojaks were smart enough to stay away from an untethered demon.

Mason's hair was plastered to his head, clothes soaked in water and blood. He shook out his sword arm and frowned at Kester, who stood rigid with his head thrown back, eyes wide despite the rain. Every muscle in Kester's body strained. Veins popped from his throat and forehead. His back arched at an angle that was painful to watch.

You have to help him. I have nothing more to give. My lips moved to say the words, but no sound came out.

Mason frowned. As always, his first thought was for me. He closed the distance between us and tried to slip his arm under my shoulder. I pushed it away.

"Help him," I managed to croak.

Emil returned carrying Terra on her back like she weighed no more than a pack. Almarick scrambled over the debris behind them.

"Call them!" Terra shouted. "Call the ghosts to you now!"

Mason closed his eyes and instantly, Janey appeared. Over Emil's shoulder, Terra reached for Mason. Her hand lit up as she touched his shoulder.

"Take her hand, quickly!" Terra urged. Light surged through her as she linked Mason and Janey like a conduit. More ghosts shambled forward. Some held onto Janey in a chain. Others simply huddled against the growing ball of spirit energy.

Terra glowed, faintly at first, then her brilliance outmatched the overcast sky. I shielded my eyes, but that did no good. The light was behind my eyelids, inside my brain and suffusing every blood vessel, every skin and bone cell. I'd felt this divine magic only once before—the night that Shar transformed.

Terra screamed. It was the sound of the sky tearing. Light pulsed from her into Mason who bucked like he'd been electrocuted, then it streamed into the waiting spirits. They let out a collective sigh that sounded like my banshee's wail.

Then the god paled. She sagged against Emil's back.

"Holy shit!" he said. "What was that?"

The afterglow blinded me. I grappled with fear of the dark until my eyes adjusted, and I saw Mason standing taller and with more assurance than I'd seen in him in months. He smiled, and for the first time since Dodona blessed him, the smile was free of pain or worry.

Terra lost her grip on Emil's shoulders and fell backward. Almarick caught her before she hit the ground. He sat in the mud and pulled her into his lap. Tears flowed down his cheeks into her hair.

The demon shrieked. Kester's shadows were dissolving.

"Now!" I shouted to Mason, even as I pushed deeper, seeking green magic farther and farther away, stretching myself to a thin thread.

Mason turned to face the demon. The ghosts were primed by the last of Terra's magic. They swirled around him like a tornado of blue fire.

He uttered one command. "Destroy it and be free!"

Ghosts swarmed the demon. The shadows burst and dissipated. Kester's body went limp and he fell to the ground, unconscious.

The demon yowled. Ghosts plowed through her chest, each one taking a bite of the darkness within. One after another, thousands of them. Each was a victim of opji hate and oppression. Each was a death that found vindication in the heart blood of the demon, the opji's greatest weapon.

I'd read tales of the Flood Wars and how humans and fae banded together to kill demons that came through cracks in the veil. Deaths that were paid for in thousands of lives. It always seemed surreal to me. People had lived through those extraordinary times, doing inconceivably impossible things just to survive.

And now I understood—truly understood at a level of blood and bone—the sacrifices they made.

The demon's shrieks faded, became petulant gasps, then her body folded in on itself as if the weight of time collapsed it.

And the demon was no more.

A cry went up from the army of ghosts, and as one great host they rose into the sky and disappeared, leaving Mason and I clinging together in the wake of their storm.

"That was some light show." Emil was standing right beside me, but he sounded far away.

Mason caught me as my legs gave out.

"Steady."

"Kester," I gasped.

"I'll see to him. You rest a minute." He lowered me to the ground and strode over to Kester who'd collapsed in the mud.

Unlike me using my green magic or Kester using his shadow magic, Mason seemed rejuvenated by his brush with the light of a thousand souls. He lifted Kester into his arms as if the man weighed no more than a child.

"He's alive, but barely. Let's get you both to Nori."

"I'm…fine." My teeth were chattering.

"You're not. Lean on me."

Once upon a time, that simple request would have raised my self-reliant-woman hackles. But Mason had taught me that being a team was so much better than trying to go it alone.

I tucked my hand into the crook of his arm.

"Let me." Emil offered and Mason handed over Kester. Almarick carried Terra. The fighting had ended, at least here, and we staggered across the field littered with bodies and bits of broken vehicles.

A figure loped toward us. My eyesight was blurred. I couldn't tell if it was from tears, rain or exhaustion. Within moments the figure resolved into Huyn. He was naked to the waist and covered in blood and mud. He hefted an axe and let out a whoop.

"They called the wojaks back behind the ward! They're holed up there while they regroup. We hit 'em hard." He grinned fiercely. "Made it hurt."

I nodded, but I knew it wasn't enough. And the walk back to camp proved it. Bodies were everywhere. Many of them were wojak and opji, but too many were our allies.

A green dragon lay inert, half sunken into the mud. Kalindari and her thunder had flown away once their fire burned out, and the fighting was too close for them to easily pick off wojaks. I wished them well, and vowed a respectful burial for their dead.

My feet stopped at a body, a face I recognized. Anni, the newest Freya of the Valkyrie lay dead in the dirt. I couldn't take my eyes off her face. Rain had washed it clean but her beautiful blond hair was matted with mud.

"Come on." Mason tugged at me.

My emotions were frozen. I hadn't always agreed with Anni or even liked her, but she'd come when I called. Because we were kin. And kinship had killed her.

"We should…b-bury her." My teeth were chattering so hard now, I bit my tongue.

"We will. But you need rest and food first."

I lifted my hands, surprised that my blade still clung to my fingers. It felt heavy in my grip, as if all the blood it had soaked up weighed on it. I scratched a line across Anni's hand. Her ghost rose like a will o'wisp, slowly forming into a brilliant beauty. She bowed to me, then faded away like smoke.

I limped on, leaning heavily on Mason now. Others were roaming the desolate field, turning over bodies, looking for loved ones. We found Soolea lifting the body of a wojak to look at another one underneath.

"Come with us," Mason said. "Get some food and water."

She shook her head. "I will. But not yet. I want to find Father Hewitt first. I'll bury him. For his namesake." Her eyes were vacant as if she walked in her sleep.

I made a feeble noise of protest, but Soolea was already pushing another body aside.

We left her to it.

The camp was a bustle of activity as survivors straggled in and wounded were carried to the hospital tent. The rain had finally let up. People sat around smoky fires, but there was no conversation. We had neither won nor lost today. We'd only survived.

Joe Mountainclaw saw us coming and ran from the hospital.

"Let me." He took Kester from Emil's arms. Mason slumped against me. He was more worn out than I realized. I tried to catch him but my arms felt like jelly. We would have fallen, but suddenly Raven was there.

"Mom! I got you!" His shoulder propped me up and I propped up Mason. We were dominos ready to topple.

Another aide came for Mason and they led us inside.

Raven helped me onto a cot. "Are you hurt?"

"I…I don't think so."

"You're covered in blood!"

"N-not mine. Maybe." I sounded breathless, and the alarm on Raven's face made me wonder if I was injured. I felt nothing but numbness. When the adrenaline wore off, would I suddenly feel a dozen wounds I didn't know I had?

I'm fine. I tried to speak, but my lips had gone numb.

"Just rest. I'll get Nori." Raven's voice came from the end of a long tunnel.

Later—Minutes? Hours?—hands dug into my already bruised shoulders and I mewled in complaint.

"None of that now." It was Nori's voice, but my eyes failed me. "Drink this. Come on. Be a good girl."

A cup pressed against my lips. Something hot burned down my throat. The convulsion from my cough hurt all the way to my toes.

"A little more. Good. Now rest."

Mason?

I cried his name in my head, and then blessed blackness took me.

CHAPTER

26

turned my head. The pillow was scratchy, but there was softness under my hands. I strained to open my eyes. They felt glued shut. I finally pried them open and lifted my head. Princess sat on my right, with her great head on the cot, propping up my hand. Jacoby held my other hand and peered at me with anxious eyes.

"Kyra-lady is awakes?"

It took me two tries to respond with a croaking, "Yes."

Jacoby jumped up and ran away.

Huh. Not the welcome back I'd expected. I let my head drop to the pillow.

Princess let out a woof and wagged her tail, nearly knocking over a glass on a table behind her. My blanket was wet with dog drool and I didn't care.

"Come here, you." She put two paws on my cot and washed my cheek with her massive tongue. Someone had beat her to it. My hands were clean. So were my clothes. I touched my head. Yuck. The sponge bath hadn't done much for the mud in my hair.

Jacoby returned with Avie. She smiled to see me awake.

"There you are. Cece's brews are truly magic."

I struggled to sit up, and Jacoby jumped onto the bed to help. His spindly arms were more hindrance than help and he was soon tangled in my blanket and the IV line that was giving me fluids.

Avie gently grasped his flailing arms and set him on the floor. Then she helped me sit up.

"Am I hurt?" My body ached in every corner, but I couldn't pick out one ache above the others.

184

"Only in spirit, but quite literally. You nearly drained your well of magic. Do you have any idea how dangerous that is?" Avie adopted her mom tone to scold me. "It nearly killed you. And Nori has been worked off her feet since the battle started. There was no way she could replenish it. Thankfully, Cece sent plenty of help." She held up a bottle of gold liquid, then poured some into a cup and handed it to me.

"Drink all of that down."

I obeyed her without question. The liquid burned a familiar track through my chest, like a good whisky. It warmed the tiniest crevices in my soul.

Avie nodded and handed me the bottle. "Good. I want you to take another sip every hour, and then we'll see about removing that IV."

I tried to hand the bottle back to her. "What about the others? They'll need it just as much as me."

"Do you think I was idle all the months while you were planning your little invasion? Cece and I have been stockpiling concoctions and charms. She sent an entire crate of this by boat. She calls it liquid magic. And as long as I'm needed, I'll be here to make more."

"You should be home with the kids."

Her face lost its usual animated humor. "I'm doing this for them. I can't fight vampires. But I can make potions. I can heal you and the other fighters. For my kids, for you and for Trevor." She paused. "Did you...see him out there?"

I shook my head. Tears suddenly blurred my vision and I gripped her hand.

"I didn't see him."

Avie drew a deep breath. "Good."

Being held captive by the opji was a terrible fate, but as long as we didn't find him among the wojaks, we could still hope he was alive.

Avie nudged the bottle. "Now drink up. You have other visitors to greet."

"Mason?" I finally asked.

Avie nodded. "He's in much better shape than you are. I'll tell him you're awake."

A few minutes later, Mason limped over to my bed.

"You're wounded!" I sat up straighter.

Mason waved away my concern. "Just a sprain." He sat on the edge of my bed, and pulled me into a deep kiss. I gently pushed him away, and nodded to the little spectator. Jacoby sat in a chair beside my bed. He hadn't left my side since I was brought in, and it seemed even a marital moment wasn't going to faze him.

"Hey buddy, why don't you see if there's anything to eat in the mess tent?" I asked.

"I nots hungry." Jacoby settled himself more deeply in the chair.

"But I am. A good apprentice would fetch a bowl of soup."

Jacoby dashed off.

I sighed. "I should feel bad about manipulating him."

"He wants to be useful. Let him."

I scooted over and Mason crawled onto the cot. It was narrow and I had to drape myself over him so I didn't fall off. Oh, well. There were worse things in heaven and earth. We spent the next ten minutes just being close. It was enough. We didn't need to rehash the fight. That was done. We didn't need to plan for the next one. That would come. And we'd face it together like we always did.

For now, I just needed the feel of his body next to mine and the sound of his heart beating in my ear.

"So did we win?" I asked. "It feels like we won."

He kissed the top of my head. "We won the first battle. And that was truly a miracle."

"Terra's miracle." I shuffled in the cot so I could see his face. "What did it feel like to channel her magic to the ghosts. Tell me it was awesome."

He grinned. "Really awesome."

"Where is Terra?"

The light of Mason's smile dimmed. "She's with Almarick and the other priests. She hasn't woken up. Nori doesn't think she will. I'm sorry."

I nodded. We could do nothing for Terra now, except get inside that ward.

Jacoby returned. His tongue poked from the side of his mouth as he carefully balanced a tray with a mug of soup and some bread. I discovered I was starving.

Mason wanted to check on Kester and he left me to my meager meal.

With a bit a food in my belly and another swig of Cece's liquid magic, I felt surprisingly better.

I got up and tested my legs. Not too bad. Jacoby was right by my side, in case I needed to lean on him, but even being able to walk seemed like a win, considering I'd just been in a battle with an army of wojaks and a demon.

Grim sat in front of the wood stove, baking his backside while he washed a paw. When he saw me up and moving around, he gave me a slow blink. I nodded back. A little piece of the rock that sat in my gut broke away. The night sun jaguar had made it through the battle.

I begged a nurse to remove my IV, then found Mason in a chair beside Kester's bed. Kester didn't fair as well as either of us. He slept like the dead. His breathing was so shallow I had to study his chest to see it rise and fall. Lying on his back, his already bony features seemed skeletal, like his bones were ready to burst through his skin.

Nori was checking his vitals. She looked haggard. I knew what healing took out of her and she'd been at it all night.

She saw me coming and her eyes narrowed.

"You shouldn't be out of bed."

"Will he be okay?" I asked.

Nori looked down at her patient and shook her head. "I don't know. His magic is…special. I can't really help him for fear of…" Her voice trailed off and she glanced at the patients in nearby beds.

"It's okay." I knew what she wanted to say. She couldn't touch Kester's magic without the risk of his dormant demon latching onto her.

He might have a demon inside him, but Kester had never given into it. He fought it everyday and won. I just hoped he had the strength to keep fighting.

From outside, I heard the noises of a busy camp. I glanced at the tent opening. I had to get back to the business of running a war, when all I wanted to do was crawl back into bed.

I sank into a chair and took Kester's hand. It was hot and dry like sand in the sun. If he didn't recover, I'd have to tell Lisobet about his end. She would take it stoically of course, and for some reason that thought undid me.

A little sob escaped my lungs. I pressed my hand to my eyes, but they were dry as if my well didn't even have enough for tears.

Mason squeezed my shoulder. He didn't bother with inanities like "What's wrong?" or "Don't cry." When I finally had control of myself again, I met his gaze. It was sure and steady, like rock. My gargoyle.

I took a shaky breath and whispered so the patients in nearby beds couldn't hear. "We can't win this, can we." It wasn't a question.

"We just need to change our tactics a bit."

I ran a hand through my matted hair. "I need to get inside that ward. I need to get to Shar and then we can worry about the opji."

To my surprise, Mason smiled and held out a hand.

"Come. I have a surprise for you."

I squinted at him. "Surprises on the battlefield are rarely a good thing."

"I think you'll like this one."

I took another swig from my little bottle and followed him. Already, my muscles were feeling looser. I was tired, but most of that exhaustion came from the loss of magic. As my well slowly filled, I felt stronger.

Sunlight cut a sharp path at the tent's door, and we stepped into a bright, muggy afternoon. Puddles misted in the sudden heat.

A caravan of trucks, vans and cars was parked at the edge of the camp.

Captain Glenda Lowe stood like a rock in the middle of a stream, directing people as they came and went from the vehicles. They were setting up more tents, unloading supplies and weapons.

I watched it all like a gaping fish out of water. I'd given up hope of backup from Hub, and even in my most optimistic hour, I'd expected a handful of disgruntled soldiers from the barracks. Instead, there were hundreds of fresh recruits making camp.

Glenda saw us and handed her tablet to a waiting Hub officer. She strode over and stood at attention before me. I half expected her to salute. Instead, the block of granite that was her face cracked and she smiled.

"Your reinforcements have arrived."

A little flutter of hope was burgeoning in my chest. We'd lasted the day fighting against the opji, but I'd held out little hope for the next battle. And now?

"How many?"

"Two hundred Hub soldiers, kitted out with ballistic rifles and blasters. Fifty non-combatants, twelve nurses and three doctors among them." Her smile grew. "Plus another four hundred civilians, most of them wardies, not homesteaders. It seems your call was heard and answered."

"My call?" It wasn't possible.

"Your blog. You have a bigger following than you know. Even I read it from time to time. And it seems enough people stopped doom-scrolling to think about their actual doom and do something about it. There's another hundred Hub soldiers on their way. They should arrive by tomorrow, but I think we're going to take care of your little vampire problem before then."

Oscar jumped down from a truck at the front of the caravan. He lifted a hand to wave us over.

"You made it," I said.

"You look like you slept in a ditch." Oscar frowned at me, then turned his scrutiny to Mason, who said with a deadpan expression, "there was a ditch involved, but no sleeping."

I rolled my eyes. Men.

"We fought the opji this morning."

Oscar's expression darkened. "I heard. And I'm sorry we didn't get here in time, but I had to secure a little present for you." He winked and opened the sliding door on the side of the truck.

"From Merrow Farsigh, with compliments."

A dozen golems sat on benches inside the truck, silent and unmoving. They wore black armored uniforms and helmets that reflected back at us, but I knew what those visors hid—monstrous, faceless heads with the GenPort logo etched into them.

The golems were killing machines engineered by Gerard Golovin, the one-time Alchemist Prime Minister who'd tried to start a war between Montreal and Manhattan. He'd created hundreds of golems. Some had been workers in his excavation sites for the train that now ran between the two wards. Others had been outfitted with mechanical arms that switched between blasters and blades. They were hard to kill and strong as giants. Hack off an arm and they just kept coming.

"Where did you get these?" I asked.

"Alchemists were sent in to clean up Gerard's little disaster with the trains a few years ago. You might remember that I was acting PM at the time. I wanted to study the golems, but Merrow insisted they be given over to the fae because of...well, you know."

I did. The golems had been brought to life by stolen souls, most of them

189

fae. I glanced at Mason. He had strong opinions about this dark magic. In his young and ignorant days, he'd used the same magic to create a gargoyle— Angus. And the green man still struggled with the contrary magics inside him. All gargoyles did.

Oscar saw the blood of anger rush to Mason's face and forestalled his outburst with a raised hand.

"Now before you get your knickers in a twist, these golems aren't that."

"What do you mean?" I keened Mason's agitation and gripped his arm before he said something he'd regret.

"I mean the bloodstones that fueled them in Golovin's time have been removed. Merrow, ah…disposed of them with all the proper and respectful rites."

I felt Mason relax. "Then what powers them?"

"Apex stones. Just chips really. And we don't have any backups, what with the shortage and all." Apex stones had been at a premium since Golovin's railroad came about. They were gems made of compressed magic, the way carbon could be compressed into diamonds. It wasn't an easy process, and making an apex stone of any great size was difficult. But I was impressed that Oscar had reverse-engineered the golems to take the stones.

"They won't last all day," he said, "but you'll get one good skirmish from them."

"Let's hope it's enough."

Despite the morning that had been washed in blood, the day suddenly felt brighter.

Once again, we had a fighting chance.

CHAPTER

27

s soon as the sun set, the Guardians woke, fresh from their day of rest. Along with some of the new recruits, they scoured the killing field, piling wojaks to one side and laying out our dead too.

I'd insisted that everyone would get proper funeral rites, even the wojaks. As Soolea reminded me, they'd all been someone's mother, father, brother or sister before being taken by the opji.

As Mason, Glenda and I surveyed the Devastation, Angus half hopped, half flew over the mess of burned out landscape to join us.

"Looks like you scared those vamps into stiffs," he said. "They're all hiding behind their ward."

I nodded. "We knew that would happen." They'd taken their shot at killing us and now they'd fallen back to protect the city—protect their king while he worked his dark magic.

Glenda surveilled the field through binoculars, then lowered them to address us. "I must admit, you did a fine job for civilians. Over five hundred dead, mostly opji and wojaks."

"But...?" I could hear it coming a mile away.

Glenda turned to me. Over the years, I'd been the subject of her close scrutiny a few times. It never got easier.

"But I'm taking over this operation. My soldiers won't answer to you."

I grinned. If she expected me to protest, she was wrong.

"Absolutely." Glenda could have the army. All I wanted was a shot at Ichovidar.

"Good. I'm glad we understand each other."

"So what is the plan?" Mason asked.

Glenda gazed over the Devastation. "Tomorrow, we hit that ward with everything we've got. The golems aren't the only presents from Hub. Parliament gave us six flash bombs from the strategic reserve."

Holy hell. I'd seen what one of those bombs could do.

The magic incendiaries had been outlawed after the Flood Wars. Certain outspoken critics believed these bombs were the reason the veil had been torn in the first place, letting in all manner of alien creatures, including demons. Even if this wasn't true, bombs launched during the war still affected the Inbetween, causing rogue pools of magic that could freeze entire villages at the height of summer or swallow unwary travelers in sudden sink holes. I'd seen both those phenomena and more during my travels. I'd also seen the effectiveness of flash bombs when I used one to decimate an entire armored train car full of golems.

What I hadn't known was that Hub kept a reserve of these weapons.

"Those are supposed to be illegal," I said.

"They are. But we're far from Montreal territory now."

"So what? You're just going to lob bombs at the ward?" Mason asked.

"Of course not. That would be foolish," Glenda said. "We're going to pack that tunnel the bluecaps have been digging. Blast the ward from below with the bombs and from above with the tanks. We'll light up the sky like nothing anyone alive has ever seen."

There was a slight maniacal shine to Glenda's eyes that made me uncomfortable, but I had to admit, it was a good plan.

"Just get me inside that ward," I said. "So I can get Shar back."

"I understand your concern for your pet, but there are other things to consider, like stopping this Ichovidar character. All our intel points to him being the head of this operation."

"Shar is not a pet." I kept my voice low but put the full weight of my convictions behind me. "Shar is a world seed. Do you have any idea what that means?"

Glenda opened her palm, inviting me to elaborate.

I took a moment to compose myself. Avie had warned me that volatile emotions were a side effect of draining and replenishing my well so quickly, and I could feel myself shaking.

Mason stepped in and took my hand. He put himself between me and Glenda and said, "It means that Shar holds a kernel of magic inside her potent enough to change the landscape of this world. The dinosaurs had their meteor. Our extinction will come at the hands of the opji if Ichovidar manages to break that kernel. The Flood Wars will seem like a minor skirmish in comparison."

Jacoby crept to my side. The fringe around his eyes stuck out like a bristle brush and he glowered at Glenda. No one put his Shar-baby in the corner.

Glenda glanced at the dervish and dismissed him. She considered me. She lived in a world of magic, we all did. But some humans still clung to the belief that magic was only a fad, that the mundanes would one day rule again and all this madness would pass. I could see Glenda try to wrap her head around the idea of a creature with the magic potential of a nuclear bomb. I saw her try and fail.

"Well, then." Already she was trying to put some distance between herself and the crazy people who thought the sky was falling. "I'll get you inside that ward and you can bring me Ichovidar's head."

"Deal."

"The bluecaps tell me they'll have dug right up to the ward in the next hour. Get ready to leave," she checked the time on her widget, "at 22:00 hours."

She turned away before she saw my exaggerated salute.

"Don't be a smart ass," Mason said quietly.

"Better than being a dumb ass."

"Glenda's not dumb."

"No, she's just willfully ignorant."

Mason rubbed my shoulders with both his hands. "Not everyone has walked between worlds, talked to gods and demons, or even dragons. You sometimes forget what a charmed life you live."

"Charmed. That's one way to think of it."

"Glenda-lady is means." Jacoby kicked at the dirt.

I sighed. Seeing my own petulance played out didn't sit well.

"She's not mean. She's responsible for a lot of people. That's never easy."

"But whats about Shar-baby?"

"She's our responsibility." I petted his soft head. "And don't worry. We won't fail her."

It was a warm, damp night, but the liquid magic made me jittery. I shivered and hugged my arms to my chest.

"You're cold." I felt Mason's arms circle me.

"I'm just wired. Ready to go. This delay is killing me."

"I know, it won't be much longer now."

I leaned back against him.

Angus stood up from a crouch. He'd been so quiet, I'd forgotten him in the shadows.

"You know, firepower isn't the only answer," he said. "There's also green magic."

"You think it could break the ward?" I asked.

"I do. The opji rely too heavily on the magic of death. Oh, it looks scary and powerful, but life always wins out in the end. Why do you think they keep this field burned around their ward? It's because they're afraid of the power of life."

I leaned my head against Mason's shoulder and sighed. "I don't think I have it in me, even with Cece's magic elixir."

Angus jabbed a finger at his chest. "You don't, but I do."

I pushed away from Mason and took Angus's hand. "It's a good thought, but you heard Glenda. She's in charge now. I don't think she'll give up her firepower for hocus pocus."

Angus looked affronted. "It's nay hocus pocus!"

I patted his hand. "Of course not. I know it and so do you, but Glenda doesn't."

"Ah, well, you're right in that. I'll keep the idea in my back pocket then. Come on, wee laddie." He held out a hand to Jacoby. "If we're going to fight, you'll be needing a bigger knife." Jacoby took his hand and the two disappeared into the night, leaving Mason and me standing alone on the edge of the Devastation.

A shudder ran through me.

"What are you thinking?" Mason asked.

"I can't shake the feeling that we're going to be too late. And…"

I let the thought drop. It was too selfish to speak aloud.

"And what?" He prodded me by tucking his chin over my shoulder and kissing my cheek.

I leaned against him. "And I just want to go home. With you. And Shar. And Jacoby. And Raven and Princess. I want to find Holly and Gita waiting for us. I want to have dinner on the patio and listen to Gallivant and Clover nicker at us from their pens."

"I know. We will."

I turned in Mason's arms.

"Our time is up, isn't it?"

He kissed the end of my nose. "Our time is just beginning. I promise."

CHAPTER

28

The camp was in full muster. I stood in the flow of moving bodies dreading and anticipating the next few hours. If we actually got through the ward, it would be a blood bath. But getting through the ward also meant getting to Shar, and I set all my focus on that one task.

The bluecaps had done their job well and dug a tunnel right to the opji's front door. We'd hit the ward with blaster fire from above and flash bombs from below.

Gods help us all.

With that thought in mind, I went to check on Terra. She still hadn't woken up. I'd told Almarick to set her up in my tent.

Six priests knelt in the dirt outside the tent, heads bowed. I wondered who they prayed to. Who answered your pleas when your immortal god was dying? They didn't look up as I passed.

Inside the tent, one candle lit the scene. It cast a harsh light on the figure sleeping on the cot. Almarick sat beside her, his fingers laced and hands clamped together.

"How is she?" I asked.

Almarick looked up. Tears had stained his face red. He straightened and wiped one cheek with his palm.

"No change."

"We're leaving now." I laid a hand on his shoulder. "I'm going to get her spirit jar back. I promise."

Almarick nodded. It was his job to believe.

"We will bring her to the edge of the battle and wait for you. It is our sacred duty to bear her in her time of need. But Kyra, please hurry."

Then there was no more time for goodbyes. I'd said them all anyway. Raven waved to me from outside the hospital tent. At his side, Princess raised her nose to the sky and cried, "Aroooo!" It was a fitting farewell.

Everyone else was loading into transports or onto horseback. Mason had our horses saddled and waiting. Spencer strained his lead to munch on grass from the edge of the clearing.

Cletus came through the crowd with his pick-axe over one shoulder. He had a jaunty step and whistled a tune that reached me before he did. Leave it to a bluecap to find joy in warfare.

"Our special package is all locked and loaded," he said.

I nodded, but I must have looked worried because Cletus took my hand in his blackened grip. "Don't worry, missy. We'll get this done. There's enough firepower in that tunnel to bring down any ward."

"Don't underestimate the opji. Their magic runs deep."

"Yeah, we saw as much, and it stinks like death rot too."

I shuddered at the thought. The opji had built their village on the bones of their victims and watered it in blood of the innocent. Breaking it would take powerful magic.

"How're you going to set off the bomb?" I asked.

"A lit arrow right in the center of the package ought to do the trick. The hard part is deciding who'll fire the arrow."

"I see. That would be dangerous. The whole tunnel could collapse. Do you have any volunteers?"

"Oh, sure! That's the difficulty. Everyone wants to be the one to light the opji's asses on fire."

Of course.

Mason waved at me and I left Cletus to get back to the tunnel. I mounted Spencer and let the gelding follow the others out of the camp. Behind us, Angus drove a cart with Emil and Jacoby riding in the back. A small cage sat on the flatbed beside Emil, holding my squamice. Errol was with them, ready to ride his little mouse-lizard taxis into the fight.

The procession was full of nervous energy. The bluecaps had put down their shovels and picked up their axes, ready to fight. Huyn, the Knackers and the yetis had survived the first battle. I even spotted Ken Okorafa leading a troop of Anansis and Olympians. Hundreds of other foot soldiers I didn't know waved to me or called out as I passed them on horseback.

They'd come because of my blog. Because I'd called them. The weight of that responsibility was suddenly overwhelming. I sucked in a breath. And another. One more and I was hyperventilating.

"Take it easy." Mason reached for my reins and Spencer crowded closer to his mount. "Breathe."

I closed my eyes and began the slow breathing technique my mother had taught me all those years ago. When I finally opened my eyes again, we were stalled on the edge of the Devastation. The crowd of soldiers and civilians was quiet. This was the first time many of them had seen the battlefield.

The moon was full and the sky cloudless, giving us a clear view of the killing field. It was an ugly sight. The ground had been churned up in yesterday's skirmish. Blackened trees jutted toward the sky like accusing fingers. Deep ruts had filled with murky rainwater and other fluids. And it was impossible not to stare at the clouds of black smoke rising from the two great pyres that burned the dead.

Across the field, the ward of Vioska shimmered in a faint red light. The town beyond was dark except for the dome of the Hall of Mages. Light shone from its roof like a laser beam shooting into the heavens.

We left the horses tied up at the edge of the Devastation and walked in on foot behind Hub's slow rolling tanks. The night was calm, the air heavy and clammy. Shadows concealed holes, bracken, and dropped weapons from the previous fight—all traps for unwary feet.

Jacoby's tongue jutted from the side of his mouth as he leaped over debris. Sweet Pea, one of my squamice, followed close behind him with Errol riding his back. The bodach had insisted on accompanying Mason tonight and I'd agreed. After this morning's fight with the demon, Mason's keening was already on the brink of overloading. Errol was there to boost his wards as needed. I consoled myself that no one, not even the opji would notice the little creatures darting among the debris.

A command center was set up inside the Devastation just out of arrow shot range from the opji archers who were mostly hidden behind the writhing throng of wojaks. The standing army stopped there. The tanks lined up in front of us like a shield, with the golems behind them.

Glenda's soldiers were well disciplined and stood silently and with guns ready. The civilian troops around the command center were less still. They paced and chatted with nervous energy. It was easy to pick out those who'd fought the day before. Like me, they were cowed by knowing what lay ahead and stood silently, some with heads bowed.

Behind the opji ward, the wojaks paced liked caged animals.

Angus whistled. "Well, damnation and roses, that's a sight to make this old heart thump."

How could there still be so many? We'd killed hundreds the day before, and yet their ranks didn't seem depleted. The sight of so many enemies took the heart out of the civilians. Some wept. A few turned and walked back the way we'd come. No one tried to stop them.

Glenda stood off to one side, talking into a walkie-talkie. Mason and Emil were with me, along with Angus and Captain Sawyer, Glenda's second in command. No one spoke. I shivered and wrapped my arms around my chest. Mason stepped closer to me, adding his meager warmth to mine.

After what seemed an eternity, Glenda joined us. "The bluecaps are ready. We're moving out."

I nodded. This was it. One way or another our fates would be decided tonight.

Glenda gave the signal and the tanks started to roll again. The golems marched behind them. As soon as they were within range, arrows shot from Vioska. They pinged uselessly off the armored vehicles. A golem took a hit in the chest. It staggered back a pace, then kept marching.

A minute later, the tanks were within firing range. They halted. The golems stopped too. They stood like statues, but if the ward came down, they'd be the first through the gap to take on the wojaks.

Guns pivoted so that all tanks targeted one square meter of the ward. The entire crowd seemed to hold its breath and the silence was oppressive.

The tanks blazed as one, pounding out streaks of red fire that arced toward the ward to hit with precision and the sound of thunder. Red crackles of light flared across the ward but it held. Mason tensed beside me as a recoil blast of magic washed over us. I gripped his arm, willing calm into him.

Opji returned fire, but their blasters were homesteader castoffs and had a much shorter range. Their fire flamed out a hundred meters before their targets. A few ballistic bullets pinged off the tanks. Guns weren't the opji's preferred weapon. They would hide behind their ward until it fell. That's when their true might would shine—in hand-to-fang combat.

The tanks fired at will now, all targeting that one spot in the ward, hoping to weaken the magic enough to punch through. Bright red veins sizzled across the ward. On the other side, wojaks parted to let opji mages through. They stood in a semi-circle around the blast zone with cowls thrown back and hands linked. From this distance, I couldn't see their lips moving but I knew they were chanting.

"They're trying to boost the ward," I said. Mason nodded grimly. His face was ashen and he swayed against me.

"Errol!" I called out, but already the bodach had jumped from Sweet Pea's back onto Mason's shoe. I keened the cool soothing cocoon of magic he pushed outward. Mason relaxed and we continued to watch the fireworks.

The tanks hadn't slowed their bombardment. Glenda was talking into her walkie-talkie again. Her free hand gestured wildly. I strode over to her as soon as she ended the call.

"What's the problem?"

She lifted her hand as if to rub her face, then checked the gesture, denying herself even this small weakness.

"Cletus says they're having trouble. The lit arrows aren't working to detonate the bombs."

"Damn. That means someone's going to have to go down there."

Glenda nodded slowly. "He volunteered."

Oh, All-father protect him.

Cletus who'd led his people through fifty years of imprisonment on Grandill, only to come home to this mess. It didn't seem fair. None of this was fair.

Glenda's mouth was pressed thin and hard as metal wire.

Another call came through the walkie-talkie, and I listened to her override a commander's objections when he wanted to cease firing.

"Keep going!" She cut off the call before he could protest. "They're running low on ammo."

Like blasters, the tanks ran on apex crystals, and the parliament ministers had been stingy with their allocation of resources. Part of me understood their reluctance. It seemed risky to clean out the city's store of apex stones for one fight. But if we didn't win this fight, it wouldn't matter.

"Fools," I said under my breath.

Glenda nodded as if she understood exactly what I'd been thinking.

The next minutes now seem like a blur, but at the time they dragged on for an eternity. The tanks pulsed out fire at regular intervals while we waited for one bluecap to hike through the underground tunnel and set off a bomb. I couldn't imagine what it would be like to take that long walk and honestly didn't know if I would have the courage to do it.

Finally, the guns fell silent. One tank fired off a last round, then no more. The apex stones were dead.

I found myself praying to Odin—who'd never answered my prayers—for Cletus to hurry. Then I checked myself. It was simply wrong to be wishing for my friend to hurry up and die, but every second that passed meant those opji mages were boosting the magic that held their ward.

I grabbed Mason's hand and squeezed until my fingers hurt.

An explosion rocked the ground and I stumbled into him. A geyser of dirt blasted into the air at the base of the ward, sending rocks and blackened tree trunks spiraling in a cloud of smoke. Debris pummeled the tanks and golems, burying the lead tank. Instinct had the spectators ducking as magic blasted over the rest of the field.

"Hail to the brave warrior," I whispered. Mason's face was sheened in sweat, but he seemed to be holding it together. His eyes were bright with unshed tears from the smoke, or for our lost friend, or both.

We waited a tense minute for the scene to clear, but I didn't need my eyes to tell me what my keening already knew.

The ward held.

As the smoke dissipated, cries of alarm, fury and despair went up from our army.

Glenda was arguing into her walkie-talkie, but no amount of angry words would get those tanks firing again.

Angus, who'd been sitting on the end of a farm cart, rose and dusted off his pants.

"Well, saints and hellfire, that was something to see. I guess those soldier boys had their chance at glory. Now we're going to see what real magic looks like." He rubbed his woody hands together.

"I'm going with you," I said.

"You're not." Mason pulled on my arm. I rounded on him, anger making my words harsh.

"If Angus is going in. I am too!"

Mason just shook his head. I almost blasted him with ill-placed rage, but Angus stepped between us and took my hand. He held it, gently, the way one might hold a wounded bird.

"Now lassie, there's no need to bind yer knickers in fetters. You're the first to show off your green power, but you're needed elsewhere and you well know it."

I scowled at Angus, then Mason. Each held my gaze with calm reason that only fueled my fury. A sharp spike of pain in my shin had me cursing and hopping on one foot.

"Grtltbrgth!" *Stand down, foolish woman.* Errol held up his walking twig, ready to stab sense into me again.

"Ow!" I rubbed my shin. "Okay, I get it."

Angus squeezed my hand again. "You let us handle this. Your job is to get in and save that wee coconut."

"I know. Be safe." I wanted to say more but the words lodged in my throat. I hugged him instead, not caring if his brambly beard scratched my face.

"And besides,"Angus said, "I'll have help." He leaned down, scooped up Errol and tucked him into the branches of his hair.

I grabbed Sweet Pea before she thought to take off, and dropped her into the cage with Niblet on the farm cart.

I took another moment to wipe tears from my eyes and put on a brave face. When I turned back, Angus had rounded up Cricket and the other hidebehinds. They were the green squad, the only magic users in our army who could manipulate the power of green growing things. Other than me and Terra.

Oh, what I wouldn't do for a little pith of the gods right now.

Out of options, Glenda was forced to go along with Angus's plan, but I could see her heart wasn't in it. She thought we'd already lost, but I convinced her to call a tank back to pick up Angus and the others.

As soon as they rolled toward the ward she said, "I don't like this. They'll be too exposed."

"Move the tanks forward like a shield," Mason said. Glenda nodded and spoke into her walkie-talkie. The tanks approached the ward and closed ranks around Angus's vehicle. Immediately, I understood Mason's reasoning. With the tanks so close to the ward, the opji archers had to shoot through the wojaks instead of over their heads.

Angus stepped from the lead tank. The golems surrounded him and they all walked forward until Angus crouched beside the ward right next to the crater made by the bomb. It had to be hot with live magic, but Angus was counting on that. Errol's specialty was being a magic conduit. He would draw on the loose power to call the green.

"It just might work," I said. Mason gave me a cold, sharp smile. Angus was like a son to him. He had to be feeling a hot and cold mixture of fear and pride right about now.

We watched with hands clasped tight as Angus spread his arms. Errol would be focused now too. The hidebehinds stood ready. Nobody moved.

Arrows flew over their heads, the angle too high to hit them, but still a frightening menace.

A tendril-like vine burst from Angus's mane. And another. They wrapped around the hidebehinds, tangling in their twiggy limbs.

Roots shot from his legs and dove deep into the bomb-churned ground.

An explosion rocked the night and fire lit up the town behind the ward.

"Did Angus do that?" I asked.

Emil was suddenly beside me. "No. It's the Bunters! That's our signal. The armory exploded. They're fighting back!" He punched the sky with a fist.

Angus blossomed like a hedgerow. His head fell back and a primal scream burst from him.

"I need to get out there," Mason said. He gripped my hands and forced my eyes to meet his. Was he asking permission or forgiveness? It didn't matter. He needed to be with Angus just as much as I needed to get to Shar. They were our children, our family.

I nodded and Mason pulled me into his arms, not caring if we made a spectacle. His lips met mine in a kiss that seemed to draw a bit of my soul into his for safekeeping. He pulled away to cup my face and press his forehead gently to mine.

"Be safe."

I nodded again, not trusting my voice. Then he kissed me one last time and jumped into one of Hub's armored vehicles.

The truck was equipped for off-road travel, but the field was a mess of root balls and burned stumps. It hit a pothole and stuck. The wheels spun on muddy ash. Mason jumped out and ran the final hundred feet, zig-zagging across the field to avoid the arrows raining down on him.

I pressed a knuckle to my lips to keep from screaming.

"He's going to get himself killed." Glenda handed me her binoculars.

I banged my nose as I jammed the glasses to my face. Mason ran through the hail of arrows, hopped over a burned log and slid, covering his boots and legs in muck. He gripped a fallen log to hoist himself up, and an arrow pierced the wood inches from his hand.

He ran until he butted up against a wall of Angus's branches, and then I lost him among the leaves.

I lowered the binoculars and studied the immense hedgerow growing from Angus. Mason, Errol, and the hidebehinds were all lost within its vast foliage.

I'd seen Angus react to magic like this only once—when we'd fought Polina. Back then, Angus had contained the witch with a ring of brambles so tight, we'd had to cut him out.

That feat was nothing compared to tonight. With all the rogue magic in the air, Angus's hedge grew like a tower of brambles. From this tower, two arms of wood shot forward and latched onto the ward.

I lowered the binoculars. Even from this distance, I keened Angus's strategy. One of the arms sucked death magic from the ward. The other fed it pure green magic. Angus had set himself up as a magic dialysis machine. As he purified the opji's magic, the ward weakened. Already, I could see cracks.

A shout went up from the opji. Something was happening in the town.

Emil shook my arm. "That's them! They're fighting the mages. This is our chance."

I could see it now. The opji were brawling among themselves. A mage fell to a sword strike from behind. Emil's Bunters had come through with more than taking out the armory. One by one, the mages were being cut down.

Other opji jumped into the fight, recognizing that only the mages stood between them and the army on the other side of the ward. The wojaks ignored the mutiny. Whatever hold the opji had on them didn't falter.

Only three mages remained, not enough to keep boosting the magic. The ward flared with light. I suspected that even those without the keening would see that brilliance. Fractures appeared like crackles on old glass.

The mages were losing the battle. Angus's hedge tower now topped two stories high. He'd been sucking magic from the ward and from the overheated environment, and he could no longer hold it all.

A wave of pure magic blasted from the hedge and flashed through the waiting army.

The ward shattered.

Angus turned to stone.

ithout their cage, the wojaks streamed across the field. Some met golems or tanks, but most ran past Angus's hedge, straight for the foot soldiers.

And the screams of battle began again.

Opji archers sent burning arrows flying. Some hit golems, setting the automatons ablaze. Others struck humans and vehicles. The sound of clashing blades nearly drowned out the shouts of pain and rage.

I stepped in front of Glenda as she shouted orders.

"I need to get into the city!"

She looked right through me, then ran toward the melee shouting into her walkie-talkie.

I would get no help there. Emil looked poised to run into the fray, and I was ready to join him.

A jagged bolt of lightning lit the sky.

Oh, no. That was no storm. The full moon still shone in a clear sky. Another flash of lightning streaked across the darkness.

Emil pointed. "It's hitting the city." I followed the line of his finger to the dome on the Hall of Mages. Lightning struck it again.

We were out of time. Ichovidar had started his dark rite to break the world seed.

I stared at the impenetrable wall of skirmishing bodies before me. There was no easy path through them.

Where was Mason? I'd promised him that I wouldn't face Ichovidar without him, but he was lost in the mess of fighting beside Angus.

Something bumped into me. I turned and the horse head nudged my shoulder again. Velvety lips parted in a snarl, showing off two rows of sharp teeth.

"Perri? Is that you?" The kelpie nodded.

Dennet stood nearby, nervously pawing the ground. Perri bowed and stayed there. I recognized the posture from Gallivant. She was offering me a ride.

I took it. Never look a gift horse in the mouth be damned.

"Come on!" I shouted to Emil. The battle was full on now. Screams and blaster fire filled the night.

I threw my leg over Perri's back. Emil mounted Dennet and we took off at a gallop.

Riding bareback isn't easy. Riding bareback over uneven ground and through hostile enemy lines was nearly impossible. But I'd flown a Pegasus. I wasn't going to let a kelpie throw me. I wound fingers in Perri's mane and tried to mold myself to the flow of the horse. Bowed over her neck, my legs firmly wrapped around her sides in a pose that used my soft inner thigh muscles in a way they were never meant to be used.

A wojak lunged at us. Perri screamed and dodged. I slashed at fingers before claws raked the mare's flanks.

The fighting raged all around us. Perri lurched and stumbled over bodies and burned logs. I clung to her back, my eyes scanning the fighting, looking for opji ready to spring, but hoping for Mason. We rode past Angus's massive monument to magic. It was bigger than I'd thought, wide as half a city block and fifty feet high. It was an intricate weave of branches, vines and leaves, all glistening white stone in the moonlight.

I had my personal wards wrapped so tightly around me, I couldn't feel the magic left in the blast zone.

An opji leaped and I cut him down with one strike. We were through the main tangle of battle and halfway to the city before I felt the tiny hands gripping my waist. I twisted to see Jacoby hanging onto me for dear life.

Damn the apprentice! In the confusion of the battle, I'd forgotten to make sure he stayed safe in one of the vehicles. Without my direct order to stay put, he'd interpreted his apprentice duties as sticking to me through all hell.

Perri loped past the crater in the ground—Cletus's grave—and then past a ring of fallen mages. The Bunters were still fighting a small group of opji. I couldn't tell the good guys from the bad, and didn't dare stop and sort it out.

I urged Perri past them.

Behind us, Dennet screamed.

Perri slammed her hooves into the dirt in a bone jangling stop. I tumbled off her back and hit the ground. Air whooshed from my lungs. Jacoby danced around me with a knife ready to attack anyone who dared to come near. By the time I could breathe again, Dennet lay bleeding out, while Emil fought the opji who'd taken him down.

Emil raised a blade. The opji hissed in their guttural language. I didn't have to understand the words to know he was cursing Emil as a traitor.

Seeing her brother-lover dead, Perri turned and kicked the opji in the head. He crashed. The mare reared up and slammed her front hooves through his chest, again and again. When the opji was nothing more than a pile of mushy bones, she paused, her flanks heaving and nostrils flaring. She bowed and sniffed Dennet. His eyes were wide and still. A pool of blood spread from the wound on his neck. Perri flung her head back, whinnied out her rage, then took off into the night.

Emil reached out a hand to help me stand.

Jacoby was still slashing at shadows.

I grabbed his elbow, pressed my lips to his fuzzy ear and whispered, "When we find Shar, you get her out. Teleport if you have to. No fighting. You run. Understood?"

He nodded vigorously.

Good.

Emil took the lead. He'd spent months in Vioska and knew the way to the Hall of Mages. We crept through the dark streets with the sounds of fighting behind us. It was a surprisingly tidy little town. I'd always thought of opji as disgusting filth and imagined they lived in squalor, like giant rats squatting in crumbling castles. But the streets were wide, free of litter, and lined with cottages that were solid, if utilitarian in style. They were also eerily empty.

The further we crept into town, the quieter it got. Soon, the only sound was the wind lashing dust off the road.

The lane ended and we came to a kind of town square. It was a massive open space of hard-packed dirt. I could imagine hundreds of opji training here, but for the moment, it was empty. The Hall of Mages stood at the opposite end, flanked by smaller stone buildings.

The first movement we spotted was from a pen of wojaks along the right edge of the square. They were crammed into a yard that had only one small shelter like a run-in shed for horses. Most of the pathetic creatures squatted in the dirt and seemed catatonic. A few paced around the pen with waspish energy.

These were young wojaks, newly made. Not too long ago they'd been homesteaders or refugees. Their clothing was mostly intact, if torn and dirty, and they didn't yet have that desiccated look that aged wojaks took on.

I wondered if being freshly undead made them more volatile. Is that why Ichovidar held them back from the fight?

We kept well away from the wojaks. I didn't think they were intelligent enough to raise the alarm on purpose, but their need for blood would be all-consuming and even the hint of fresh prey would send them into a frenzy that would surely be investigated.

We inched along the far side of the town square, keeping to the shadows. That forced us to slink past the other pen.

A pen of humans.

As soon as they saw us, a cry went up from the captives. Emil rushed over to the fence. Large bony fingers reached through the chain links.

Emil grasped them.

"Raymond, you have to keep them quiet!" Emil hissed.

The man on the other side of the fence looked dazed and beaten. He was a tall black man, painfully thin with blocky shoulders. Sunken eyes were framed in dark lashes and a fresh scar cut across his cheek and nose.

"Ray!" Emil urged. The man shook his head as if to clear away cobwebs. Beside him a boy, no older than twelve tugged at his sleeve but Ray seemed lost in his daydream. It was probably better than waking to this nightmare.

Another figure pressed against the fence.

"Get us out of here," the man said. "You promised."

Emil nodded. "I will. The army is at the door. Hear that?" Another explosion had just rocked the night. "I need a few more minutes. Keep everyone quiet and I'll come get you soon."

The man studied Emil with a frown. My mind raced back a dozen years. Was it possible? He was older, leaner and covered in filth, but there was no mistaking those eyes and that downward tipped smile.

It was Liam, the man I had almost become a homesteader for.

Liam's eyes flicked over me without giving anything away. If he recognized me, he didn't show it.

"Go on," he said. "I'll keep everyone quiet as long as I can."

Emil's eyes never left Raymond's face. He took an extra minute to hold the fingers pressed against the fence. When he finally let go, I heard Raymond give a small choking sob.

It seemed Emil had been busy during his time in Vioska.

Liam was good to his word. It didn't surprise me that he had a voice of authority in the krowa pens. When I'd first met him, he'd been a gangly twenty-three-year-old, but already he'd known his own mind. I had no doubt that he'd become a leader in his village.

That thought brought me up short. If Liam was captive, it could only mean that the opji had overrun the little fishing village of Ors. Their wards had been good for keeping out marauders and wildlife, but they wouldn't have stood a chance against an opji invasion.

My feet followed Emil along the pen's fence. My heart and my eyes searched for Liam, but he'd disappeared back into the crowd of prisoners. Instead I found only desperate faces pressed against the chain links. They were dirty and wasted. Their eyes were hard and piercing or glassy and unfocused. These were people who'd long since lost all hope, but now the sky was lit up with explosions and humans were walking freely into the den of the monsters. Something had changed. Hope, that most fickle emotion, was starting to infect them with a nervous spirit that wouldn't go unnoticed by any nearby guards.

"Quit gaping and move." Emil's sharp voice brought me back to the reality of our situation and the danger we were in. If the opji discovered us, we'd be dead long before Glenda broke through the army of wojaks.

Jacoby clung to my hand and bobbed along beside me. His eyes were huge in the dim light, like doorways to every night terror I'd ever had. I squeezed his fingers, to reassure him as much as me.

We crept toward the Hall of Mages, slinking past shops that were dark and shuttered. Every moment I expected to be discovered, but no one came out and no lights came on. It seemed like the whole town had turned out for the big battle.

One block from the Hall of Mages, we ducked into a narrow alley. A pile of crates gave us enough cover to study our target.

The hall was a large pantheon style building. Two massive columns flanked a set of wide double doors. Dozens of stairs led from the square to the entrance. Whoever walked out on that stage would stand high above any gathered crowd. The doors were open and a pale flickering light came from inside. Fifty wojaks stood on the stairs leading up to it. Behind them opji held their invisible tethers, as if they controlled snarling dogs on magical leashes.

I leaned back against the stone wall of the alley. "So many."

"Too many," Emil agreed.

"And you're sure that's where Ichovidar is?"

Emil nodded, but I already knew the answer. The Hall of Mages was his seat of power and his laboratory all in one. If that wasn't reason enough, the undead honor guard on the steps confirmed it.

On my best day I couldn't fight that many wojaks, not even with Emil's help.

"We need a diversion," he said.

I pointed toward the sky to the east where the fires burned and the battle for Vioska raged on. "That *is* our diversion." Could we wait long enough for backup? Would there even be backup coming once the opji army was finished with Glenda's troops?

I peeked through a crack between crates. Something was going on in the hall. The light coming through the front doors was brighter, and the wojaks paced in agitation.

Lightning struck the dome again. I keened a surge of magic. A beam of light shot from the roof, straight into the sky.

It was starting. Whatever dark rite the vampire king had planned was already underway.

I grabbed Emil's arm. "What kind of diversion?"

"Nothing short of total chaos." He grinned and his fangs seemed bright white in the reflected moonlight. "Come on."

We dashed back the way we'd come. About halfway to the krowa pens, we ducked down another side street. The smell of fresh manure hit me. Emil threw open the door to a barn and we were greeted by the quiet whinnies of a dozen horses.

"I didn't know the opji kept horses." I'd never seen one ride.

"Plow horses," Emil said. He was sorting through a bunch of keys on a hook until he held one up. "Found it!"

"Is that for the pens?"

"Yes. It used to be my job to go in and clean them. It was supposed to be a punishment." His eyes glittered with menace. Once again, I really wanted to know what he'd endured here. But we were out of time.

We ran back into the night.

And straight into a pack of opji.

My sword came up by sheer muscle memory. The lead opji hissed and crouched low, ready to spring. I widened my stance, left foot slightly ahead, ready to bring my blade around in a powerful strike and take off his head. A dozen more vamps ranged behind him. They would fall on me the instant I struck, but I'd go down fighting.

"Stop!" Emil pushed me aside and lunged at the opji. They gripped each other's arms, wrists to elbows.

"Teo!" Emil clapped the other opji on the back. "I wasn't sure you'd come through."

The opji spread his thin lips in a smile. "I wasn't sure either, my friend. We did what we could. The mages are dead, but the battle rages on. What can we do?"

"We need a way inside the hall." Emil held up the key. "I'm going to free the krowa. Find us weapons."

Teo nodded and the opji ran off.

Emil turned to me and I shoved him toward the krowa pen.

"Go. Set them free. I'll try to create a bit more chaos here."

I could smell smoke, so as soon as Emil was away, I threw open the first stall door. The old draft mare inside snuffled me but had no inclination to leave.

I clucked my tongue. "Come on, girl. Go!"

With Jacoby's help, we opened each stall. A barn cat hissed and arched its back.

The fur around Jacoby's eyes sprang to attention, and he hissed right back. The cat darted out the front door. None of the horses wanted to follow. Barn rest and fresh hay was much more enticing than running outside and possibly into fire.

I haltered the first mare and tugged her outside, then set her free. She clip-clopped down the lane toward the square. The other horses followed her lead.

Once the barn was empty, I lit the hay in several stalls with matches from my belt kit. The hay was damp and smoldered. Smoke soon filled the barn.

I grabbed every weapon I could find—pitchforks, shovels and rakes—and ran outside, coughing into my sleeve. Jacoby followed with smaller tools spilling from his arms.

Shouts came from the town square. Emil had released the captives.

I ran with the awkward load in my arms and skidded into the square, right into a group of captives led by Liam.

"Here!" I dumped the tools on the ground and Jacoby threw down his too. They pounced on them. Liam grabbed a spade and hefted it, testing its balance.

A wojak appeared as if out of nowhere and attacked one of the captives. The woman fell under its weight and screamed as fangs bit into her shoulder.

Liam swung the shovel hard. The spade head bit deep into the wojak's skull. The human woman ran away, clutching her bloody throat. Liam yanked the shovel, bringing the wojak up with it. Even with its skull caved in, the wojak hissed and its fingers strained for Liam's throat. He slammed it to the hard ground. Repeatedly.

When the shovel split its head, I stepped in. "Liam, leave it!"

Liam yanked his spade free. Then he turned and met my eye.

"So you do remember me." There was no gentleness to his tone.

"Of course I do."

We studied each other for a brief moment, each trying to find that softer person we'd once shared a bed with.

He looked like a warrior, a far cry from the young fisherman I'd once known, and I wondered what battles life had thrown at him in the last twelve years.

"Here." I handed him my hunting knife. It didn't have the reach of my sword, but it was better than a shovel. He hefted it in his right hand, but kept the spade in his left.

I turned to assess the situation. Smoke filled the air and the barn was in full blaze now. Buildings on either side had flames shooting from their roofs too. The wojak pen was empty. Someone had let them loose.

Sounds of fighting came from ahead. Most of the captives had joined Emil and the Bunters at the steps of the hall, but a handful remained in the pen, sitting catatonic in the filth.

My eyes scanned the melee. How could I get inside the hall? I sat back on my heels and bumped into Liam. Instead of watching the fight, he was gazing east, toward the lights of the main battle.

"Did you really attack the vampires with an army of humans and fae?"

"And dragons."

Liam shook his head, but the small grin on his face said he was more incredulous than anything.

I shrugged. "It seemed like a good idea at the time."

"When Emil started chatting up Raymond, I thought it was a trick. A few of the krowa had been fighting back against the guards, and I thought Emil had been sent in to ferret out information. And then he told us about his boss, a crazy woman named Kyra who was sending in the most mismatched army in the history of the world. To free us. And I knew it had to be you. No one else would be that crazy."

I swallowed past the lump in my throat. "I figured you wouldn't even remember me."

His brows lowered. "If you ask my wife, she'll say I never forgot you." A dark moment spread between us. I thought he might kiss me. Then he stepped away. "Asked her, I should say."

"Janey? She's dead?" I thought of the vibrant young woman I'd met in Ors. Another life snuffed out by opji madness.

Liam nodded once. "They turned her. She's probably lying dead out there." He lifted his chin as if he could see the killing fields.

I had nothing to say. Janey *was* dead. I'd seen her ghost, but I wasn't sure if that knowledge would soothe Liam or enrage him.

The village square had turned into a blood bath. Newly-turned wojaks hit the melee of weakened captives and Bunters like an arrow through the heart.

I'd never understood the magic that kept wojaks under opji control. Every time I'd faced them in the Inbetween they acted like dogs on an invisible leash. The opji had some kind of mind control over their minions that let them strike with ferocity and precision.

But there were no opji at the helm now. The wojaks killed and fed with abandon. As I watched the wanton destruction and listened to the screams of the dying, I wondered how had our plans gone so terribly wrong?

A wojak leaped on me from behind. His teeth bit down on my shoulder but found the leather harness for my sword.

Jacoby gaped at me as the wojak tried to gnaw through my harness.

"Hide!" I yelled. Then the wojak spun me around and I lost sight of the dervish.

Claws dug into my arms, and I screamed as I fell and rolled to crush the wojak against the ground. We grappled and I ended up on top with the flat of my sword pressed against his throat. I couldn't turn the blade to slice into skin, not without letting him up. My knees pinned his flailing arms.

We were frozen in a deadly pose. His jaws snapped, inches from my nose. Spittle flecked my face along with the stench of undead meat. I strained to shift the grip on my sword, and his claws raked my shoulder.

A shovel came down like a guillotine on the wojak's skull. His arms spasmed, letting me free and I jumped back.

Liam stepped on the corpse to tug his spade free.

"Th…thanks." My hand went to my parched throat.

"Duck!" Liam swung the shovel again as I hit the ground. He took out another wojak. I rolled and came up to fight.

A female wojak flew at me with grabbing claws. I severed her arms and spun away from her shrieks to come face-to-face with another. This one was male and freshly turned.

And I knew him.

CHAPTER

31

Newly-turned Trevor was a rabid, crazed version of the Trevor I remembered. In life, he'd been a handsome man with long dimples that had run amok, leaving deep creases on his cheeks. They showed up when he laughed, which he did a lot, usually at the antics of his kids or when Avie poked fun at him. Now skin hung on his face like it was melting. In another few years, that skin would desiccate, whither and shrink to the bone, and he'd become unrecognizable.

I'd spent many evenings with Trevor and Avie, around dinner tables and afternoons in the park with our kids. I'd hoped beyond hope to find him in the krowa pens. Alive and uninjured.

My sword arm faltered. The blade dipped giving wojak-Trevor a chance to slip under my defenses. I faced his fangs and manic glare as unchecked bloodlust drove him onto the tip of my sword. It pierced his chest just above the heart. The blade sang and I added to its voice with a cry of my own as I dragged it downward. Magic let it easily slice through muscle, sinew and bone, down to the only spark of life in his undead body. I cleaved into his heart.

His eyes widened and he snarled in defiance of his end. I pulled my sword backward, freeing him for an instant. He swayed. His fingers grappled for my throat. I swung and severed his head from his carcass. It fell and rolled into the dirt coming to rest against the krowa pen.

My right knee buckled. After too many fights and too many injuries, it was never strong, but this time it gave out because my heart gave out. I knelt in the dirt and had the unreasonable urge to put Trevor back together, to tuck his head back onto his shoulders as if that would somehow make things right. But I couldn't bring myself to touch his head with the wide, sightless eyes. Instead, I lugged his corpse over, choking back sobs with each strain of my muscles, until body and head—heart and mind—were lined up together.

And then I put my head on my knees. I tried to cry for Trevor and all the others lost that night, but my heart was dry.

The fighting raged on. I felt a small furry body press against me and smelled Jacoby's distinctive scent, like burning coal and wet dog. I hugged him.

I don't know how long I sat there. It felt like hours but couldn't have been more than minutes. A shadow eventually blocked out the light of the full moon.

Liam stood over me with a frown. The shovel in his hand was streaked with gore. Blood dripped down the side of his head and matted his shirt. He saw me clutching Trevor's corpse and frowned.

"I knew him. He had nine kids." It seemed like the only epitaph worth anything. Liam just nodded and reached for me. I drew energy from my blade, still gripped in my right hand, and leaned on it as I clasped Liam's hand and rose.

Another surge of magic erupted from the hall, filling the sky with light and power.

Liam was ready to charge into the fight, but I stopped him.

"I need to get inside." I pointed wildly at the hall.

He hesitated, glanced at the people—his people—who struggled for their lives with the wojaks, then back at me. I could see need in his eyes. He wanted to go to them. I shook his arm again.

"Ichovidar is in there! Stopping him is the only way to stop this madness!"

Liam's sharp eyes focused on me, as if seeing me for the first time. He nodded once and we ran.

Emil had said there was another door into the Hall of Mages, around the back, but the building was as big as a city block. Screams from the fighting and explosions faded as we ran along the side wall. So did the light. The full moon was nearly overhead, but the building cast a deep shadow—deep enough that my eyes had to adjust, and I stumbled the first few feet in the gloom.

Liam took the lead, pressed against the stone wall. Ahead was a small garden with shrubs, a dry fountain and benches set in a semi circle around it. Nothing moved, but we approached slowly, expecting wojaks or opji to jump on us at any second. Liam slung the shovel over his left shoulder and held the knife in his other hand.

Jacoby tugged on my sleeve. "Crazy-sword is noisys!" His whisper was too loud and I made a shushing noise. I could do nothing about the screaming blade in my hand.

For two days, my sword had been drenched in blood. Now its song rose to a fevered pitch, and I hoped there was no one around who could keen its call.

We crept from one shadowed recess to the next. After each hop, we waited to be sure we hadn't been seen. It was a slow process and I itched to run, to shout, to storm the castle and have done with this entire fight.

About halfway down the length of the building—and it seemed to go on forever—a sound stopped us. Liam dropped into a crouch and tensed. I pressed my back flat against the wall. A garbled wail sounded again. A bird, maybe? I didn't know any kind of night bird that made that noise.

The cry repeated, louder now. Liam rose and lifted his gaze to a closed window that interrupted the line of brickwork above us.

It was a baby. Now that I recognized it, there was no mistaking that newborn mewl.

Liam ran. Ten meters along the wall was a door—solid wood and locked. He threw himself against it in a frenzy, not caring if he drew attention to us.

"Stop!" I hissed and jumped between him and the door. Momentum kept him coming, and I got a shoulder in the face as we slammed against wood.

I shoved him aside. His hands pressed the door, his eyes frantic as he looked for any flaw in its solidity.

"Stop!" I said again. "Let me do it."

I glanced into the shadowed lane. If there were any opji watching, they'd already have shown themselves. I squared myself and studied the door and its lock.

Nori had warned me about using my well-magic so soon after nearly draining myself, so I primed my sword with a bit of magic pulled from the environment. There wasn't much. The opji had scorched the earth for miles around Vioska. But green magic is always there, humming along the mycelium and root systems even after a great purging. I pulled on this energy and jabbed the tip of my blade into the crack between door and jamb. Wood and metal smoldered and fell away as easily as melting ice. When I felt the lock break, I kicked the door and it swung open into a dark hallway.

Liam glowered at my sword. He'd once watched me jab his brother's corpse in order to release Sean's spirit. He hadn't understood Valkyrie magic, and in his grief, he'd given me no chance to explain. I hadn't blamed him at the time, though it saddened me. We'd shared something precious for a few days, a burgeoning of possible love. But Sean's death had blighted us and there was no going back.

It had been a hard lesson for me to learn and unlearn when I finally met the man who understood all my quirks—understood and accepted them without question.

Liam hadn't been able to do that. And by the look he gave my sword, he'd never gotten over his disgust or distrust for it.

I gave him a tight smile and strode past him into the Hall of Mages.

IT WAS DARK AND quiet. The air smelled stale. Like a tomb. Our boots made soft padding noises on the stone floor. My eyes went right for the end of the long hall where I could see flickering light.

Jacoby scampered by me. I hissed out a warning and he stopped short. I beckoned to him. He fell back and pressed against my shins like a cat. I stood still, letting my keening flow through the building.

Ichovidar had a lab somewhere and he was already starting the ritual that would transform Shar into a weapon of mass destruction. I needed to find him, and fast.

Follow the magic.

Liam had other ideas.

I ran lightly down the hall with Jacoby close. After only a few steps, I realized we were alone. Liam had stopped at the first door along the wall. I turned back to see him standing in the open doorway.

"Liam!" I whispered, hoping I wasn't calling every opji in the house down on our heads.

Liam didn't answer. He didn't move.

A baby cried, in a short burst, then went silent.

I trotted back. He blocked the entire doorway. I nudged him and he moved forward. Ducking around his broad frame, I stepped into a large room filled with row upon row of bassinets, each cradling a swathed newborn. More cribs lined the far wall for older toddlers. Most were asleep, but a few were standing up, gripping the crib bars, their eyes hollow and lost.

I let my keening out to sweep the room and found not one opji magic signature in the place.

The babies were human.

Dear All-father. My thoughts froze. Words evaporated from my brain.

Of course, I'd known about the opji breeding pens. Everyone knew. But my horror had always been focused on the poor women and men who were forced to endure such a life of captivity. Why, oh why had my concern never been for the children bred for one purpose only—to be turned into undead killing machines?

I was concerned now. And horrified.

The room was silent. I couldn't tell which of the babies had been crying. They all looked so beyond hope.

Liam gripped the edge of the open door like a lifeline. "One of these is mine."

Oh, gods.

"He or she—I don't even know." His voice hitched. "They would be a year old now. Janey almost died giving birth. And when they found out she couldn't *breed* anymore, they turned her." He said *breed* like a curse word.

"Kyra-lady?" Jacoby tugged on my arm. "Why ares the babies so quiet. Nones of them cries."

"Because they know no one will come," Liam said. His eyes were shuttered, all emotion locked away.

One of the newborns still had hope for salvation and made a strangled cooing sound. Liam lurched forward like an automaton. He picked up the bundled child and started to weep in chorus to its cry.

I left him there, rocking the baby. I wanted to stay, to pick up every one and tell them they were loved, but if I didn't find Ichovidar before he split Shar's shell, none of us would survive the night.

I slipped out of the nursery and ran toward the light at the end of the hall.

32

Finding Ichovidar's lair wasn't hard. At the end of the long corridor, I came to an atrium. From there it was a matter of following the sound of thunder and the flash of lightning as it hit the dome. I ramped up my wards, ready for any spill-over magic and let my sword lead the way. The blade sensed a coming fight and vibrated in my grip.

I skidded around a corner with Jacoby right behind me. My boots screeched on the stone floor and I froze. Jacoby slammed into the back of my legs. Ahead, two great wooden doors were thrown open, letting blue light bleed into the hallway.

Thunder crashed and lightning struck the dome again. I flattened myself against the wall. The rolling boom seemed to go on forever. It disgorged magic that suffused the hall and tried to latch onto me with grabby fingers. It claimed my breath. My heart skipped a beat as it tried to match the thunder's toll. I ramped up my wards again and choked as I reclaimed my own heartbeat. The thunder died, leaving a deep silence in its wake.

"Come in, Valkyrie," said a soft, oddly accented voice. "I have what you want and more, I suspect. Come in and claim it."

Good. I didn't want to hide anymore. I sucked in a frayed breath and turned into the room with my crooning sword held high.

I stumbled over a body lying just inside the door, and went down on one knee. The woman lay on her stomach, head turned toward me and cheek pressed against the cold floor. Human. And dead, though there was no sign of trauma. Unlike the captives in the pen outside, her clothes were clean and simple. A house servant? I stepped over her legs and moved deeper into the massive room.

To the left and right, I spotted more bodies sprawled around a circular pool in the middle of the room. The water in the pool was black and frothing. A giant glowing globe, like the bulb on a blazing alembic, was suspended above. I didn't know its exact purpose, but I could guess. It was some kind of magical hub, like a giant bonfire doused with gasoline and primed to be lit. And I had no doubt that when the opji king ignited it, it would mean the end of Shar and possibly our reality.

The ceiling was open to the sky. The moon's glare hit the globe and reflected into every corner of the room.

I counted at least another six bodies, but the pool was so massive, I couldn't see the far side. There were probably more. Had their deaths served as some kind of catalyst to ignite the magic? Whatever had happened to them, they hadn't been the main show. I could still keen magic growing, tensing like a predatory beast, readying itself to strike.

I shielded my eyes and peered past the bright globe. The moon was inching its way to crest in the sky. In a few minutes it would shine straight down. I knew enough about magic to know that Ichovidar was waiting for that connection between moon and alembic to fuel his mad spell.

Thunder pealed again and galvanic magic crackled across the globe like blue lightning. I braced myself against the onslaught of magic, but the globe contained the worst of it.

Beside me, Jacoby whimpered. His soft hand slipped into mine. I briefly considered splitting up and sending him clockwise around the pool while I continued counter-clockwise, but his fingers gripped mine so tightly, I decided it was better to stay together.

We stepped over the woman's body and deeper into the hall.

The globe pulsed and crackled.

I strode around the edge of the pool, no longer creeping or hiding.

"That's right, little Valkyrie. Come to me." The voice taunted.

"Why are you hiding?" I stepped over another dead servant. "Are you afraid? Bock-bock-bock." I let go of Jacoby's hand and flapped my arm like a chicken wing.

That's right, Kyra. Taunt the big scary monster. See how that works out for you.

The vampire hissed. "You are the one who should be afraid. I will take everything from you. And then I will remake the world to my order."

Steam billowed up from the pool. The water was opaque with bits of twigs and leaves floating on its surface. It boiled, releasing clouds of steam as it flowed around the pool in a swift current. A foul smell rose on the steam. Sulfur. The perfume of choice for demons and other lowlifes.

Another few steps and another dead body.

A silent prayer came to my mind as we stepped over it, but I suppressed it. The All-father had never come to my aid, and the god of all Earth lay dying in a tent back at camp. The gods couldn't help me.

Instead, I prayed to my feet to keep moving in the gloom. And to my hand to hold fast to my sword. And to my heart, begging it not to implode as the foul magic in the room pressed down on me.

Wind blew in through the open ceiling. It smelled of blaster fire. Only a sliver of the moon's corona peeked out from behind the globe now. The alembic crackled like a blue ember.

Time was short. I picked up my pace and nearly stumbled over the last body lying next to a throne-like chair.

Ichovidar, King of the Opji, sat on the chair, leaning forward with his elbows resting on his knees. He wore the typical black homespun opji jacket with wide lapels and a white shirt underneath. His pointed nose was framed by long cheeks and a strong chin, all clothed in that alabaster opji skin. A crown of white-blond hair cascaded over his shoulders like a waterfall. I registered all that in a moment and tossed it aside. Ichovidar didn't matter because gripped in his hands and dangling between his knees was Shar.

She didn't squirm. Her eyes were closed and her feet hung limply from her shell.

Jacoby shrieked and launched himself at the opji. Ichovidar had been eyeing me and had barely registered the dervish until he was latched onto Shar with both hands. Ichovidar jerked his hand. Jacoby bit down on his wrist. The opji hissed. He tried to fling Jacoby away, but the little guy had wrapped himself around Shar. His eyes glazed over and smoke streamed from his ears.

Ichovidar held Jacoby three feet in the air and shook him, but Jacoby refused to be dislodged. His feet churned like he was trying to pedal a bike.

He was about to go nova. The poor, sweet little dervish had only tried to do what I asked—to protect Shar.

Gods, I will kill that vampire a hundred times over.

Ichovidar ignored the dervish drama and showed me his fangs. They caught the moonlight and shone like opals. He bent his head, never taking his eyes off me, and breathed in the scent from Jacoby's neck.

"Mmmm. I don't usually indulge in beast-kind, but this little creature is so full of heat. I think it would be like drinking the sun, don't you?"

"You've never seen a dervish, have you?" I inched closer.

"Is that what it is. How extraordinary. I'm sure he'll taste like chicken."

"Why don't you leave them alone. Take my blood instead." I arched my head back, exposing my neck. I was close enough now that I saw his eyes dilate at the thought of my blood, so freely offered. Bloodlust seemed to overtake him for a moment. He lowered Jacoby and Shar and leaned in to take my scent.

And that's when I saw it. A crystal vial hung from a leather thong around his neck. It was three inches long and tapered to a point like a tooth. Like a fang. Cut edges made it glitter and a green substance swirled inside it.

I got only a glimpse before Ichovidar leaned back and the vial was lost in the folds of his shirt, but I had no doubt. This was Terra's spirit jar.

Ichovidar was no baby vamp, just turned and easily swayed by his lusts. He brought his need under control and snarled, "There is no instead. I will bleed you both dry." He glanced at the opening in the ceiling. The moon was about to be eclipsed by his monstrous machine. Galvanic magic crackled across the globe constantly now, and it whined like an engine revving.

He wrenched Jacoby away from Shar and carried them both to the edge of the pool. Jacoby hung like a limp rag in his grip, but Shar was awake now and staring at the opji with wide frightened eyes. He was going to dump Shar into the pool and start whatever magic he was calling on to crack her shell like a coconut.

And that breaking would break the world.

"Nici thought she could crack the shar-lil too," I shouted. That stopped him in his tracks with Jacoby and Shar dangling over the black, churning water. He turned dark eyes on me.

"Yeah, Nici. She was what, your daughter? Your lover? Both?"

A muscle ticked on his cheek.

"What a bitch, though. Am I right? And kind of dumb too. Didn't she screw up your plans twice? First when you tried to invade Montreal on the fae prince's coat strings. And again, when you tried to enthrall the entire godling population."

Smoke rose from Jacoby in billows that met with the steam from the pool. He'd gone rigid and his eyes had rolled back. But Shar watched me intently.

Good baby. Keep still. Mama's coming for you.

I kept up my stream of babble, inching closer to Ichovidar.

"I was there when she died, you know. My husband snapped her neck like it was a twig." Ichovidar hissed. He wasn't giving up so easily. But as long as I kept his attention, he wasn't working his magic.

"And that other opji? He looked just like you. Another child or maybe a little brother? He went missing in the Inbetween, didn't he? On a raiding mission near Mount Saint Savior? I bet you've been wondering what happened to him."

I leaned in and whispered, "I stuck my blade through his heart. He squealed like a pig as he died." That was a complete fabrication. The opji prince had died in the melee with the Winaskwi fighters, but later, when I had time to examine my actions, I found that I was okay with lying to opji scum.

And it pushed just the right buttons. Ichovidar leaned away from the pool. His muscles bunched, ready to lunge for me.

"Did you feel your ward break earlier tonight? Of course you did. That was my husband and my friend too. Just like the hundreds of humans and fae who are now working together to kill your wojaks, your opji and your mages. It's over. You lost. Give me my children back and I'll let you walk out of here."

I beckoned to him with one hand while I pointed my sword at his throat with the other.

Jacoby woke from his trance and yanked the cord holding the spirit jar. "Kyra-lady!"

Ichovidar thrust Jacoby away at the same moment the dervish tossed the jar in my direction.

My fingers skimmed its edge but I missed. It crashed to the ground with a shatter of crystal.

Jacoby landed with a smack on the stone lip of the pool and slipped into the water. The current took him away.

Magic boomed at the release of the god's spirit. It shook the hall like an earthquake.

Ichovidar gaped. Terra's pith pooled on the floor between us. It rose and swirled in a green cloud. Spinning faster and faster, it shifted and cut through Ichovidar like a ghostly saw blade. He choked, dropped Shar and clawed at his throat.

The green mist exploded outward in a wave of power that picked me up and tossed me against the wall. I landed hard. Air was pounded from my lungs and I lay on the stone floor too weak to even gasp.

When my lungs finally remembered to fill with life-giving breath, I sat up, leaning heavily on one elbow. My sight was blurred. Sound came only in vague rumbles. Pain shot through me in spikes.

The room was dimmer. The globe blazed with primed magic, and it swung from only one chain above the turbulent water.

Jacoby! He'd gone under. I shakily rose to my knees, then to my feet. I keened my sword whining nearby, picked it up and leaned on it like a staff.

I had to find Jacoby and Shar.

My vision was black around the edges, and I groped my way toward the pool.

An unseen power grabbed my shoulder and spun me around.

Ichovidar stood ten feet away, panting. His coat was torn and blood dripped into his eyes. His raised hand clenched into a fist and the invisible force squeezed my windpipe. I was lifted into the air. My feet kicked, but found nothing to hit. My blade flailed uselessly. I felt the invisible magic loosen on my throat only to seize my right wrist and shake it, until I dropped the sword.

Ichovidar stepped forward. I was stuck in his magic chains. He hissed into my face, spraying me with spittle and the stench of death. His invisible claws squeezed my throat. I scrambled for my belt, pulling out the only other weapon I had.

The Thorn of Vidar.

I was too weak, too far gone to strike with any real power, and my underhand angle was all wrong, but I drove the stake deep into his gut. He reeled backward, and the force holding me let go.

I dropped to the ground and sucked in air.

Ichovidar grabbed the stake and yanked it out.

His eyes went wide, not from the sight of his blood, but because of the weapon.

"You recognize it, don't you?" My throat was raw and voice rasping. "The Thorn of Vidar. Killer of kings."

Ichovidar's lip curled. His wound would already be healing. "You don't believe that old myth that a wooden stake can kill a vampire?"

A swamp monster rose from the pool, cutting off my response.

Jacoby held Shar in a tight embrace. Weeds and muck clung to them and dripped into the water. Jacoby rose higher, floating above the pool. His head was thrown back and eyes rolled to white. Steam rose off him. His poodle fur sizzled and popped. The weeds draping his shoulders dried out and burned away.

He might have rallied before, but the explosion, the vampire, the near drowning—it was all too much for the little dervish. He was seconds away from going nova.

Shar burned with an inner light. It was her magic that held them suspended. The light grew until it circled Jacoby and grew some more until I had to shield my eyes against it.

Just as he'd protected her, Shar was now protecting him from Ichovidar and from Jacoby's own fire that would decimate him.

Ichovidar wasn't giving up his prize so easily. The Thorn of Vidar clattered to the floor. He shoved me aside, and I fell backward as he made a grab for Shar.

The fall put me within inches of my sword. My fingers scrabbled on the floor as I reached for it. I yearned for my sword, yearned so hard that the blade reacted to my need and shot forward to settle in my grip where it belonged.

I slashed the air wildly. I only needed one cut.

Ichovidar gasped as my blade sank into his calf. He kicked me aside and clutched his chest, eyes bulging from his head.

I dragged myself onto my knees. I was shaking badly. Something wet dripped into my eyes. I wiped it and my hand came away covered in blood.

"Feels weird doesn't it?" My voice was shaky and barely above a raw whisper. "That's your dead heart coming back to life." I'd seen other opji react to my sword's magic. They gasped and choked and usually gave me a chance to finish them off, but Ichovidar got his fear and surprise under control quickly. Instead of cowering, he backhanded me across the jaw.

My neck snapped back and I slammed to the ground, losing all sense of time and space for precious seconds. But I couldn't stay down. It wasn't a choice. I rose painfully to one knee. The room spun like a carousel. I wiped blood dripping from my nose. I couldn't feel my limbs and my ragged fingers clung to my sword. My body felt broken, but it didn't matter. It only mattered that I stand, and I did. One painful, creaking joint at a time, I dragged myself to my feet and raised my blade.

Ichovidar held Shar in front of him like a shield of light. Jacoby lay crumpled on the floor, dead or unconscious.

Dear All-father or any god left to listen, please don't let him be dead.

Ichovidar licked blood off his lip "Now you will see the true power of the world killer. It's not too late. The shar-lil is already primed. It is ready to break the veil and set this world free!" He dangled Shar over the pool that churned with magic.

"Why?" I rasped. He paused and shot me a glance, confident now that he held the position of power. "Why would you want to tear the veil? What could you possibly gain?"

Ichovidar grinned. His fangs were red with blood, probably mine. He opened his mouth to answer and I cut him off.

"You know what? I don't care. Your motivations are as insignificant as a cockroach's." I pretended to relax and Ichovidar tossed Shar into the water. The alembic exploded.

In the same moment, I found whatever iota of reserves I had and leaped, plunging my sword into his chest. The blade speared him like a shish kebob and stuck. Ichovidar toppled into the pool, taking my blade with him. The momentum of the thrust had me falling too. I clambered over his body, frantically searching the pool for Shar.

My hands closed around her shell. I raised her up just as blue light shot from her in a column that burst through the open ceiling and speared the sky.

Magic flowed off her in wave after wave, but instead of burning out my magic reserves, she filled me. I laughed in drunken delight as magic lifted my spirit and suffused me with light.

I gazed down on the baby god, the world seed…the world killer. And she gazed up at me. Her three-pronged nose snuffled through her lattice shell and all the love I had for her was reflected in her eyes.

My Shar. My baby. She was safe. *I* was safe in her light.

"It's time for Shar to go home." The voice came from far away. Reluctantly, I dragged my gaze away from Shar to find Terra leaning against the rim of the pool.

CHAPTER

33

erra gripped my arm. Gone was the frail old woman. In her place stood the Terra I remembered from my dreams. She was tall and strong and ageless. Almarick lurked behind her.

"Her magic has been ignited," Terra said as she reached for Shar. "It will grow exponentially now. You know what you must do. Quickly! Before she takes root in this world!"

"No!" I clutched Shar to my chest. "It's too soon." She was just a baby. She needed me!

"It's past time. You must open the veil. I have no strength."

"But your spirit jar. It broke…" My words and thoughts stumbled away as Terra shook her head.

"Breaking the jar wasn't enough. It helped, but to regain my full power, I needed to consume it." She pointed to the floor and the broken shards of crystal.

I didn't know what losing her essence meant in the grand scheme, but all I cared about was the small scheme, the one where I cradled my baby and never let her go.

Terra's fingers wheedled under mine, trying to loosen my grasp.

"Look!" She pointed to the ceiling and I saw what I hadn't seen during the last moments of my fight with Ichovidar. The blazing alembic had exploded. A fragment of the globe hung from its chain. I stood in the pool and the water frothed around my feet. Thunder tolled and lightning hit the roof some thirty meters above my head.

Shar called to it. I could hear her song now. It drowned out even the raucous call of my sword. And it was growing.

"Kyra, look at me."

My thoughts were fractured and scattered, and Terra's voice was like an irritating itch that I couldn't scratch.

"Look at me, child."

I turned to her. She seemed to be wrapped in a bubble of green energy that rebuffed the blue light streaming off Shar. She dipped her head, meeting my gaze. With or without pith, there was still power in those eyes. They steadied me, and the room stopped spinning.

"We don't have much time. Shar's magic will grow faster now. Soon it will overwhelm everything in its path. If you won't do it for us, do it for those soldiers out there." She pointed vaguely in the direction of the fight still raging outside. "Or do it for Shar. How do you think it will corrupt her, to kill millions of souls?"

I hadn't thought of it that way before.

I looked down at Shar who watched me with pure trust in her soft brown eyes.

"I know her magic feels benevolent now, but the gods cannot survive on your world without breaking its laws. So much death! It will twist her magic in ways we can't even predict." Her hand squeezed my arm painfully. "If you truly love her, you won't do that to her."

Tears fell from my eyes to splash on Shar's shell. She cooed and pushed out even more magic. Thunder cracked overhead.

I sucked in a breath and stood tall. I wasn't a destroyer. I was a rescuer. It was time to start acting like one.

My cold fingers found the pendant hanging on the cord around my neck. I turned the opal moon a half turn. From the seething waves at my feet, a seam split upward. Like a zipper opening, a crack appeared with a shredding sound that rocked the building. The crack widened to a portal. On the other side, the landscape was dull gray and lifeless.

"Quickly!" Terra reached for Shar and I let her go. They disappeared through the portal. I turned to follow, but the water at my feet rose up.

Ichovidar latched onto my leg.

In the turmoil, I'd forgotten him, just as I hoped history would. He strained to pull my sword from his chest. I grabbed the hilt and yanked. It came free with a gleeful song.

The vampire king hissed. Water streamed off his ghost-white face. I swung my blade and lopped off his head. The momentum took it sailing through the portal to land on the virgin soil of Shar's new world.

Something exploded. Light burst through the open portal. A flash so bright, I was momentarily blinded.

I stumbled forward, hands reaching. My passage through the veil felt like warm oil washing over my skin. Then my feet crunched on gravel. I tripped over something hard. As my eyes adjusted, I saw Ichovidar's head—mouth gaping open and fangs still red with blood.

I kicked it.

Then I thought better, and reached down to pick it up, planning to chuck it back through the portal. It didn't belong here.

"Leave it," Terra said.

I blinked several times in the bright light. This world wasn't as gray as I'd anticipated. Clouds thinned to let through the rays of a brilliant orange sun.

I glanced at the vampire head. "It shouldn't be here."

"Let it stand as a reminder," Terra said. "The opji are part of Shar's making."

"Shar! Where is she?"

"Come and see." She took my hand and I was glad for the comfort of another's touch.

In the distance, a deep purple sea shone like a jewel. The ground started to slope upward, and rocks gave way to blue-green grass, dotted with white flowers. As we climbed, the flora increased. Shrubs and new saplings grew in tangled bunches. At the top of the hill, we stopped.

Shar sat on a grassy knoll as if on her throne. Her eyes were closed. A crown of tendrils grew from her shell and plunged into the dirt beneath her. The bright glow around her had dimmed. She was feeding all her magic into her world.

I crouched and laid my hand on the ground, feeling the current. This was green magic on an epic scale, but Shar wasn't calling to the green like I did. She was producing it. She was filling the well of this new world, filling it with light and life. Even as we watched, shrubs and flowers burst from the ground, creeping down the hill toward the sea.

And when it reached the warm waters? Who knew, maybe Shar's magic would suffuse the oceans and spark life of a different sort.

I was watching the birth of a planet, not the geological birth, but the spiritual birth. So, why did my heart ache so much?

I turned back to Shar. She was nearly lost in her nest of vines and roots. In a few years, the forest would consume her.

"Can she hear me?" I asked.

Terra frowned. "Perhaps. But your voice will be one among thousands now. Already she will be listening to the voices of the lives she creates."

I laid my hand on her shell. It was warm and smooth and humming with energy.

"Thank you." My voice hitched. I breathed deeply and tried again. "Thank you for letting us care for you. For letting me hold you when you needed someone to love. And thank you for letting me witness this miracle. You are truly beautiful, despite the horrors inflicted on you." I smiled. "Or maybe because of those horrors. Always remember where you came from and remember the difference between love and hate. Because I love you."

I had more to say. So much more. I had words that could fill a world just as Shar's magic was filling this one. But she knew what was in my heart.

I led Terra down the hill and back to the portal. We ignored the vampire's head that was already being smothered by green growing things and headed toward the rift. My heart felt like a ball of lead in my chest—heavy, hard and toxic.

A shadow crossed in front of the rift, and then Mason was there blinking in the bright light of the new world. He swept me up just as the dam of fear, sorrow and exhaustion burst inside me. He held me and I finally cried. Not for Shar. She was fulfilling her destiny. I cried for me, the one who had to let her go. I cried for Trevor and for Liam's lost wife. For Carmen and Dennet. And for all the souls taken that night.

stumbled through the portal with my eyes still blurred by tears, but my heart feeling lighter. Mason had lived through the battle. That was something.

The Hall of Mages was a mess. Ichovidar's carcass bled onto the stone floor that was covered in broken glass. The torches in wall sconces had mostly burned out. Only one still flickered with light.

"Jacoby!" I clutched Mason's sleeve. With Ichovidar bearing down on me, I'd left the little dervish for dead.

"He's fine. A little disoriented, but fine. I sent him to find water."

I felt one more burden lift from my heart. There would be many such moments of relief and grief in the next few days as we sifted through the wreckage of battle.

I had one last job to do here before I left the hall to face that wreckage.

I turned back to the portal. The world on the other side was already vastly different from the wasteland that Terra had once shown me. Shar's uplifting magic drifted through the rift along with daffodil-yellow sunlight. I breathed in her magic, willing myself to never forget the feeling of its touch on my skin.

I twisted the moon on the pendant and the portal slammed shut. Shar's magic winked out and the night suddenly seemed deathly silent. I pulled the leather cord off my neck and handed it to Terra. She pushed my hand back at me.

"I gift it to you, so you may visit your child." She raised one eyebrow and gave me a stern look. "But use it wisely. Do not open the portal in the same place more than once, lest the veil decide to make the opening permanent."

She closed her hand around my fist. "And keep it secret."

"Kyra-lady!" Jacoby burst into the hall, carrying a single cup. Water sloshed over the sides as he bounded nimbly across the debris-strewn floor. I crouched to catch him as he flung his arms around my neck, spilling the last of the water down my back. I didn't care. I hugged my dervish.

He pulled away and bounced. "Dids you see? I tricks him good. Nasty old vampire! I tricks him to thinks I could explodes him!"

I laughed. "Is that what you did? You were quite the actor."

Jacoby gave his best theater bow, then he looked stern. He cupped my face with both hands. "Kyra-lady cries?"

My breath hitched in my chest. I had to tell him.

"I'm sorry, but Shar has gone to her new home."

His eyes were huge and nearly black in the dim light. "Is she deads?"

"No! She's alive. Very much alive." I gripped his hands. "But she can't come back here."

Jacoby shook. He was trying his best to hold it together. After a long moment he took a ragged breath and said, "She tolds me about her new home. She saids she wants to go." He thrust out his chest and straightened his bony shoulders. "And we're rescuers. Rights? Sometimes we has to let them go."

By the One-eyed god. My apprentice had just graduated.

"Yes we do." I hugged him again.

Almarick held out his hand for Terra to hold as they picked their way through the debris and out of the hall.

Mason surveyed the room with the massive pool full of black steaming liquid and the jumble of parts hanging from the open ceiling. He rubbed a hand across his neck and upward, a gesture so familiar, I had to smile. He looked exhausted. The dark stubble on his chin seemed to emphasize his pallor. Blood covered the front of his shirt, some of it his. An oozing wound showed through a tear on his sleeve.

His gaze finally came to rest on the remaining shard of the globe hanging from a chain.

"Blazing alembic?" he asked.

"I think so."

"I would have liked to see it in action."

"It was pretty cool." I rose, keeping one of Jacoby's hands tucked firmly in mine. "But I think we should dismantle it before we leave, just in case."

"Agreed. I don't know what will become of this place, but it's not a good idea to leave hot magic lying around for anyone to find."

I turned to face the door of the hall. Out there was destruction. So much destruction. I had the irrational idea that as long as we stayed here, in this hall of shadows, none of that would be real.

But of course, we couldn't stay.

I sucked in a deep breath and let it out slowly.

"I guess we have to face the music." I started toward the door.

"Kyra wait. There's something I need to tell you."

Vioska was burning. Acrid smoke filled the air. I pulled my bandana over my nose, but it did little to help. The taste of burning wood, metal and flesh seared my throat. The opji's former captives and a few soldiers milled about the main square, but the fighting had petered out. The survivors were too tired to do more than sit in the dirt and watch the town burn.

Someone would have to organize the cleanup and care for the wounded. Someone meaning me and Mason. And maybe Glenda if she survived.

"Glenda?" I asked.

Mason nodded as he led me through the alley toward the town's edge. "She made it."

"And Soolea?"

"I'm not sure. I haven't seen her."

There were a lot more people I wanted to ask about, but not now.

Now I needed to see Angus.

Magic hung on the air. The opji had been abusing this space with their dark rites for months. Add the flash bombs and the breaking of the ward, and you had the recipe for a potent magic stew.

My personal wards were frail and battered too. The magic buffeted me like a wind that scoured any exposed skin. Mason's jaw was clenched as he also warded his keening with his last strength. He stalked through the town like a man on a mission, his eyes scanning the shadows for threats. Jacoby bounded along at his side.

More activity centered around the crater from the flash bombs. Hub soldiers were picking up pieces of golems and tossing them into a truck. Others piled bodies to burn.

In a dramatic backdrop to this gruesome scene, Angus's stone hedge spread two stories high and a hundred feet wide.

Oh, Angus.

His face was lost in the mass of stone brambles. I approached slowly and laid my hand on a branch. It was cool under my touch. I glanced at the sky. The moon had long since set. In the east, the sky was just starting to lighten from black to purple. Sunrise was in a couple of hours. He shouldn't have turned to stone until then.

I laid my head against him. "He used too much magic, but the sun always heals. Isn't that what you told me? It's a gargoyle's life. He'll be fine come sundown. We might have to cut him out of there, but—"

"Kyra, stop."

I was rambling as I gripped the stone branch with clenched fists. I often did that to avoid a harsh reality. Mason knew it too. He knew all my foibles. He laid his hands on the branch beside mine.

"Your keening is better," he said. "If I can feel it, so can you." He covered my hand in his, and I faced what I had willfully ignored.

There was nothing to keen. The stone was cold and silent and inert.

Angus was dead.

"How?" I blurted the question, but I already knew the answer.

Angus had emptied his well of magic to save us all. It wasn't the only act of pure selflessness in this war, but it was one that would stand as a monument to the lives lost on this day—a warning to future generations about the dangers of taking too much from the Inbetween.

I pried myself from Mason's grip and grabbed the stone hedge again, willing it to hum with Angus's unusual and discordant song. His magic had come from two halves—a small piece of Mason's spirit and the soul of the fae that brought him to life. The two magics had never melded into one coherent spirit. Some gargoyles couldn't reconcile that dissonance inside them. Their magic jangled like a bag full of screws and bolts, eventually driving them to suicide or madness. Angus had embraced the jangle and made it his song.

And now that song was silent.

Mason pulled my hand away and forced me to face him. "He gave everything he had to tear down that ward. I was there. He knew what he was doing."

Jacoby popped up between Mason and me, his eyes huge and worried. "Is Mister-Angus sleepings?"

I smoothed the frizzy fur away from his brow. "Not sleeping. He's gone."

Jacoby made an odd trilling cry that I'd never heard from him before and buried his face in my stomach. His shoulders heaved and I patted his furry back. He'd been brave for Shar, but Angus was one too many losses. For me too.

I did the only thing I could do. I lifted my sword and dragged it across the stone branch.

I felt no rush of power, no release. Angus didn't need me and my Valkyrie sword. He knew the way home all by himself.

The next hours went by in a blur. Terra presided over the pyre of bodies, giving out last rites to opji, wojaks, humans and fae without prejudice. No one questioned her and I suspected they thought she was a priestess.

Mason left to help put out the fires, and I saw to as many wounded as I could, hauling those who could walk back to the tent and marking others so they could be brought in on stretchers.

I found Dekar limping through the slushy ash of the Devastation. He half carried another man whose bloody shirt was wrapped around his head. Dekar didn't look much better. Blood soaked his right pant leg, and every step brought a grimace of pain to his face.

I took the load of the wounded man off him, and we all hobbled back to the infirmary. Dekar wanted to go back out right away to bring in more wounded.

"Come on, Kyra. I made it through the battle. Now let me help."

I pressed his shoulders down onto a cot as he tried to rise.

"Not until you get looked at."

I didn't need to explain to Arriz that his son survived the fight only to die from sepsis. I waved Joe Mountainclaw over. He'd been through a battle of his own, treating wounded for thirty-six hours straight. And he looked it.

He smiled wearily when he saw me.

I pointed to Dekar. "Sedate him if you have to. I don't want him back in the field tonight."

Joe gave a small laugh and nodded while Dekar scowled. A moment later, Muzzy appeared and threw himself into his brother's arms.

The rest of the day continued with the same bittersweet mix. I lost track of the number of wounded I lugged back to camp, and the bodies I stacked in front of Terra's pyre. Every friend I met was one more I could check off the list of the lost.

A yeti had brought his fallen brethren back to camp. He dropped the body next to the infirmary. It was clearly dead. Nori tried to explain to the yeti that there was nothing she could do for his friend. He lifted the arm of the corpse and let it drop, then the shaggy beast beat his chest and let out a primal roar.

Nori didn't shrink away.

"Can't you do something?" I asked.

She shook her head. "Do what? Sedate him? I couldn't even guess at the dosage to put out a yeti. And if I got it wrong, he could go berserk and rampage through the camp."

The yeti knelt. He touched his forehead to the corpse's forehead and held that pose for a silent minute. Then he rose and loped off into the trees. I didn't see him again.

The bluecaps left that afternoon. They tacked up their mules and piled their carts high with every possession they owned. Glenda gifted Neva with food, gear and weapons from Hub's stores.

"It's the least I can do," she said. "For your sacrifice."

Neva bowed her head but didn't answer. I knew that look on her face. It said, *if I speak now, I won't be able to hold in the grief.* I'd been there before.

I watched their train of carts wind through the camp until the last bluecap disappeared into the forest.

The dragons returned to claim their dead. After a silent vigil that lasted through the night, the dragons incinerated the green who'd fallen in battle. When the body was little more than ash and bone, Kalindari let out a shrill cry and the thunder took off as one. As the others swept into the sunrise, Ollie swooped low over the camp. It didn't feel like goodbye, only a farewell for now.

240

And then it was time to face up to something I'd been putting off. After breakfast on the second day, when the blue caps were gone and the dragons were gone and all the wounded brought in, I sought out Avie.

She'd given me a brief hug when I first returned after the battle, but she'd been busy with the wounded. Now I found her in the mess tent, standing by a coffee urn with a mug in her hand. When she saw me coming, she poured a second mug and handed it to me.

"Thanks." I took the cup and sipped the dark, bitter coffee. It warmed my soul like nothing else. "So good."

Avie smiled. "It was Carmen's contribution to the cause. She said an army can't run without coffee."

"To Carmen." I raised my mug and gently tapped it against Avie's.

"To Carmen."

We took a moment to remember the vibrant woman who loved coffee and adventure in equal parts.

"I'm wiped." Avie turned to set down her cup. "I don't think I've slept for two days."

"Before you go, there's something I have to tell you. It's about Trevor."

Her mouth froze, lips half-parted to speak. I felt like a heel. I'd watched her all night. As every new patient came into the hospital, her hope had surged and died. It was never the patient she wanted to see.

My mouth was suddenly dry. My fingers squeezed the coffee mug until they hurt. How did I start? How did I find the words that would shatter Avie's world?

In the end, I kept it simple. I told her how I'd seen him in Vioska as a wojak. I didn't detail the fight, but only made it clear he was dead.

Avie crumpled. I caught her before she hit the floor and led her to the bench beside a mess table.

"I'm so sorry." I patted her shoulder while she wept into her hands. Then she went catatonic, just staring wide-eyed at nothing as tears cut rivers in her cheeks.

Raven found us like that and ran for Joe Mountainclaw. The big man came and scooped up Avie.

"I'll take care of her," he said, and I thanked him. Avie looked like a doll in his arms. Raven and I watched them leave. He shifted nervously from foot to foot, as he dealt with pent up feelings. Princess bowed and whined, not sure why her humans smelled like sadness.

"Will she be okay?" Raven asked, and I knew he was really asking if we would be okay.

"Eventually." I beckoned him to sit, and he didn't argue. My kid was taller than me now, but I didn't care. I tucked my arm under his elbow and pressed his head to my shoulder. He rested there and let out a breath that was somewhere between a sigh and a sob. He'd seen a lot in the last two days. Too much for one so young. I wished I could have spared him that trauma.

Princess put her muzzle on my knee and whined. I scratched the thick ruff behind her ear.

We'd lost loved ones, but my family had come through mostly intact. I'd have to find a god to thank for that.

CHAPTER

35

The next day, only a handful of opji remained in town. Hub soldiers hunted down the wojaks. There was no saving them. Without opji mages to control them, the wojaks were nothing more than mindless killing machines.

My job as leader of this expedition had mostly ended, but I used my influence for one last demand. All wojak got decent funeral rites. Every face was recorded in case family came looking for them, and no one was left for the scavengers.

Hub soldiers also found four opji elders cowering in a closet in the Hall of Mages. The crowd of civilians wanted them executed on the spot, but Glenda insisted they should be taken into custody instead.

She and I watched the soldiers lead the elders away and lock them in an armored vehicle to be transported back to Montreal.

"What will you do with them?" I asked.

"They will be debriefed."

"And then?"

"And then they are no longer your concern."

Glenda's eyes narrowed as she looked over the town square and the shelters that were being set up to house the krowa refugees.

I knew she was right. This war might have been mine to start, but Hub and the Parliament ministers would finish it. I suspected that once the opji elders had worn out their usefulness, they would be quietly dispatched, and I found I couldn't muster the will to care about that.

The rest of the opji underlings fled into the Inbetween, preferring their odds against the monsters of the wood to the mercy of Hub.

Only Emil and his Bunters remained, and after much questioning, they were released, mostly because certain krowa factions intervened on their part.

What was left of the krowa and the Bunters would rebuild Vioska. Prejudices on both sides would be put aside. The Bunters would learn to live among humans, and the humans would have to trust them. No one expected it to be easy.

Vioska had mostly burned to the ground. Only the Hall of Mages, now renamed the Hall of Victory, and a few outer buildings still stood. Hub had set up a camp in the town square for the krowa. Some were too frail to make the journey back to Montreal. Others wanted to stay. They had no homes to go back to.

Glenda gave them all the supplies at her disposal, and vowed that more would be coming. Then there was nothing left for the Hub soldiers to do and they left. Most of the wardies who'd come to fight followed them home. I didn't envy Glenda the hours she would spend debriefing Parliament.

Emil and I walked along an avenue lined with burned out buildings. He was making a survey of which ones needed to be torn down and rebuilt first.

"You're really going to stay?" I asked.

He made a note on his widget without looking at me.

"My home is here now."

"Because of Ray?" Emil had fallen in love in the krowa pens. That much was obvious. He spent every evening nursing Ray, who'd been injured long before the fight came to Vioska. Ray's little brother helped, and together the three of them looked like a family.

Emil put down the widget and looked at me. "I have never fit in. Not at the fae court, not later when I went off on my own. I was always the odd man out, the feared wolf among the sheep." He paused and looked back at the ruin of Vioska. I suspected he saw more than burned out shells of buildings. He saw what it would become with hard work and cooperation. "But here, I'm the link between humans and opji. My unique perspective finally has worth." He looked at me again. "Here, I can be something."

I nodded. It looked like I'd be interviewing candidates for a new office manager. Again.

We headed back to the Hall of Victory. Nori had moved her hospital inside. Avie and the Hub doctors had gone home with Glenda, but Joe Mountainclaw remained. Together they treated those too wounded to move.

I left Emil to his survey and headed into the hall. I spent most afternoons changing bandages and offering help where I could.

Nori was sitting on the bed of a man whose head was completely wrapped in bandages. He'd suffered a terrible head wound and Nori feared even her magic wouldn't be enough. He hadn't woken since he'd arrived.

"How's he doing?" I asked.

"I'm not sure. I think he moved." Nori felt his pulse then lifted his hand. It flopped down, but twitched when it landed. "It's time to change those bandages. Would you help me?"

"Of course." I found a basin. Nori unwrapped the patient's head and dropped the old bandages in the basin. He groaned. Nori picked up the pace as he tilted his head on the pillow. With all the bandages removed, she peeled back the pads covering his eyes.

His wound was still so raw that it took me a moment to notice anything else. It snaked a jagged line from his jaw up through his ruined left eye. I hadn't seen him when he came in, and even now, he was barely recognizable.

The man groaned again and opened his one good eye, and I was sure. It was Jeremy Hewitt.

"Jacoby!" I called out. The dervish had been busy restocking towels and he nearly dropped them. "Find Soolea and bring her here. I think she's building the new garden. Hurry now!"

He dashed away, not questioning. The garden was on the far side of town, away from the magic hotbed left by the flash bombs.

Twenty minutes later, Jeremy was sitting up in bed. Nori had re-bandaged his wound to hide the worst of it. He was coherent, if disoriented.

Soolea burst into the infirmary like a wild animal in flight. When her gaze fell on Jeremy, she froze. One hand went to her mouth. The other punched the air above her head, and she let out a whoop like a battle cry.

LATER THAT AFTERNOON, I found Liam in the nursery. He sat in a rocking chair with an infant in his arms. I'd checked on him often over the last few days and each time I found him here, feeding or rocking a different child.

I brought him a cup of coffee. It was the last of Carmen's stash. I sat beside him, suddenly aching for my own Holly. He sipped his coffee without disturbing the sleeping child.

"I came to say goodbye," I said. "We're leaving tomorrow."

Liam nodded.

"What will you do now?" I asked.

"Stay. Take care of this mess. One of these children is mine. I may never know which one, so they'll all become mine. Your Hub friend said she'd help with supplies and doctors as long as we need them."

"Is there no one left in Ors who's waiting for you?"

"No one." He ran a hand over his face. "Many of us krowa have no homes. We're going to stay, rebuild and take care of the children." He smiled sadly. "The children of the krowa."

I liked the name. It took the power away from the horror done to them by the opji and put it firmly in their hands. I wouldn't be surprised if in a few years there was a ward here big enough to rival Montreal.

That gave me another thought.

"My friend Soolea lives in a village with some pretty potent wards. Even the opji couldn't breach them. I can have her show you the basics to get you started." I paused. "You'll need some ancestral bones though."

"I think we can find those." Liam smiled wryly. Both our minds flicked back to the Devastation and the pyres that were still burning the dead.

"I was approached by a witch from Montreal. Avalon something or other. She wants to relocate here too. Maybe she'll tackle the ward." Liam saw the shock on my face and said, "Are you okay?"

I took a deep breath. It was a week of losses, but that one wasn't expected. "It's just that Avie is a friend. She didn't tell me she was leaving Montreal."

Liam pinched his lips as if he was holding in a smirk. "It seems you have a lot of odd friends, Kyra Greene."

I squeezed his arm. "I hope there are a few more in Krowtown or whatever you plan to call it.

"Krowtown." He smiled, the first genuine smile I'd seen on him yet. "I like it. What happened here should be remembered. The children of the krowa will never forget."

I took a deep breath and straightened.

"I'm not here just to say goodbye."

Liam gave me a side-eye. I'd been so exhausted and the past few days had been a blur, but last night, sleep had eluded me despite my muscles screaming for rest. And so I'd walked under the waning moon and gone over everything that had happened. Everything I'd done or not done. And one tiny detail stuck in my thoughts like a thorn.

"Janey's dead."

You'd think I would have been better at delivering bad news by now, but it was a talent I hoped never to master. I just laid it all out for him.

"Her spirit helped to defeat the demon, but she's at rest now. She was very brave. I just thought you should know."

Liam bowed his head. After a long moment, he raised it, leaned in and kissed me. A soft, wistful kiss. It was over before I could react. He leaned back, licked his bottom lip and said, "Yup." Then he stood up and placed the sleeping baby into a bassinet. He turned to leave and walked right into Mason.

Liam grinned. Mason's expression was impassive, like a flat black sea at sunset. Liam gave him a good-old-boy punch on the shoulder and stalked off.

"He didn't mean anything by that." I braced myself for push-back.

Mason shook his head and sat in Liam's vacated seat.

"Poor guy." A small smile flirted at the edges of his lips.

"You're not mad?"

"How could I be. He's the lesson, I'll never forget."

I squinted at him. "What lesson?"

"The lesson of what might have been, if I'd let my own fears and arrogance get in the way of this." He pulled me toward him and covered my lips with his in a deep kiss. A reclaiming kiss. A confirmation of everything that had brought us to this place in time. I leaned into him and rode it out, then tucked my head on his shoulder.

"It's time to go home," I said with a sigh.

I felt Mason's deep voice rumble through his chest. "It's time."

I PACKED UP OUR tent and stowed it on the cart. We'd come here with a job to do and now I couldn't get home fast enough.

Terra appeared wrapped in a heavy cloak and carrying a wooden staff, though she didn't need to lean on it.

"Walk with me." It wasn't a request. She turned and headed out of camp toward the Devastation. She no longer needed Almarick to lean on and he trailed behind us out of earshot.

She walked with strength in her back and stealth in her legs. She was tall and vibrant, perhaps not beautiful but striking. Her long brown hair hung in a glossy wave down her back. A few days ago, her skin had been wrinkled and her joints swollen. Now she seemed ageless again, with smooth skin and an old soul peering from her eyes. Still…there was something off about her, something lacking as if I were gazing at her reflection in a mirror instead of her real self.

I desperately wanted to know what had happened to her, but I was wise enough not to push. We reached the burned out ring of land around the city before she finally spoke.

"Almarick will be coming with me, but I will leave the other priests here to help rebuild and to tend the wounded. It will be their service to me."

I'd known she would leave, but hoped she would stay.

"Where will you go?"

"I don't know. Here. There. Everywhere." She favored me with a small smile. "I would like to experience life for a bit, before this body fails me." She ran a hand along one hip.

"I don't understand what happened. Your spirit jar…"

"It broke." She frowned and it felt like the sun dimmed just a bit. "Had I consumed the essence in that jar, I would have been all powerful." For a moment, I had a glimpse of the old divine Terra, then she seemed to dim. She smiled. "In retrospect, it's probably a good thing the jar broke. The essence dissipated. It's everywhere now. In you and me and all around us. Freeing it restored me somewhat, enough that I'll enjoy a long mortal life. And when I die?" She shrugged. "I'll be reunited with my spirit just as we all are. Until then, I plan to enjoy this body and all its talents." She winked. "I shall walk for a while, I think. Come along Almarick."

She picked a path through the burned out debris with her brown-robed priest in tow, and where she stepped, green shoots poked through the ash.

EPILOGUE

June 2085

I hung up the phone with Adam Marat. The new Valkyrie Bestiary office was officially under construction. Adam and his team had laid the foundation that day. In the end, I had decided to tear down the whole structure and rebuild it. Let the ghosts of the past rest in the past. Adam promised we'd be in the new building by September.

Raven finished out his year at Bremmer Academy and had been accepted at Montreal's Institute of Alchemical Sciences, the finest alchemy school in the city. He'd start in the fall.

Since Jacoby had graduated from apprentice to full critter wrangler, I set him the task of interviewing candidates for our new office manager position. I figured, if they could sit through an interview with a dervish, they were probably a good fit.

But all that business was put on hold because today was Holly's third birthday. It started at breakfast with a food fight between Holly, Raven, Mason and me. The winner was Princess who got to eat all the ammunition off the floor. We'd laughed so hard, I didn't care that guests were arriving and I had muffin stuck in my hair. Funny how little things like that didn't matter anymore.

In the afternoon, we had a lovely picnic in the yard within sight of the old cemetery. No one seemed bothered by the gravestones. They were part of the family too.

Everyone was there. Herne and Charlotte had arrived the day before from Annequin Lodge. Soolea and Jeremy came with baby John who was already walking. So did Joe Mountainclaw. The goblins were there and Cricket, Grim and Errol riding on a squamus. Avie and the kids had made the trip from Vioska along with Emil and his new partner, Ray. Only Nori had stayed behind because there was a flu outbreak in the nursery. Lisobet had stayed on to celebrate Holly's birthday. Later in the week, she'd make the long trip home to Bosk with a stop in Manhattan to bring Kester's ashes back to his family. Even the Guardians had lined up on the roof of the gatehouse the night before so they could be included too.

Holly launched herself into my lap. "Mama, cake now!" She was red and sweaty from playing ball with the goblits.

"You already had cake," I said. "How about some juice instead? And then I have a surprise for you."

"Surprise!" Holly shrieked and bounced on her toes.

I poured her a drink and wiped her face. Mason watched us from across the yard where he chatted with Emil and Joe. He saw us get up to leave and nodded.

I'd promised we would be back before anyone realized we were gone.

"Come on, birthday girl." I took Holly's hand. We skipped along the path, through the cemetery and into the field where the bluecaps had once camped.

"Right here seems like a good spot."

"Good spot?"

"For visiting Shar."

Holly's face lit up.

I reached inside the collar of my blouse, fishing for the pendant I usually wore on a leather cord. It wasn't there. I'd taken it off to shower before the party and forgotten to put it back on.

"Oh, honey, we'll have to wait for Shar. I forgot the pendant."

"I want Shar now!" Holly's face screwed up, ready for tears.

Uh-oh. She was already tired from the party and hyped up on sugar.

"Come on. We'll run back to the house and get the pendant. It won't take long."

But there was no reasoning with an over-stimulated toddler.

Her face turned red. Tiny hands clenched into fists. She thrust them over her head and let out a veil-tearing scream. Leaves rustled on nearby trees.

And then, the veil actually tore. A ragged portal opened in front of us.

Holly stopped screaming and smiled.

"See, Mama. I want Shar right now."

"I see that."

Holy mother of all that is sacred. My child just opened a door between worlds.

"Shar!" Holly squealed. She grabbed my hand in her sweaty fingers, and we stepped into the lush green landscape that waited for us.

September 8, 2085

VALKYRIE PEST CONTROL AND ANIMAL CARE FACILITY GRAND RE-OPENING!

Come join us today from 1-5 p.m. for our grand re-opening in beautiful Sayntanne. To celebrate our new expanded facility, we'll be hosting an open house with a BBQ and carnival games. Try your aim at "Dunk the Kraken" and win prizes!

Do you have brownies nesting in your potting shed? Or electricity leeches in your basement? Did you find an orphaned screech? Valkyrie Pest Control and Animal Care Facility can take care of all your fae animal needs, including:

- Humane pest removal
- Rehoming of venomous and non-venomous species
- Fostering of injured or orphaned fae animals

No creature is too big or too slime-covered for us! Free quotations.

ACKNOWLEDGMENTS

Over ten years ago, I started a story about a baby gargoyle alone in the rafters of a Montreal cathedral. I didn't know it then, but that was the beginning of what would become the Valkyrie Bestiary. I actually wrote four complete novels before hitting on the story that I published as *Dragons Don't Eat Meat*. Along the way, I deleted certain characters (such as the baby gargoyle) and added others (like a baby dragon), but two characters remained through all incarnations: Kyra and Mason.

They became family to me. Having worked in animal rescue myself, I could relate to Kyra's desire to save ALL the critters. And her grief when that didn't happen. Kyra turned her passion into a business and then into a family.

Love has always been at the center of the Valkyrie Bestiary—romantic love, but also love for family, community and oneself, and I believe that is why the story resonated with readers. I am more grateful than you can know to have found those wonderful readers who responded to Kyra's found family too. Your continued support and enthusiasm have been the fuel that kept my ideas flowing and my fingers typing for all these years.

From the very beginning, I planned nine books in the Valkyrie Bestiary Series. Many readers have asked me to continue Kyra's story, but I think this is a good place to end it, before she wears out her welcome. But as a thank you to my readers, I penned one more novella, *Thorn of Vioska*, which tells the tale of Emil's journey into the heart of Vioska to spy on the vampires. You can find out more information about that on my website.

It seems impossible and strange to even consider writing about new characters and different worlds, but I am excited to try. I already have two new series in the works, and I invite you to visit my website or join my newsletter for more information on those.

For now, I want to say thank you for sticking with Kyra to the very end. Your support has contributed to making the series a success, and that success has meant that I can fulfill a life-long dream to continue telling my stories.

I would also like to thank Elaine Jackson, my tireless editor who has never failed to make each book better.

The series began before AI art was even a thing, and I thank the One-eyed Father for that. My cover artists have inspired me over the years, and I always enjoyed the creative flow between us. So thank you to Pamela Francescut, Sergey Velikoluzhskiy and Kayla Schweisberger.

I also want to give a big shout out to my Advance Review Team. There are too many names to list here, but I am grateful for your patience when I don't get ARCs to you on time and your generosity in sharing reviews of new books. Your diligence has gone a long way to getting these books noticed.

And finally, I would like to thank my family: Louis Chatel, Genevieve Chatel, and Claire McDougall. You are my first readers and a big reason why I continue to write.

Kyra's wrangling rule #21 says sometimes you have to let them go. And I think we owe her the same. I like to think that Kyra's story going forward is full of sunshine and cute critters, but without the vampires and monsters.

I hope you'll join me on other worlds because I have a lot more stories to tell.

Kim McDougall

DEAR READER

Be sure to sign up for the Readers' Group at KimMcDougall.com/Readers-Group to get updates on new releases. When you subscribe, you'll get a free eBook, *Tales from the Inbetween*, that includes deleted scenes from Valkyrie Bestiary books and a short story from everyone's favorite dervish, Jacoby. This story won't be available anywhere else, so be sure to join the Readers' Group to claim your copy.

You probably know that authors love reviews, but do you know why? Reviews are important because they help other readers know what to expect from the book, they let me know how my books are received by readers, and they help booksellers decide which books to show to new readers.

If you enjoyed this book I would be grateful for your honest review. It can be as short as you like. Even a few positive words will go a long way. And I'll try to make it as painless as possible. Use this link, KimMcDougall.com/Review-Worlds-Don-t-Collide to find the review site of your choice.

Thank you for reading *Worlds Don't Collide* and for supporting Kyra on her nine-book journey.

Kim McDougall

WANT TO FIND OUT MORE ABOUT KYRA'S WORLD?

- Learn more about the Valkyrie Bestiary series and other books by Kim McDougall at https://kimmcdougall.com.

- Poke around at Kyra's blog at http://valkyriebestiary.com.

- Find all the Valkyrie Bestiary books (including prequels and novellas) along with deleted scenes and series FAQ at https://kimmcdougall.com/valkyrie-bestiary.

OTHER PLACES YOU CAN FOLLOW KIM MCDOUGALL BOOKS:

- Facebook: https://www.facebook.com/KimMcDougallBooks

- Instagram: https://www.instagram.com/kimmcdougallbook

- Amazon: https://www.amazon.com/-/e/B002C7CI2M

- Bookbub: https://www.bookbub.com/authors/kim-mcdougall

- Goodreads: https://www.goodreads.com/author/show/1432797.Kim_McDougall

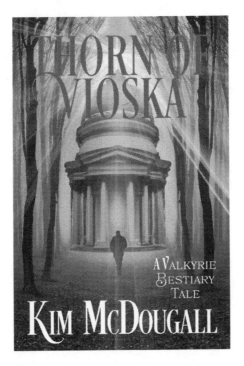

Thorn of Vioska is a companion novella to *Worlds Don't Collide* told from Emil's point of view.

When Kyra asks Emil to infiltrate Vioska and spy on the vampires, he jumps at the chance for revenge against the creatures that killed his one true love.

If the vampires discover him, they'll kill him or worse—they'll turn him into an undead lackey. He expects and even welcomes the danger. What he doesn't expect is to find a new purpose in the slave pens of Vioska.

Thorn of Vioska will be free to Newlsetter Subscribers for a limited time before going on sale. Subscribe at <u>KimMcDougall.com/Readers-Group.</u>

Books By Kim McDougall

Valkyrie Bestiary Novels
Dragons Don't Eat Meat
Dervishes Don't Dance
Hell Hounds Don't Heel
Grimalkins Don't Purr
Kelpies Don't Fly
Ghouls Don't Scamper
Devils Don't Lie
Unicorns Don't Cry
Worlds Don't Collide

Valkyrie Bestiary Novellas
The Last Door to Underhill
The Girl Who Cried Banshee
Three Half Goats Gruff
Oh, Come All Ye Dragons
Thorn of Vioska

The Hidden Coven Series:
Inborn Magic
Soothed by Magic
Trigger Magic
Bellwether Magic
Gone Magic

Writing as Eliza Crowe
The Shifted Dreams Series:
Pick Your Monster
Lost Rogues

ABOUT THE AUTHOR

If Kim McDougall could have one magical superpower, it would be to talk to animals. Or maybe to shift into animal form. Definitely, fantastical critters and magic often feature in her stories. So until she can change into a griffin and fly away, she writes dark paranormal action and epic fantasy tales, from her home in Quebec, Canada. Visit Kim Online at KimMcDougall.com.

Manufactured by Amazon.ca
Bolton, ON

40679573R00150